D0507756

ROGUE OFFICER

Previous Titles in this series by Garry Douglas Kilworth

SOLDIERS IN THE MIST
THE WINTER SOLDIERS
ATTACK ON THE REDAN
BROTHERS OF THE BLADE
ROGUE OFFICER *

* *available from Severn House*

ROGUE OFFICER

Garry Douglas Kilworth

This first world edition published in Great Britain 2007 by
SEVERN HOUSE PUBLISHERS LTD of
9–15 High Street, Sutton, Surrey SM1 1DF.
This first world edition published in the USA 2007 by
SEVERN HOUSE PUBLISHERS INC of
595 Madison Avenue, New York, N.Y. 10022.

British Library Cataloguing in Publication Data

Kilworth, Garry
  The rogue officer
    1. Crossman, Jack (Fictitious character) - Fiction 2. India
    - History - Sepoy Rebellion, 1857-1858 - Fiction
    3. Historical fiction
    I. Title
    823.9'14[F]

ISBN-13: 978-0-7278-6535-9   (cased)

All Severn House titles are printed on acid-free paper.

Typeset by Palimpsest Book Production Ltd.,
Grangemouth, Stirlingshire, Scotland.
Printed and bound in Great Britain by
MPG Books Ltd., Bodmin, Cornwall.

This one is for David Ross.

Acknowledgements

Thanks go to Major John Spiers of the Light Infantry Museum, Winchester, for his assistance.

Author's Note

Whether the uprising of 1857 in India was a mutiny, rebellion or war is hotly debated by historians. This work of fiction is seen through the eyes of British soldiers while they are still currently involved in the action and therefore it is regarded as a mutiny by them. It began at a place in northern India called Meerut on the 10th of May, 1857, when 85 members of the 3rd Bengal Light Cavalry were thrown into prison for refusing to use cartridges they believed to be greased with either pig or cow fat. The Hindu soldiers were revolted at the thought of the latter, the Muslim soldiers at the idea of the former. Whether the cartridges were indeed greased with animal fat was almost irrelevant to the outcome. A number of grievances had gathered to a head at that time: a belief that local religious practices were being threatened; the growing arrogance of British officers of the East India Company; fear of having to do duty overseas – and the situation in India was ripe for explosion.

At Meerut the Indian troops rebelled, releasing their comrades from prison and killing British officers in the process. The rebels then marched on Delhi, which was the home of the Bahadur Shah, the aged Mughal Emperor, who was a figurehead for the mutiny. The rebellion gathered momentum, drawing into it Indians who were not sepoys but civilians, ranging from disaffected land owners to opportunist vagrants. Delhi fell to the rebels and British families were slaughtered. The British rallied at this point and a siege of the city began. There were in fact only around 35,000 British troops in the whole of India and they were vastly outnumbered by Indian troops, but a force of 4,000 men were in position by June, two thirds of them consisting of Sikhs, Punjabis and Gurkhas. This number increased to nearly 10,000 by September, including General John Nicholson's reinforcements from the North West Frontier. Eventually the city was stormed, desperate and bloody street fighting ensued, and finally Delhi was retaken with the loss of John Nicholson and many other lives on both sides.

Further east, in Cawnpore, rebels under their leader Nana Sahib massacred British soldiers and their families. Reprisals, once Cawnpore was retaken in June, were swift and devastating. Many innocent Indians were caught up in the fury which followed and were either hung or dismembered by being blown from cannons (a method of execution adopted from the Mughals). The British troops were in no mood for leniency or mercy and the thirst for revenge continued for some time afterwards.

In the meantime the mutiny had spread to Lucknow, where the rebels began attacking the Residency in July 1857. The Commissioner of Oudh had been forewarned and had gathered supplies and fortified the Residency ready for a siege, having only 1,500 troops at his disposal, half of them Bengal sepoys who had remained loyal to his command. The Commissioner, Henry Lawrence, was killed in the first fighting and command passed to the colonel of the 32nd Foot. The battles were fierce and unrelenting and many died on both sides. A relief force under Major-General Havelock arrived, but this new force was unable to free the defenders of the Residency. Finally General Sir Colin Campbell arrived and on the 16th of November his men stormed the rebel enclosures. Campbell's British soldiers had received news that at Cawnpore British women and children had been butchered and thrown down a well. Their blood was up and they massacred the Indian mutineers in the grounds of the Residency. Tantia Topi, a leader who had risen amongst the rebels, then attacked Campbell with a large force in December, but was defeated with the additional help of Gurkha troops sent by the King of Nepal to aid the British in recapturing Lucknow.

At the opening of *Rogue Officer* it is April 1858 and mopping up is taking place in Central India. Lieutenant Jack Crossman and his men are in Rohilkand, where there are battles still to be fought, notably Bareilly and Gwalior, and rebel leaders still to be subdued, amongst them that fierce female warrior, the Rani of Jhansi. The East India Company itself is in deep political trouble back in Britain, where there is talk of abolishing it and transferring the government of India to the British Crown. The Company's Army is about to be reorganized under direct British rule and its Indian troops will no longer be commanded by East India Company officers.

One

Oudh, India, 1858

'Gentlemen, are you ready?'

'I will be when I get these damn boots on,' snarled Captain Deighnton, one of the three duellists about to indulge in single combat with fellow officers. He was sitting on the stump of a tamarisk tree allowing a sweating Indian servant to force his feet into a pair of brown leather boots. 'Damn your clumsiness, you oaf,' shouted Deighnton. 'Get those bloody boots on.'

'The captain's feet have swollen,' murmured the servant.

Deighnton struck the man around the side of his head with his fist, knocking him off his feet.

'I'll tell you when my feet have swollen.'

Captain Deighnton had arrived in slippers, but insisted on changing his footwear before fighting, as if it mattered whether he killed or died in outdoor footwear.

His efforts were watched impatiently by three clusters of officers. Captain Deighnton had elected to fight two duels on the same morning, such was his crowded timetable in these matters. The army was just about to march and there would be no space for duelling once they were on campaign.

Deighnton finally rose from his seat only to find his trousers were covered in a white sticky substance known as manna, which tamarisk trees exuded after they had been attacked by insects.

'Hell and damnation!' roared the cavalry captain.

Lieutenant Jack Crossman, waiting in the wings for his turn to have his head blown off by the captain, remarked mildly, 'Well, as I see it you have three choices. You can fight with dirty pants, you can change 'em, or you can take 'em off and fight bare-bottomed. Which is it to be?'

Deighnton ignored him. Instead the captain indicated that the first duel should begin. This was with a much younger man than the captain; a boy not beyond two decades. The youth's father had purchased him an ensigncy. Naturally this was in an infantry regiment, a section of the British Army Captain Deighnton despised. In his opinion the only true warrior was one who went into battle with a thoroughbred horse underneath him. Those infantry officers who had made the rank of field officer – majors and above – were nearly acceptable since they were permitted steeds. Any officer of foot below that rank was fair game for his spitefulness, which of course engendered fury.

Deighnton's youthful adversary was deep in conversation with two brother officers, about the same age as he. They were all Indian Army – John Company's men – another reason for Deighnton to pour scorn on them. Jack Crossman could see the boy was afraid. He was pale, shaking a little, and obviously anxious. It was right for him to be so. The captain was a notoriously good shot with a pistol. He had already dispatched two opponents in previous duels and should have been court-martialled long ago.

One of Deighnton's seconds went to the group of young men and asked whether Ensign Faulks was ready.

'I – I am as ready as he,' said the young man nervously.

'Gentlemen,' called the adjudicator, 'please take your places.'

White shirts, tight trousers, brown boots. Both men, dressed alike, stood back to back. In the branches of bare trees, standing just forward of the village huts, some local children were sitting and watching silently. Adults too, stood in the shade while their breakfasts were cooking on open fires. This early-morning activity was entertainment. Would that all *firinghis* killed each other in these strange rituals and rid them of masters. Of course the Moguls would then return, but at least change was interesting.

A cavalry officer Jack did not know took him to one side. 'I'm sure he'll just wound the boy in the arm. There's no great honour in killing a youth of his years. Deighnton is quick enough and a good enough shot to do so without danger to himself. Yes, I'm certain he'll just wing the stripling before the boy can get his shot off.'

Jack fervently hoped so.

'Just a minute!'

Deighnton's opponent began fiddling with his belt. All could see his fingers were shaking madly. Jack felt a lump forming in his throat. The boy was terrified. He, Jack, felt afraid for the young man, and afraid for himself. He was next up to face this madman Deighnton. There ought to be a name for officers like him, who enjoyed killing, who seemed to have not a jot of compassion in their souls. Young, old, inept, stupid, it mattered not to Deighnton, a serial duellist. It seemed to be like a drug to him. How he managed to avoid censure from the high command was beyond Jack. The man must have had very powerful friends in very lofty places.

'All right,' croaked the young ensign, 'I'm ready now.'

There was nothing wrong with the boy's belt. Jack had seen his lips moving rapidly. He had been saying a prayer.

The commands were issued in a clear, calm voice.

'Walk.'

Deighnton strode, the youth trotted.

'Turn.'

The ensign actually turned first.

'Fire.'

A single shot echoed in the morning sending birds into a panic in the bushes and trees.

Deighnton was still standing like a statue, his smoking pistol at a stiff arm's length.

His adversary fell backwards. As he did so, he spun round. All the witnesses could see a large jagged hole between his shoulder blades where the bullet had made its exit. Blood had soaked the whole of the back of his silk shirt. His body hit the ground sending up a puff of dust.

'Help!' A plaintive cry went up. 'Help! Help!'

It came not from the mouth of the young man, who was now stone dead, but from one of his horrified companions. An equally youthful friend bent over the body. Tears were coursing down his cheeks. He cradled the limp corpse in his arms, rocking with it.

Deighnton stared in scorn at this exhibition of sentiment.

The dead boy's friend wailed. 'Danny, Danny, what will I tell them?' Others bent down, solicitous. Faces were pale and drawn, turning to haggard.

A shaken surgeon unfroze and stepped forward, but in such a way as to indicate his services were useless. The young ensign had no life in him. His chest spurted blood on to the breeches of his seconds who tried to lift him up. Others began to assist. They carried the body off, away to a cluster of mango trees, into the shadows. There they could grieve outside the glare of disdain from the other camp.

Jack felt the shockwaves coursing through him. Shock and fear. How swift it had been. One moment alive, the next gone. Quick, and then dead. Such a young man. He had probably been goaded into the duel. Now, because of a flash temper or a high sense of honour, his parents and sisters and brothers would be mourning. What a stupid thing to die for. Yet here was Jack, facing the same fate, for equally stupid reasons.

Deighnton had turned away from the carnage he had caused and was chatting idly to his cavalry friends. It was as if he had simply shot at bottles. There was not a spark of remorse evident. And now he planned to kill Lieutenant Jack Crossman with equal contempt for his life.

Jack's legs felt weak. He could hardly find the strength to step forward to where his seconds stood. Could he do this? He had been in many battles, many skirmishes, where death was present. But this? It seemed like tossing life away. He was an idiot for agreeing to the duel.

Jack Crossman had tried everything to get out of this duel with Deighnton. However, the cavalry captain would have none of it. He had Fancy Jack Crossman in his sights and was not going to allow him to get out of them, unless of course Crossman trod his own honour into the dust, something the lieutenant could never do.

Out here in India honour was everything, even more so than at home. A man without honour lived a miserable friendless existence, rejected by all but the most understanding of close friends and family. A man without honour was nothing but a walking shell.

'Have some coffee ready, Raktambar,' said Jack as he stepped forward. 'Not too bitter, if you please.'

He hoped his voice did not betray his fear.

The Rajput, who was acting as his second, nodded and signalled to one of the local men outside the village: a vendor carrying hot coffee in a container on his back. Raktambar was Jack's 'protector', sent by the Maharajah of Jaipur, and since none of Jack Crossman's men were of officer status, he was the only one permitted to attend the duel. Of course Deighnton had at first objected to him being present, but on reflection decided that it would be entertaining to shoot Crossman dead in front of his own man. Deighnton had scores to settle with Raktambar too. The captain had imprisoned the Rajput on false charges, but to Deighnton's fury Jack Crossman had managed to get Raktambar released.

Deighnton now turned and stood on his spot, a fresh single-shot duelling pistol in his fist. He did not look at Jack and this made Jack wonder whether his opponent was also afraid. Surely he had to be? Yet Jack knew that there were some men who were completely fearless. They were very rare, but they did exist. It seemed that Deighnton was one of these.

A velvet-lined box was thrust under his chin.

'Here.'

Jack stared at the pistol inside.

'Take it,' whispered the officer holding the box. 'Quickly, before he sees you're in a funk.'

The officer was not being unkind. He was being helpful.

Jack's only good hand closed around the butt of the duelling pistol. He lifted it out. It was surprisingly light. A quick check revealed that it was ready to fire. What a pity. He might have claimed cheating. At the very least he would have gained another few minutes of precious life while he or someone rammed home a cartridge.

But the pistol was already primed.

Jack then took his place, his back to the broad-shouldered but shorter man. He could smell Deighnton's sweat. Jack's head began to spin. He shook it quickly, horribly worried that he would swoon.

'Sir? Are you all right?' asked the adjudicator.

'Perfectly fine,' croaked Jack. Then cleared his throat. 'Let's get this farce over with.'

'Walk. One, two, three . . .'

His stiff legs moved mechanically. The lump in his throat turned to concrete.

'. . . ten! Turn.'

He tried not to crouch as he turned around, tried not to cower, managed, thank God, to remain straight and tall.

'Fire.'

He snatched at the trigger, dear Lord, when he should have squeezed it with great deliberation.

The shot went wide, over the left shoulder of his opponent.

A fatalistic feeling then swept over Jack. He expected to die and was now strangely at peace. He waited calmly for the pain to arrive.

It never came.

It was a full minute before he realized that Deighnton had already discharged his pistol. A misfire? Deighnton was at that moment inspecting his weapon with an annoyed and frustrated expression. Relief and dismay met in a confluence within Lieutenant Jack Crossman. On the one hand he was unharmed, on the other he would no doubt have to go through the whole thing once more.

He was just so glad they were Deighnton's pistols, and not his, or the other officer would be bellowing about cheating by now.

'Crossman,' called Deighnton, looking up. 'Apologies. We need to do it again now.'

Jack's stomach turned over. *Do it again now?* He could not. It was impossible. His courage finally failed him.

Jack gripped the empty pistol hard. The point of the trigger at the end of its gentle curve was sharp. He pressed his finger harder into this, piercing the skin. Having gone so far he went further, until he reached the bone. The pain felt good. It meant he was alive and going to stay alive. Then he let the pistol fall from his hand to the ground and presented his hand to the adjudicator. Blood was pouring from the hole, covering his palm, his fingers.

'An old wound,' he said, lying. 'It opens on occasion. I'm afraid I can't continue today. As you see – ' he held up his left arm with the missing hand – 'I can't use the other even if I wanted to.'

The elderly officer nodded.

'The duel is over, gentlemen.'

Deighnton, still busy with his pistol, looked up sharply.

He cried, 'It's over when we say so. You, sir, will simply do your duty.'

The lieutenant spoke in measured tones. 'Captain, I may have remained only a lieutenant but I am nearing my middle fifties. I have witnessed more duels than you have drunk bottles of port. I *know* when a duel is over. This man's hand is not fit to hold a pistol. Besides, you have each had the opportunity to fire your weapon and both have done so. The fact that your pistol failed is neither here nor there, sir. One cannot continue to load and fire at will until someone is either dead or wounded. The duel has been fought, you have both come out of it alive with your honours untarnished, and there's an end to it.'

He spoke with finality in his voice. As he had said, he might only be a lieutenant, but he was quite senior in years, and therefore entitled to the respect those years should bring to him. This was not the battlefield. This was a private affair between gentlemen. Captains could not order lieutenants about in a mango orchard as they might on the parade ground.

These facts did not prevent Captain Deighnton from trying to bully him.

'I shall have satisfaction, sir.'

'Not today,' remarked the lieutenant, 'and if it must be it will on someone else's time, not mine. Good morning.'

'You will regret this, lieutenant.'

The older man turned and smiled wearily.

'You threaten me too? Captain, I'm too long in the tooth for such games as these. You'll need to find another playfellow.'

Deighnton must have known then that he was beginning to look the fool, for he turned and threw his pelisse over his shoulder. There was no glory, no elan to be had, in forcing into a duel a passed-over lieutenant with grey hair and lank beard. Besides, the high clear notes of a bugle were sounding over the forest scrub. Deighnton had to be with his troopers. Before he left though he wagged a finger at Crossman, saying, 'We will do this again.'

'Go to hell, you pompous fart,' Jack said under his breath. 'I've had enough of you for one war.'

'Connaught Rangers,' Deighnton was still muttering to himself. 'Irish Regiments of foot. Bloody peasant army of potato eaters.'

'And it's pronounced *Connocht*,' Jack corrected him, for Deighnton had called it Con-nort. 'Connaught, as in the Scottish loch. Time you went back to school.'

However the last word was not to be Jack's.

'Damn cripples,' snarled Deighnton, making reference to Jack's missing left hand, where the sleeve was pinned back towards the elbow. 'Chuck 'em out, I say. Send 'em back to their maters.'

The original quarrel between Jack and Deighnton was both complicated and simple.

Before Jack had married his wife Jane, she had been attached to an aristocrat by the name of Hadrow, a rake who eventually cast her aside. In deference to Jane's wishes, Jack avoided any encounter with Hadrow, but the man had decided otherwise. Hadrow and two others from his club had followed Jack through the streets of London intent on conflict. The conflict indeed took place and ended with Jack drawing Hadrow's cork with his wooden left fist, letting the claret flow on the flagstones.

There ended the complicated part.

The simple part was that Captain Deighnton claimed to be a 'good friend' of Hadrow and was determined to right his friend's wrong. In Delhi, Deighnton had challenged Jack to a duel, which Jack had thought ridiculous and refused the offer. The captain persisted however, in front of witnesses, insulting Jack until he was honour-bound to accept the challenge. Jack suspected there was more to the thing than Deighnton simply acting for his friend Hadrow – Jack had never heard of a duel fought in proxy – but could not for the life of him think what it was. He had no recollection of ever meeting Deighnton before their encounter at Delhi and was completely bewildered by the man's hostility.

Someone came up to Deighnton and told him that General Martlesham awaited him in the officers' mess. Deighnton trudged off, followed by his servant, who cradled the captain's slippers, one under each arm, as if they were newborn twins.

Jack took a cup of coffee from his Rajput's hand. Surprisingly his own bloody fingers were now steady. The body could lie too.

The coffee scalded his tongue; bitter but so welcome.

'You will kill him next time,' said Raktambar, his eyes revealing nothing. 'When your hand heals.'

'Yes – yes, I will.'

He looked towards the part of the orchard where they had taken the corpse of the young ensign. It was empty. They had gone.

The magnificent blood-red dawn that flowed across the sky above Oudh began to fade. In the bungalows and the palaces the servants had long been awake and busy, while those they served were just stirring in their warm beds. Mosquito nets were thrown back, copper washing-bowls were carried into bedrooms, the scent of tea was in the air. Inside the relatively cool mud or marble dwellings life was tolerable. Outdoors the heat would rise to savage levels bringing with it hot dry winds and choking dust storms. Any business not related to war was best done before the sun rose any higher in the heavens. Even killing another man, if it was a necessary thing, was carried out more comfortably in the early dawn.

Jack walked back to his tent with Raktambar at his side. Both men were silent. Jack wondered whether the Rajput had guessed what had happened. Did Raktambar know of Jack's cowardice? The fear had gone now, of course, with the removal of the threat. Now Jack simply felt appalled at his actions. To have faked a wound in order to avoid a duel? It was unthinkable. There was a hard lump in his throat. Guilt. It would clog his brain for a long while to come. Perhaps for ever? How disgusting of him. How despicable. Yet he *was* still alive, if indeed a coward.

A horrible secret. Was it worth it? Surely it would have been better to die marching into the mouth of a cannon than give that bastard Deighnton the satisfaction.

Yet that ugly word remained – coward.

That poor but honourable young man with a hole in his chest: at that moment Jack would have changed places with him.

Jack and Raktambar made their way towards the tents where Sergeant King, Corporal Gwilliams and King's adopted son Sajan were waiting for them. There was relief on the faces of his waiting crew. Jack was touched by that. He and King did not always see eye to eye and though Gwilliams, the North American, was loyal enough, Jack believed the corporal did not have a sentimental bone in his body. He felt sure news of his death would have drawn a shrug at the most from both of them. Yet here they were, seemingly concerned for his well-being. Yes, he was touched.

'Didn't he even hit you *anywhere*?' drawled Gwilliams, his eyes running over Jack's form, presumably looking for signs of blood. 'I thought he was supposed to be a dead shot?'

'He is. He certainly mangled the poor boy who went before me.'

'Then how come you're all in one piece?'

Jack said, 'Don't sound so disappointed, Gwilliams. His pistol misfired.'

'What about yours?'

'It went off.'

Light came into Gwilliams' eyes. 'He's dead then?'

'No – he's unharmed.'

The light faded and Gwilliams now spat in disgust. 'You missed!'

'I missed.'

'You should let me go next time – I'll blow the bastard's head off.'

Jack smiled at Gwilliams' enthusiasm. 'You can't, you're a peasant. Deighnton won't duel with peasants.'

'We don't have none of that malarkey back home,' snarled Gwilliams. 'Don't matter whether a man's a king or a cobbler.' He paused before adding, ''Cept them so-called Southern gentlemen can be a bit picky sometimes. Mostly though, you can fight who you like. I'd sure like a crack at this prig of a captain, sir, if it can be arranged.'

Corporal Gwilliams was North American. Sometimes he claimed to be a Canadian. Other times he said he was from the United States. At all times he claimed to be the barber who had shaved every famous frontiersman from Kit Carson to Jim Bowie. Certainly he was very good with a razor, as Jack had found out when he'd sent the corporal sneaking into enemy camps at night. Gwilliams was also a crackshot with a rifle. His prowess was not confined to weapons. Raised by a preacher, Gwilliams had read all the classics in his adopted father's bookshelves and reckoned he could 'out-classic' any Englishman he met. His association with Jack's spies and saboteurs was not yet a long one: he had joined Jack's peleton a short while before the end of the Crimean War and Jack's eventual posting to India, but he had proved himself very able in that short time.

'It's my problem, but thank you for the offer, corporal.' Jack turned his attention to his sergeant. 'And you need not apply, Sergeant King, we all know your lack of prowess with a firearm.'

King stiffened. 'I'm getting better all the time, sir.'

'Glad to hear it.'

'But I wouldn't fight a duel if I was the best shot in the regiment. I think it's the stupidest thing I ever heard. What's wrong with settling an argument with your fists?'

Jack sighed. 'It's not permanent enough for some people,' he said. 'Nothing but my corpse will satisfy Deighnton. Now, you heard the trumpets and drums, let's strike camp. It seems we're off to Rohilkand at last. The sooner this rebellion is quelled, the better. Civil war is so ugly. We seem to commit more atrocities against friends than we do enemies.'

'This is not civil war, sahib,' interrupted Ishwar Raktambar, who was unhappily torn between two sides. 'This is a war to drive you foreigners from India.'

The reluctant Rajput bodyguard of Lieutenant Fancy Jack Crossman had been raised in a village in Rajputana, the son of a poor farmer. When he was eight years of age, his uncle, a gardener at the palace of the maharajah of Rajputana, sent for him with the promise that he would assist the boy in becoming a palace guard. When his father packed him off to the palace, his uncle simply used him as a personal slave until Raktambar reached the age of eighteen. He was by that time a muscular youth with a fine physique due to the hard work his uncle had put him through. Finally, the boy rebelled and wrestled with his uncle in the courtyard of the palace, a scene which was witnessed by the maharajah's vizier.

The Grand Vizier was impressed by the youth's strength, as he saw him bodily throw his uncle, first into the goldfish fountain, then into some thorn bushes. Having come to the notice of the vizier, Ishwar Raktambar was then taken on as personal bodyguard to the maharajah himself. However, his good looks and natural ability with weapons also made him a favourite in the maharajah's harem, a fact known to the maharajah himself, and when a British officer visited him he saw a way of ridding himself of this tall, handsome young warrior, without having to execute him and upset half his wives and most of his concubines. He offered the young man as a bodyguard to the lieutenant, hoping the pair of them would be dead within a few months from the bullets or swords of rebel sepoys.

'As you say,' replied Jack, not wishing to argue the rights and wrongs of the matter with Raktambar. 'Now, Gwilliams, will you get the mounts up here. We need to join the division.'

There were five of them altogether, including the boy Sajan. These intelligence-gatherers, being independent of the rest of the division and needing to move rapidly in the area of the fighting, had been provided with horses by their colonel. There had been some grumbling amongst the staff officers regarding the boy being mounted, but Jack pointed out that Sajan was sometimes an invaluable gleaner, being able to slip into a market place or village and listen to the gossip amongst the local population.

As they were preparing to join the rest of the division in Lucknow, commanded by Brigadier Walpole, two young Eurasian girls came running up to greet Lieutenant Jack Crossman. These were daughters of a corporal drummer named Flemming and his Punjabi wife. To Jack they were a perfect nuisance. The older one, Silvia, a mere seventeen years old, was besotted with him, and the younger one, Delia, a year behind her, followed her big sister everywhere. They wore saris, ran around without shoes on their feet, and both had long black coils of hair hanging like a thick rope down their backs. They were slim, lithe and incredibly beautiful.

'Captain, captain,' called Silvia as they both rushed up to Jack, tears in their eyes. 'You are going away from us. Please, please stay to protect us from the badmashes.'

'Girls,' he said in despair, as the square-faced Sergeant King's face split with a grin, 'please don't bother me now. I'm trying to get ready to march with the rest of the division. You know what your father told you. You must stay away from me. I'm – I'm a *bad* man.'

'No, no, you are not,' cried the lovely Silvia, grasping his sleeve with her slim fingers. 'Those cavalry officers, they are the *bad* ones.' She and her sister both spat into the dust to physically register their disgust of officers of horse. 'They want to steal the flower from us. You are a good man, sir. We will come with you. Delia and I cannot stay here while you are fighting war. We must be by your side, Captain.'

'Yes, we must,' cried Delia dutifully.

This younger one had convinced herself she too was in love with her sister's 'captain'. If Silvia was so madly in love with this tall one-handed officer with the black hair and scarred but handsome face, there must be something very special about him. Thus Delia Flemming was also moon-struck. The pair of them were driving Jack mad. He had told them countless times he was not a captain – and indeed they knew it – but they had decided they were too proud to be in love with a mere lieutenant, so they had promoted him and insisted on that rank. He

was their captain and even though he had informed them he
was a happily married man, they were convinced he would one
day come to hold them in high regard. All this because he had
once shown them simple kindness by acknowledging them with
a 'good morning' and a smile. Had he but known what he was
bringing on his head he would definitely have snarled at them.

'Girls, please,' said Jack, 'your father will bring me up in
front of the commanding officer if you keep following me
around. Do you want to get me into trouble? This is silly
infatuation . . .'

'No, no, it is true love,' said Silvia, her large dark eyes full
of sincerity. 'You must believe it, sir. You must.'

Gwilliams glanced back and forth between the two girls,
chewing a quid of tobacco slowly. His expression told you
nothing but Jack presumed the crusty corporal was wondering
what he would do in such circumstances. Gwilliams was
absolutely sure what he would do and it was not the act of a
gentleman. King just grinned and shook his head, the bowl of
the clay pipe between his clenched teeth red hot with being
overpuffed. Sajan simply looked disgusted, and well he might
for he was just a young boy.

It was Raktambar who stepped in and saved the lieutenant.

'Go away,' he bellowed at the sisters. 'Go away or I shall
beat you with the flat of my sword! You are interfering
baba-logue.'

The girls did not like to be called 'children', and they glowered at the Rajput, who was not finished with them.

'Here is an important man! He cannot be bothered with mere
girls. Be off with you or I shall make smackings on your
backsides.'

Gwilliams' eyes opened visibly wider at this last remark and
registered expectation. But the girls were afraid of the tall Rajput
in the red turban. They made faces at him, stuck out their
tongues and waggled the tips, but they began to walk away.
When Raktambar stepped forward quickly, they turned on their
heels and ran back towards their father's quarters, yelling something unintelligible over their shoulders.

Jack heaved a sigh of relief. He let Gwilliams strap on his
sword, since there was no time for him to fiddle one-handedly,
then he checked his double-triggered Tranter revolver. He had
become quite adept at holding the weapon between his knees

and loading it with his right hand. When he felt sure they were all ready, he motioned his group forward.

'Come on, before those two nuisances come back,' he said.

They mounted and moved up to join the column. There were one or two old acquaintances in the region: people he had met during the Crimean campaign just over a year ago. Sergeant-Major Jock McIntyre was here with the 93rd. As was General Sir Colin Campbell, who had commanded the 93rd in their now infamous *thin red streak* stand at Balaclava. Sir Colin was commander-in-chief in this region. Now known as 'Old *Khabardar*' (Old Be-careful) he was the man who had ordered Walpole into Rohilkand to hunt down the rebel leader Nirpat Singh.

Some known civilians were here too: war correspondents who had been in the Crimea. William Howard Russell, of *The Times*, and Rupert Jarrard, of the *New York Banner,* were present, though Jack had not before crossed paths in India with his good friend Rupert. This was one reason he liked the army. Comradeship. These were men he respected and they had known him under fire. Some of them not well, it was true: Colin Campbell would have difficulty in remembering a sergeant standing in line with his beloved 93rd during the Russian charge, but Jack remembered, and that was the important thing. It felt like a close-knit club, but not one of those London clubs like Whites, where the *ton* snubbed the little men. He knew if he were to say to Sir Colin, 'I was there,' he would receive a warm and knowing acknowledgement. Men who had fought beside each other under adversity were welded together until death, no matter what their rank. A corporal who stood with his king at Agincourt had that hour of his life when he was level with his liege and neither would deny it.

So, joining Brigadier Walpole's column, Jack found the 93rd Sutherland Highlanders, the 42nd and 79th Cameron Highlanders were ready to move with the 9th Lancers (Deighnton's lot, who in their distinctive blue uniforms reminded Jack of the Cossacks who had hunted him down in the Crimea), the 2nd Punjab cavalry, the 4th Punjab Rifles, two troops of horse artillery, two 18-pounders and two 8-inch howitzers. He and his small group had been given the freedom to join with the column as they pleased.

Jack Crossman's group's main task in India was intelligence, with the odd foray into sabotage and some map-making on the side. These were strange times, however, and the land had been turned on its head by the mutiny of the Indian sepoys. The East India Company were outnumbered a thousand-fold by the native troops of their own army and if all the native regiments had revolted the British would have been driven into the sea by now. As it was the Company Army, along with those regiments of Her Majesty stationed in India and thereabouts, had been able to contain the rebellion thus far. It had been touch and go for John Company.

There had been some horribly ugly events at Cawnpore and Lucknow which Jack hoped would eventually fade in his mind. The slaughter of British families – women, children, babes – which had sickened his comrades-in-arms. There was some terrible retribution going on, with innocent natives being executed alongside guilty ones. The scales of justice and mercy had been knocked flying from the hands of those who held them and extreme violence was flowing back and forth, first on one side, then the other. Men were blinking away the misty blood from their eyes to find they had been part of something very grisly and awful. Some were already trying to justify it on both sides, while others were dumb with horror. This deluge of violence was a numbing thing to sensible men.

Jack and his men fell in behind some khaki-uniformed Punjabis, happy to stay out of the way of regular HM troops. They were not easy with anything that approached strict discipline, having been away from it for so long. It was better to stay out of the eye of high-ranking officers, their keen senior NCOs, and the general hard-drinking privates with their coarse ways. Not that Jack's little band were angels, but they did not indulge in the mindless swilling and swaggering that marked some soldiers.

'What are you thinking, sir?' asked Sergeant King, eyeing his commanding officer with a puzzled frown. 'It's as if you've been to chapel – you've got a look of fearful enlightenment on your face.'

Jack had actually been thinking about the recent duel and a belated wave of relief had passed through him, but he said to King, 'I was thinking about comradeship. I was recalling the Crimean campaign and those I knew there. Some are dead, of course, but a few are actually here in India. It makes for a warm feeling to have old comrades-in-arms about me . . .'

At that moment Jack caught sight of a private soldier sauntering towards him with an Enfield slung casually over his shoulder. There was something about the jaunty step of this figure that sent a shiver down the lieutenant's spine. Here was a cocky individual, to be sure, for insolence and insubordination was written in every approaching step. Jack had been in the army long enough to read the signs. Then he recognized the facings on the uniform. The man was 88th Connaught Rangers. Jack's heart sank and he let out an audible groan which brought a frown to King's features.

The approaching soldier finally arrived, a great wide smirk spread across his face. He was lean, unshaven, and had the narrow face and louring eyes of a petty criminal borne out of an unhappy childhood. He unslung his rifle, then hitched off his haversack and let it fall to the ground in a cloud of dust. Then he stretched out his left hand as if intending to shake that of the lieutenant's, only appearing to notice at the last moment that Jack had no left hand himself. A shrug and a grin and a little wave followed.

'Pleased to see me, eh, Sergeant? Sorry, lieutenant now, ain't it?'

'Private Harry Wynter,' said Jack sighing. 'Don't tell me you're with the 88th in India now.'

'Nope.' Wynter continued to smirk. 'I'm with you – sir.'

Jack's heart sank even more and he grimaced. 'With me – with us?'

'It were like this, sir. I was marching along as merry as can be with me comrades-in-arms, happy to be fightin' for queen and country like, when I sees Colonel Hawke ridin' by. Our Colonel Hawke. So that evenin', I goes to his tent and asks to see 'im. I tells him who I am and lord 'elp us, the dear old colonel recognizes me. Naturally, bein' as we got on so well together in the past, I asks him, is our Fancy Jack 'ere, fightin' for the cause? And he tells me you are, so I asks to join you again. "Wynter," he says, "the lieutenant can do with men like you, men he can trust, as he's only got new coves who don't know their arse from their elbow." ' Here the newcomer looked at King and seemed gratified to witness a twitch of anger. '"Good sir," says I, "'cause I want to help. I've been trained up to do skulkin' and blowing things to bits and that's what I want to do." And he says to me, "Consider it done."'

Wynter stood there, still wearing that sly grin, waiting for a response. When there was none, he added, 'So here I am, sir. By the by, Fancy Jack, how's the missus?'

At these incredibly insubordinate words, Sergeant King, who had been sitting in his saddle transfixed by this grubby soldier, suddenly came to life with a burst of high energy. He dismounted to confront Wynter and stuck his jaw into the man's face. Wynter lost his smile and stumbled backwards.

'Private,' barked the sergeant, making Sajan jump, 'I don't know who the hell you are, but when you approach an officer, the first thing I expect from you is a salute. Then you stand to attention and wait until you're spoken to. Pick up that pack, put it on your back, straighten that forage cap, shoulder arms and stand ready for inspection!'

'What?' cried an affronted Wynter.

'*YOU HEARD ME!*'

Wynter did as he was told, muttering under his breath all the time.

'I don't know what you're chuntering at, soldier, but let me tell you this. I am the senior NCO here. I am the man who speaks with the officer in charge of this unit. If you have anything to say, you say it to me first, and if I think it's important enough – and only then – I shall convey your remarks to the officer in an economic way, so's not to waste his valuable time. You may or may not have served under this same commanding officer . . .'

'Sergeant then.'

'What?' growled King.

The sullen Wynter repeated, 'He was a sergeant then.'

King was silent for a moment, but unfazed. 'And he's a lieutenant now and will be given all due deference and respect deserving of that rank. You, sir, are *nothing*. A weevil in an army loaf of bread, nothing more. A slug. A dung beetle.' He looked Wynter up and down. 'In all my time in the army I have never seen a more slovenly soldier . . .'

'Eh?'

Wynter looked round him. He felt justifiably aggrieved by this remark, since he was surrounded by troops who were in much the same condition and state of poor dress, having lost bits of their uniform over the past few months of bitter fighting, and having replaced official caps with turbans, and taken off coats to march in shirtsleeves. They were a motley-looking force of grubby worn-out warriors, not enhanced by the haphazard dress of the irregular forces who marched alongside them. Wynter was no more or less scruffy than the next man.

Indignantly, he said, 'I just marched a thousand miles or more!'

'And you'll march back again if I have anything to do with it – you would give an army of cockroaches a bad name.'

Wynter stored this insult away to nurse in the future, when he was planning just what he would do to sergeants like King once he left the army.

'Now, what have you to say to me, soldier?' cried King.

'Sergeant, Private Wynter reporting for duty with the spies and destructors as ordered,' yelled Wynter.

'Fall in, Wynter. We're about to march,' said King. 'I shall speak with you again later, when there's more time.'

'I ain't got no horse!' Wynter pointed out.

'Then you'll have to walk until we get you one.'

Wynter glowered at King as the sergeant remounted, then the cheery grin returned to his face as he looked up and saw Gwilliams peering down on him. He fell in beside Gwilliams, taking hold of his mount's bridle. They began to move forward and Wynter started chatting to the man he had served with in the Crimean campaign.

'Hey, Yankee, you're a corporal now! That's good. I was a sergeant for a bit.'

'Yeah?' replied Gwilliams in an uninterested voice. 'So, what happened?'

Wynter shambled forward with the rest of the column.

He shrugged. 'I got drunk.'

'Surprise me,' drawled Gwilliams.

Private Wynter had been with Jack throughout the Crimean War, from start to finish. Jack had been a sergeant in those days and Wynter had been a thorn in his side. Despite the fact that the pair of them were the only ones left serving out of the original peleton that had been formed by Major Lovelace as his intelligence gatherers, Jack and Wynter were as far apart as men could be. Jack despised Harry Wynter and Harry Wynter despised everyone but himself. Adversity normally forges friendships but not in this case. When Jack had been promoted to lieutenant, Wynter had somehow managed to get his sergeant stripes.

It seemed Wynter had not held on to his new rank for very long. Harry Wynter was from a large poor rural family, the product of having to fight for every scrap of food that passed his lips when he was a child, and had consequently developed into a conniving, sly adult who trusted no one, hated the world, and felt that property belonged to he who could wrest it from another, either by force or cunning. He was always on the lookout for those weaker than himself, so that he could crush them. This especially applied to native inhabitants of countries other than his own.

While these two were going on ahead, King rode forward to speak with his officer.

'You have a history, sir, with that individual?'

'Yes – I thank you for intervening.'

'My job. Don't forget, sir, you're an officer now, not a sergeant. You don't have to deal with the likes of him. That's for NCOs. I'll sort him out.'

'I spent almost three years trying to – and failed.'

King said, 'Well, perhaps you were born to be an officer and I was born to NCO rank, and so . . .'

'So, you'll make a better job of it?'

'It's a thought.'

'I hope you may, sergeant. For my part I was weary of the man in the Crimea and I can't see my attitude towards him changing. He's trouble from helmet to boots. He whines constantly, he gets drunk at the slightest sniff of gut rot and he continually starts fist fights he never ever looks like winning. Wynter seems to have the capacity to absorb blows and misfortunes, both physical and mental, which would cripple any other man. Yet there he stands, my nemesis, haunting my every step in life.'

Wynter was not Lieutenant Fancy Jack's only personnel problem. There were others.

For instance, he and Sergeant King himself did not always see eye to eye about things. King was far more interested in map-making than he was in spying or sabotage. He actually saw making maps as his prime duty. That was what he had been trained for and that was what excited him as a man. Jack, on the other hand, did not give an owl's hoot for map-making and he *knew* that the purpose of his crew was intelligence gathering and sabotage. Thus the two men were often at loggerheads with each other, Jack usually winning but not always. King often took advantage of the times when Jack was ill or away to further his feverish desire to create maps.

King had been foisted on Jack just before the lieutenant left the shores of Britain for India. This time it had been Colonel Hawke who had insisted that Jack take on a new man. Although he and King had fought the Indian Mutiny campaign together, they too held views to which each could not reconcile himself. King was a blacksmith's son, educated at a boarding school, and keen to raise himself above his origins. He had taken to map-making as eagles take to the air. He soared.

Sergeant King was unmarried but had been in India for a previous tour of duty. While there he had fallen in love with a village girl and had got her pregnant. His unit had taken him away from the village and when he returned she was gone, no one would tell him where. Later the girl's family had tried to have him assassinated for violating their relative, but the assassin had failed, ending his life by being shot by Lieutenant Crossman in a coffee shop in the Punjab. Since that time Jack Crossman had taken a young Indian boy out of virtual slavery – the boy Sajan had been a punkah wallah – and King had decided he was his lost child. No one knew if this was true (it was highly likely it was false) but none wanted to prise the belief from the sergeant, who had adopted Sajan as his son. The boy now went everywhere with the group and proved to be very useful in certain circumstances. King was teaching him to make maps.

'You leave Wynter to me, sir,' said King. 'I'm the man for him. If he wants to settle scores behind the trees with fists, I'll accommodate him in that too.'

Farrier King had fists as big and hard as four-pound hammers.

Raktambar, while all this was going on around him, was happy to talk in Hindi to Sajan. The Rajput was ostensibly Jack Crossman's bodyguard, but he resented the duty and only remained in the position out of loyalty to his master in Jaipur, and more recently out of respect for Lieutenant Jack Crossman. Gradually, as they had fought together against the rebels (another aspect of his duties which was not entirely in accord with Raktambar's own principles) the pair had come to like and think highly of each other. The most important ideal to Raktambar, and many others from the Punjab and various areas of India, was honour. A man with his honour intact was a man to be respected. He and Jack were both of the opinion that a soldier without honour was not worth a crow's droppings. The late General Nicholson's entourage of Afghans and Punjabis – big, fierce men who fought to the death beside him – had been at his shoulder because of their regard for Nicholson as a man with great honour.

'Who are we going to fight?' asked young Sajan in his native language. 'Is it the sepoys again?'

'Now there are more than just mutinous sepoys and sowars,' replied Raktambar. 'There are the rajahs' matchlock men, badmashes and Gujars, along with many ordinary civilians unhappy with the British. The sepoys are only a few now, at the heart of the rebellion. But that is not for you to take part in – you must stay out of the fighting.'

'Who is their leader?'

'Why, there are many hereabouts. I think this is one Nirpat Singh, but there is also Khan Bahadur Khan in Rohilkand. They say Khan has many followers, almost as many as the Maulvi. There will be many more battles before this is over, child. We must wait and see what happens.'

'You think the British will not win?'

'Who knows? There are valiant fighters out there, with Tantia Tope and the Rani of Jhansi. Men are willing to die. Perhaps it may yet turn against the British and they will be driven out?'

During their conversation they kept their opinions on the uprising neutral, both boy and man. In truth their loyalties were stretched; Raktambar's more than the boy's. A child who has been treated with much kindness, adopted by a British sergeant, and whose feelings have not yet hardened to granite, will rarely bite the hand that feeds him.

Raktambar though was resentful of the arrogance of the East India Company's acquisitiveness. They had annexed provinces like Sind and Oudh and seemed determined to extend that annexation further. He saw people like himself hanged for no other crime than standing and watching. Yet there were thousands of others who still fought with the British and saw them as the main power in a vast land which had been held by conquerors for hundreds of years. In fact, Raktambar was secretly glad the decision to choose sides had been taken from him by his maharajah.

The column marched and camped for several days, so by the fifteenth of April they were some fifty miles south-east of Lucknow and just a few miles from the River Ganges. Brigadier Walpole was heading towards a fort named Ruya, which was occupied by a small force of rebels. When they arrived they found that thick bamboo forests went right up to two sides of the fort. Inside, at the head of the rebels, was their leader, Nirpat Singh. Raktambar and Sajan, posing as itinerant father and son, learned from a nearby village that there were little more than two hundred defenders in the fort. This was confirmed when Jack managed to speak with a native trooper of Hodson's Horse, who had been a captive in the fort before escaping.

The information was conveyed to Brigadier Walpole. Unfortunately Walpole had a harsh opinion of 'skulkers'. He thoroughly disliked spying and regarded all such gathered information as dubious. Instead, the brigadier made up his own mind that there were at least one-and-a-half thousand rebels in the fort. Nothing would budge him from this view. Moreover he forbade any further reconnaissance of the area, saying he could see for himself what was before him.

On his own initiative Jack decided to reconnoitre the area and discover for himself the fort's strengths and weaknesses. He found that though it was protected by jungle north and east, there were little natural or man-made defences on the other two sides. There were shallow ditches and walls low enough to leap over should the British attack from the south or west. Jack went back with this information and tried to get past staff officers to see Brigadier Walpole, but he found himself barred.

'The brigadier does not want any further reconnaissance of the fort,' a young subaltern told him. 'He prefers to go on advice given to him before he left Lucknow.'

'Advice by whom?' asked Jack. 'After all, we are here now and can see for ourselves. Perhaps this advice was formed years ago?'

The young officer sighed. 'Perhaps – but that's how it stands. Look, who are you anyway?'

'My commanding officer is Colonel Hawke. I'm with Major Lovelace. We're an independent intelligence-gathering unit.'

Light came into the subaltern's eyes. 'Oh, I know you, you're the fellah whom Deighnton talks about.'

Jack sighed and looked away. 'Yes, I expect I am.'

The subaltern moved closer to Jack, looking about him to make sure they were alone, and said, 'Next time, don't miss.'

Then the officer was gone, back into a tent opening barred by two formidable looking soldiers of the 93rd, with legs as thick as tree trunks sticking out of the bottoms of their kilts. They turned hard Scottish eyes on Jack as he stood there, wondering whether to blunder past them, to take his chance. But he could see it would be like trying to barge through two buffaloes and gave up the thought.

As he was walking away however, the guard was changed. He turned back again, thinking there might be an opportunity to slip past two new sentries, who had not seen him ejected by the subaltern. But he found his path blocked by a short, square, very solid man with a rigid expression. The soldier, a sergeant major, came to attention and saluted briskly.

'Gud day t'ye, sir. And a pleasant day it is.'

'Sergeant Major McIntyre!' cried Jack. 'How the devil are you?'

A grin appeared on Jock McIntyre's rugged face. 'Aye, as well as could be expected, given this bloody war.' He looked Jack up and down, retaining the wry smile. 'An officer, is it? I well ken the time ye thocht officers were the dregs o' the army, sir. A wee change o' mind, eh?'

'Oh, you know how it is, Jock. I'm one of those fate is determined to thrust greatness upon, whether I like it or not. Look, Jock, can you get me into that tent? I have to speak with Brigadier Walpole.'

'Can ye no walk in yersel?' Then Jock seemed to understand. 'Ah. Ye've tried it, but . . .'

Jack's expression must have told Jock the whole story.

The sergeant-major shook his head sadly. 'Sorry, sir. I ken the problems ye'll be havin', wi' the commander. He's a wee bit deef when it comes to listening, if that's no a daft thing tae say. Ye'll have the stripes off mah arm and it took aye too long tae get them there, ah'm afraid.'

Jack nodded. 'All right, Jock. I understand. Good to see you again, anyway. I'd shake your hand but it'd look a bit unsoldierly to those two kilted Colossi, guarding the gates of the Good and Great.'

'Aye, I'd rather ye didn't, but the feeling's mutual, lieutenant. Ye deserve the rank. How's the hand?'

Jack held up the stump. 'Gone.'

'But no a bother, ah hope?'

'I'm getting used to it.'

Jack left his old friend Jock and went back to his group. King was incensed when he learned they were being ignored.

'What are we here for, sir? Just to look pretty?'

'I thought it was to draw maps, Sergeant.'

King flinched. 'Well, that's the most important thing, I'll grant, but there is this other side to our work . . .'

Despite advice, Walpole attacked the fort from the jungle. The Highlanders and the Punjabis became entangled in the undergrowth and those in the fort had a field day. They could not believe their luck. Nirpat Singh had intended to make a token resistance, then beg for terms. Instead the rebel leader took advantage of the incredibly bad tactics of the brigadier. The British took many casualties, including one popular high-ranking officer among the many who were slaughtered, and the troops were incensed. Wave after wave of infantry was halted and finally the brigadier came to his senses and ordered the withdrawal of the Highlanders and Punjabis, bringing up his cannons rather too late to bombard the fort's walls and towers.

Sajan stood by a gun crew and watched them go through their actions. The boy was as fascinated by the gunners as he was with the map-making of his adopted father. He loved mechanical devices, whether their purpose be peace or war. Most of his short life had thus far been spent as a punka wallah in a rajah's guest bedroom. Now here he was, out and about in the world, able to witness an attack on a fort. It was exciting and enthralling to a youngster of his age. He watched as the sponge-man swabbed out the barrel while the ventsman placed a leather-covered thumb over the vent's aperture to prevent any explosion from a residue of the last charge. Then the next charge and round were rammed home. He noticed that the spongestaff only needed to be reversed to provide the rammer. Once the charge and shot were rammed home the ventsman inserted a pricker down the vent aperture to puncture the charge bag. Finally the firer put a smouldering portfire to the vent and the shot was sent on its way.

Each time the gun was fired, Sajan jumped with the noise, even though he had his fingers in his ears.

'Big bang!' he kept saying. 'When I am as old as my father, I shall make a gun with a noise no louder than a *pop*.'

The artillery attack continued into the dark night.

In the morning Walpole was furious to find the fort empty. Nirpat Singh and his men had escaped during the night. It was a hollow victory. Jack knew that the troops had been close to mutiny when they realized what a mess their brigadier had made of the battle, and Walpole narrowly escaped being executed by his own men. It was clear to everyone he was no military leader and many officers wanted him replaced immediately. However, as with such situations, nothing was done at the time. Walpole ordered the column to march on to Fatehgarh, where they were joined by General Campbell and his column, who assumed command and took them on to Shahjahanpur, which was also found evacuated. Finally the combined force reached Miranpur Katra well inside Rohilkand. Awaiting them were the troops of one General Penny, who had been killed earlier in an ambush.

It was here too, that Major Lovelace caught up with his intelligence unit and briefed Jack.

'Campbell has missed catching the Maulvi at Shahjahanpur,' explained the cold-eyed major. 'We think Nana Sahib was also there. It's a great shame. We could have dealt a double blow to the rebels. You know how badly we want Nana Sahib.'

Nana Sahib was believed to be responsible for several atrocities committed against British families, one of them being the massacre in Cawnpore. There were men in the British Army who would have given a fortune to have Nana Sahib at their mercy. In fact the word mercy would not have been heard. It would have been lost in the baying of the wild dogs as they tore their victim to pieces.

'Campbell is now going to push on to Bareilly. He's going after Khan Bahadur Khan. You and your men need to ride ahead to assess the size of Khan's army, his strength in the field and the lie of the land. You'll report back directly to the general.'

'I tried that with Brigadier Walpole and got snubbed,' replied Jack.

'Walpole is an idiot,' Lovelace said. 'You and I know Campbell's worth.'

Jack turned his mind to the task. It was not an easy mission, going on ahead alone, with bands of malefactors wandering the countryside just looking for an opportunity to hang some British soldiers. The pot was boiling and several armies of rebels had fractured into smaller groups, either trying to find their way to an area where they could hide from retribution or seeking revenge themselves. Two years ago a European could have walked from one end of the country to the other and felt safe from attack – Thugs and Gujars accepted – but all that had changed since the mutiny.

'It won't be a cricket match,' said Jack.

'No, but it's necessary. I wouldn't send you out there, if I didn't believe that.'

Lovelace was a calculating man. Not thoroughly callous, but certainly uncompromising when it came to his work. Jack Crossman had seen him kill in cold blood without compunction in order to extract or protect information necessary to win battles. He was a user of men. It was not that he thought his own soldiers totally expendable – far from it; he knew that a good man saved today could be used again tomorrow – but given the opportunity he would exchange any one of them for a prize like Khan. Major Lovelace was not the sort of man you wanted to know outside the army.

Jack said, 'We'll do our best, you know that, Nathan.'

Major Lovelace gave him a rare smile. 'Of course, Jack. By the by, I hear you've been in a spot of bother.'

Jack knew immediately what Nathan was talking about.

'You mean the duel.'

'Yes – a Captain Deighnton I understand? He seems to like duelling. I'm told he's just killed his third man. Very expensive, having a chap like that in our army. Good men are not easy to find.'

'How does he get away with it?' asked Jack frowning. 'Duelling isn't exactly condoned by authority. I felt I was between a rock and a hard place. If he killed me, well then I would be dead. If I killed him, however, I feared a court martial and subsequent punishment. Yet nothing seems to happen to this man, however many duels he fights.'

Lovelace's eyes half-closed as he drew on a cigarello.

'I made inquiries,' he said, as he blew out a thin veil of smoke. 'Someone's protecting him. Those around him, his colleagues, are quite afraid of him – scared to speak out against him. Of course they're also terrified of being ostracized by their fellow officers if they break the code of honour and bear witness. There have actually been two Courts of Inquiry, but the case has petered out both times. Deighnton leads a charmed life. He's under the wing of some high-ranking official – or perhaps more than one?'

'Well, the last officer he killed was just a boy.'

Lovelace raised his eyebrows.

'You saw it? You wouldn't care to bear witness, I suppose?'

'Nathan, I'm as weak as any man when it comes to protecting my honour. I'd be a ruined man . . . even you would look the other way when I walked past. Admit it. You'd cut me dead, wouldn't you, Nathan?'

'I suppose I'd have to. Damn this culture, this upbringing. We're locked in it. What was the boy's name by the way?'

'He was an ensign. I believe they called him Faulks.'

'Faulks? Daniel Faulks?'

'I never heard him called by his first name.'

'I'm sure we're talking of Lord Holbrook's nephew. Interesting,' muttered Lovelace. 'The dispatches that went back stated that young Ensign Faulks fell in battle. Died bravely I think they said.'

'I don't suppose that's unusual.'

'Jack, what do you know of Lord Holbrook?'

Jack shook his head. 'Not a great deal. He's a friend of my father's – or was, when Pa was in his right mind. I believe my brother has met with him once or twice since he assumed control of the estates in Scotland – apart from that, no – not a lot.'

'Hmm. Well, try to stay out of the bastard's way – Deighnton, I mean. He'll get his one day. It always puzzles me how these villains manage to elude death in battle. They're seldom cowards. I've seen him fight. Plenty of elan. Always at the front. War – like golf – is dreadfully unfair, Jack.'

They shook hands and Lovelace left. The pair had been standing a little apart from the rest of the unit, who had pitched their tents. Raktambar was feeding and watering the mounts. Sajan was helping Gwilliams cook over a camel-dung fire. Wynter was ram-cleaning his Enfield. He was not normally one for polishing his kit, but he knew a clean rifle might save his life.

Sergeant King was drawing a map in the leatherbound note-book he carried. It was about half-a-yard long and six-inches wide, this notepad, with good thick paper. He was making a route map, the kind of map a marching army liked best because it was simple to follow, it left out unnecessary detail, and it revealed the shortest distance between two points. From Jack's point of view it looked like a snake wriggling down the page, with only pertinent landmarks on either side.

'I expect you miss your team of helpers, do you not?' he asked King. 'I'm sorry we haven't the time for such work at the moment.'

When they had first come to India, King had asked the lieu-tenant to recruit a band of mapmaker's men to help measure the ground. Men to stand with posts and mirrors. Men to help carry and set up the heavy mapmaker's equipment. The theodo-lite on its own needed two men to lift it. The measuring chain was also extremely heavy, being a hundred feet of steel, and there were other tools just as weighty. A whole team of men and two camel carts had been needed to drag the iron, brass and steel gadgets halfway up India. Now they had been left in Peshawar, awaiting the outcome of the mutiny.

'Yes,' said King, 'I admit it, sir.' He stuck out his square jaw. 'I know it means very little to you.'

Jack stiffened a little. 'I said I was sorry, Sergeant. Don't make me retract the words.'

King looked up from his drawing, not for the first time having forgotten to whom he was speaking. 'Oh – sorry, sir. I have a big mouth.'

'Well, that's not what I came to talk to you about anyway. Tomorrow morning, early, I'm going to take two men with me to reconnoitre the enemy defences. One of them will not be you. I'm leaving you behind with Sajan and Gwilliams. I just wanted you to understand the reasons.'

King raised his eyebrows. 'They being, sir?

'You can't shoot for love or money.'

King knew this and shrugged. 'That hasn't stopped you before.'

'No, but I think three is a good number. I'm obviously taking Raktambar. And I want to give Wynter a baptism of fire. Who knows, he might want to rejoin the regiment afterwards. I would like that. In any case, he's had it soft until now. He needs to be reinitiated into the ways of the spy and saboteur. So there's no room for you.'

'Fine. And what if you don't come back?'
'Get in touch with Major Lovelace.'

The next morning the dawn boiled over the horizon. It was one of the hottest days Jack had experienced in India, being 112 degrees Fahrenheit in the shade. The three riders headed out into the bushy landscape before most of the camp had stirred. Dull-eyed sentries watched them go, wondering if these three were getting out of something bad or getting into it. One of the riders was already complaining and not just about the heat.

'Why me?' whined Wynter. 'Why not one of the others? Gwilliams could've come, couldn't he? He's a better shot than me.'

'This is not about shooting, Wynter, this is about observing. If it comes to a shooting match, all three of us are dead.'

'Do we need this dog along with us?' growled Raktambar. 'Best if we were just two.'

'Who are you callin' a dog?' cried Wynter, kicking his horse to get up alongside the Rajput.

A dark hand flashed out and chopped Wynter across the throat. The private reined in his mount, choking on his own air for a moment. Jack and Raktambar drew up too, waiting for the coughing fit to pass. When he had recovered sufficiently to speak, Wynter gave voice to a series of complaints, all directed at his lieutenant.

'What're you goin' to do about *that*, sir?'

'Do? Nothing. You're lucky that was the edge of Raktambar's hand and not his sabre. I wish it had been his tulwar. It would save me a lot of trouble to leave you here with your throat cut. Just behave yourself. Show some respect to your betters.'

Wynter spluttered, 'I always show respect to officers.'

'I'm talking about Raktambar.'

'*Him*? Why he's a – well – he an't nothing but a . . .' Providence intervened to save Harry Wynter from digging his own grave. He pointed over Jack's shoulder. 'Look, there's some dust up ahead.'

There was indeed a dust cloud, which indicated horsemen.

'Into that clump of trees,' said Jack. 'Quickly.'

Two

The dust cloud out on the plain was being created not by horsemen but by runners. A band of around two dozen Indians appeared out of the shimmering heatwaves like phantoms from another world. They ran past the copse in which Crossman, Wynter and Raktambar were sitting quietly on their steeds. Some of the Indians wore pieces of Company Army uniform, which indicated they had probably been sepoys at one time. Others wore civilian clothes. They were all armed, though many only with bladed weapons. At least one carried an Enfield, which was puzzling since these were the rifles over which the army had mutinied. The sepoys had wanted nothing to do with weapons which needed cartridges greased with animal fat.

As the Indians were trotting by, one of them happened to look into the trees and Jack knew he and his men had been seen. However, though the observer stared for a good few moments, he said nothing to his comrades, and eventually turned away again. Jack was relieved.

'We were seen,' he told the other two, 'but not recognized.'

The reason they were not identified as British soldiers was because they looked nothing like army men. All three wore loose Indian cotton clothing and turbans. Both Jack and Wynter had been weathered and burned by the sun. (Wynter was darker than Raktambar, who had lived and worked in a palace most of his life, though the irony of that fact would be lost on him.) A close scrutiny of Jack and Wynter might reveal the European under the skin, but in the mottled shade of the trees, from a distance of fifty yards, it was impossible to tell.

'Lucky,' murmured Raktambar. 'Very lucky, sahib.'

They rode out of the trees and continued their journey. As they travelled across the Ganges plain, which lay astonishingly flat and mysterious before them, Jack voiced his earlier observation.

'Wynter, how is that your skin is so dark? You've only been in India for a short while, haven't you?'

The disgruntled soldier flashed a look at the back of his own hand to confirm the fact, then argued, 'I an't black.'

'No, I really am curious. Answer my question.'

'We marched here from the Crimea.'

Jack pulled on the reins of his mount, quite astonished. 'You *marched*? What, all of you?'

'Some of us come by ship, some by foot. I was one of them what come by foot.'

Jack knew that British troops had been hastily sent to India from all the nearest countries – Burma, Ceylon, Mauritius, Persia – even soldiers on their way to China had turned back to assist in the quelling of the mutiny. But to march from the Crimea to central India, why that was some feat. It was over 3000 miles, through harsh arid mountain regions, across deserts, swamps, over raging rivers and deep gorges, not to mention jungles.

Jack looked at Wynter with new eyes until the soldier cried, 'What?'

'You're telling me the truth?'

'Why would I tell a lie – you'd find out, eh?'

'What happened on that march?'

Wynter's sly eyes narrowed. He was thinking back to it.

'Not many of us got here. Lots of men died on the way – died of different things – some from fatigue, some was sick and just fell over an' never got up again. Some was killed by tribesmen and such-like. We was attacked a good few times, I can tell you. Some went through hunger, some through thirst. There weren't much water in a lot of places. Some was drowned though,' he added, after reflection, 'in fast rivers, which sounds kind of odd, don't it, after I say we was dead thirsty most of the time? One man, Lance Corporal McGarvey, he shot himself on purpose, not bein' able to go on. A few went mad when their brains boiled in the sun. We never left an able-bodied man behind though. Captain wouldn't let us. We carried 'em until they died, then we buried 'em, pleased they'd gone at last. I hefted Jackson, a pal o' mine, when he got sick, and I weren't unhappy when he passed on. He was bleedin' heavy, that bastard. I cursed him for a friend.'

'I can't imagine the ordeal you've been through, Wynter. Are you listening to this, Raktambar? A terrible trial.'

Raktambar nodded slowly, still smarting it seemed from the insult he had been given, and was not willing to give Wynter credit for anything.

Jack was amazed Wynter had not told him of all this before. He knew the soldier was survivor. Any man who had gone through the Crimean campaign and lived to tell the tale was a survivor. But to live through such a hard march and remain tight-lipped about it showed real character. What a perplexing creature was man, he thought. Harry Wynter was a sewer rat. He was lazy, dirty, foul-mouthed, self-serving and belligerent. He was insolent and untrustworthy. You could look for loyalty in him for ever and not find it. Yet such a man had been among the few – and there could only have been a few – to survive a death march across a continent. That showed grit and determination beyond the norm. That was an enormous achievement. Only men of great fortitude made marches like that.

'Did your captain make it?'

'None o' them officers did. Sarn Major did. He was the ranking officer, when we got 'ere. None of them commissioned ones. One lieutenant went down in quickmud. Never left a ripple on top. Another one fell off a mountain. We could see 'im, all twisted up below, but couldn't get to 'im. He might 'ave still been breathin' for all we knew. Ensign got the cholera or yeller fever or somethin'. He went off with just a sigh. Young lad, not much more'n seventeen years, I would guess. They was all too soft, way I saw it, beggin' your pardon, sir. Not like us at all.'

'Well, hard men die in extremes too.'

'Maybe. Anyways, here I am, back in the fold.'

Despite his loathing for Wynter, Jack was impressed. It was hard not to be. One day he would find out about that march, the full truth of it, and satisfy his own curiosity on the vagaries of life and death. For the moment they were approaching a small village, a gathering of dung-built huts baked hard by the sun. There was one sorry-looking camel standing under a single thorn tree. One or two children were running around, but most were lying in the shade. Jack's eyes scanned the dwellings and saw no untoward signs. They needed to water the horses and there was a well visible in the centre of the village.

'Wynter,' he said, 'say nothing to anyone. Let Raktambar do the talking.'

'Suits me,' said Wynter. 'I can't do that nonsense talk.'

They went directly to the well and dismounted. It was a mere mud hole in the ground with no brickwork, but a greasy rope attached to a leather bowl lay by the opening. Wynter took this item and lowered the bowl into the darkness of the hole. At first he could not get the bowl to take water, then Raktambar, with some impatience, told the soldier to put a weighty stone in the bowl so that it would submerge. Once Wynter did this, he was able to raise enough water for the horses to drink their fill. No one from the village came to ask them who they were or what they were doing. An old woman eyed them from a doorway and two small children stood off from them, watching their every motion. No elders came out. Only a dog came to squeeze between two of the horses and lap the water they spilt.

'Bloody dead-an''-alive place, an't it?' said Wynter. 'Who'd live in a dump like this?'

A few seconds after this a shot came from one of the dwellings, narrowly missing his head. All three men dropped to the ground. One of the horses shied and bolted. Jack reached inside his cottons with his good hand, seeking his revolver. He drew it and waited.

Raktambar yelled, '*Aapka shubh naam kya hai?*' asking for the shooter's name.

'You are not fooling me,' cried a voice from a hut. 'I am hearing you speak English.'

'*Meri samajh men nahin aaya!*' retorted Raktambar.

'Yes, you do understand me. I am hearing English from you.' Another shot and a bullet slapped into the mud near Jack's head. 'We are many here. You will make a surrender or die.'

Remaining with Hindi, Raktamber cried, 'Yes, you heard English, from our prisoner. This scum of a British soldier is our captive. I am a Rajput – can you not hear? Are you an idiot or what? I shall make the prisoner stand up. You can shoot him if you wish. But hear this, we other two are Rajputs on our way to Bareilly to join with the great Khan.'

Jack saw no alternative now but to make Wynter get to his feet. He stuck his revolver in Wynter's face. 'Get up. Stand,' he whispered. 'Quick.'

'I an't standin' up,' cried Wynter. 'You've got another bloody think comin', sir. Not for nothin' I an't.'

Jack kicked him sideways in the thigh.

'Up, up, or I shoot you myself.'

Raktambar took matters in his own hands. He got to his feet slowly, gripped Wynter by the hair and yanked the soldier to his feet. Holding him there, he invited the shooter to leave his hut and inspect the captive.

'Come on out,' cried Raktambar, still talking in Hindi. 'Come and see this squirming rat for yourself.'

There was silence for a while, then the voice said, 'I am coming out, but my comrades will be covering for me. If there is any trickery they will shoot you all down dead.'

After another few moments a small figure in a turban and dhoti came out of one of the huts, a rifle in his hands. When he was halfway across the baked-mud square of the village, Raktambar suddenly dropped the whinging Wynter and drew a pistol from his cummerbund. The approaching man's eyes widened and he raised his rifle, but Raktambar was quicker. He shot the man full in the chest. Jack was on his knees, ready to return fire at any others who opened up at them from the dwellings. No shots came.

'He was alone,' confirmed Raktambar, 'just as I thought.'

Jack got to his feet. There was no one in sight now. The old lady had vanished along with the two children. Even the dog had gone. It was as if the whole village was deserted. Jack went to the dead man and turned him over. He was quite young, perhaps not more than twenty, with handsome features and a lithe body. Yet in height he was no more than four feet eight inches. Not a child though, a grown man. Jack felt some relief at knowing this. For a few minutes he had suspected it was a child.

They went to the hut from which the rebel had emerged and there they found a dead British soldier. His clothes were torn and stained with berry juice and there were scratches – thorn bushes? – covering his face and hands. It would seem he had become detached from his unit, his comrades, whatever, and had struck out on his own trying to find a way back to his camp or column. There were many like him. Civilians too. Wandering around, some half-mad with fear and hunger, many of them naked having been robbed of their clothes.

Others, having been taken in by villagers and hidden from their pursuers, had been treated with utmost kindness. This one had found neither hospitality nor robbers but the enemy.

'Well, we know where that Enfield came from now,' said Jack. 'Some dacoit has got himself a good weapon and isn't fussy about the grease used on the cartridge. Well, there's nothing we can do for this fellow now. Wynter, go through his pockets and see if you can find any identification on him.' The lieutenant looked around him. 'Ah, there's some lamp oil over there. Once you've checked his pockets, pour some on the body.'

They left a few minutes later, unsuccessful in their attempts to find out the dead soldier's name. Raktambar set fire to the hut which served as a pyre for the corpse. The walls were fashioned from crisp palm leaves and the roof thatched with reeds. Both were as dry as kitchen-stove kindling. They went up in a great flaring blaze. The trio had to get out quickly and be on their way. The flames and smoke would be seen for miles.

Jack was aware that now they would probably never find out who the soldier had been, but what was he to do? They could not carry the cadaver with them and to leave it without burial did not seem right. Cremation seemed the only sensible option.

When they were safely outside the village again, Jack said to Raktambar, 'How did you know that rebel was alone?'

'I thought it, though I did not know it. If there were more, they would have given voice along with this one. The rebels are very excited at this time, being free from the British. They like to give voice in their liberty. They are very proud and feel they have their honour back. If he had been with others, we would have heard from them too, not just this one.'

At that moment shots began humming around the three riders. Wynter let out a loud yowl and clutched at his right ear. 'I've been clipped,' he yelled.

Jack, looking behind them, saw that the runners had returned. Without doubt they had come from the same village where Raktambar had shot the man. Perhaps they had left just one of their number behind and now they had arrived back to discover his hut ablaze. On they came now, at a very fast pace, firing their weapons but not pausing to reload.

'Up, up,' cried Jack. 'Leather your horses.'

The three men spurred their mounts and shot forward, out into the dusty plain. Wynter had blood streaming from his ear, but for the moment he was not complaining about it. There was a look of serious intent on his features: the same sort of intent that had got him through that long march from the Crimean peninsula. Raktambar, on the best horse, surged in front. Jack did his best to keep up with his Indian bodyguard, praying that none of their steeds hit an animal hole or stumbled over their own hooves.

Soon the trio left the runners behind, as the pursuers dropped off one by one, until there were none following.

In the late evening they camped in a mango grove where Wynter's ear was patched. After eating they all smoked in silence. Then, exhausted by their ride, all three simply lay beneath the trees and fell fast asleep for the night. Wynter was woken by a wildcat of some kind, which dropped on him by accident from a branch above. It ran off without scratching or biting him, for which he considered himself lucky. In the morning some women arrived to tend to the trees. The three men left the orchard, snatching a bite of salted meat on the ride.

They rode for another day before nearing the houses of Bareilly. As they got closer they could see thousands of rebels gathered around camp fires. The smoke curling up in the windless air created a thick fug. It was the end of the day, when dust, smoke and heatwaves mingled to warp the landscape. A darkening sky was blotched with deep-red smears which might have been cirrus clouds. The noise from the enemy encampments – pots clattering, men gabbling, women shrieking for their children – filled the twilight world.

A wave of stink passed over the trio as they dismounted half a mile from the enemy camp, which recalled for Jack his Crimean days. It was simply the smell of a horde of men. Their cesspits were probably open to the elements. Their urinal patches would be in constant use and the contents would have no time to evaporate. There was probably only just enough water to drink, let alone wash in. They were crowded together, farting and belching, the dregs of their meals rotting on the ground. The stench of thousands of fly-spotted cavalry chargers sweating and defecating on a plain where there was no wind to carry away the unpleasant odours they produced.

Raktambar found a hut with an aged tattooed elephant hobbled outside. The occupant of the hut, a thin and grizzled elderly man, seemed uninterested in his visitors. There were so many men – several thousand of them – in the vicinity. In which case locals like him might easily lose interest. His eyes were wary, as if expecting to have to guard his precious beast, which stood with watery eyes munching hay. Raktambar exchanged greetings with the old man, told him they were only staying the night and would not bother the elephant. This put the old man's mind at rest. He went back to stirring some liquid in a pot over a fire, completely absorbed by the task of thickening his soup.

Since Raktambar had to shout at the old man to get him to hear, they supposed him deaf.

'Well, we're here,' said Jack.

Wynter said, 'Why don't we join this lot instead? Look at 'em. There's thousands of the bastards. Let's swap over. We could be on the winnin' side for once.'

'That's too close to the truth to be humorous,' said Jack. 'I would ask you to keep your suggestions to yourself, Wynter.'

Jack could see the silhouettes of guns against the fading sky. He wanted a closer look at those field weapons, though he knew he would have to wait until dark to do so. In the meantime he could make a note of their number. The snouts of the cannons were visible between the sets of two spoked wheels. Jack counted thirty from his position out on the edge of the army. Khan Bahadar Khan's soldiers had lined them up neatly along a ridge, with exactly five yards between each, as if expecting to give a birthday parade salute to Queen Victoria in the morning. British Army training was a difficult habit to throw off, even for rebels who professed to hate their old masters. There was the gleam of old bronze in the dying sunlight: a mellow light that leapt from barrel to barrel as the day went down.

'I'd like to spike a few of those,' Jack muttered, 'but I suppose that would be too much to ask.'

'Damn right, sir,' said Wynter. 'We need to get back.'

'Unfortunately we do, or our information will die with us.'

When the last of the light had drained from the sky Jack

and Raktambar went on the prowl, leaving Wynter to look after the horses. Jack had done this sort of thing before and found his private missing when he returned from patrols, but this time Wynter had remained put. He was still there, albeit very nervous, when Jack and Raktambar returned. The pair had simply wandered through the encampments, arousing no suspicions since they were dressed similarly to the rebels and they covered the lower half of their faces, as if to escape the effects of smoke and dust. Thus they were able to walk around unmolested, with Raktambar fielding any casual questions or returning greetings. Jack's Hindi and Urdu were up to it, but he knew it was best to keep his mouth shut in case he made a tiny mistake.

'Well?' asked Wynter. 'You goin' to tell me or not?'

'In good time,' growled the lieutenant. Both knew the information had to be shared as quickly as possible, in case they were suddenly discovered. If Raktambar and Crossman were killed or captured, and Wynter survived, it would be up to him to pass on the information to General Campbell. This was not an outfit in which the officer kept things close to his chest, as in a normal unit. Espionage only worked on a share-all basis. The figures and disposition of the foe had to get back to be of any use at all.

Later, Jack Crossman briefed Wynter on what he and Raktambar had learned during their walkabout. They spent the evening counting fires and using the average number of men who might use a fire to calculate roughly the total number of troops. They had walked through the cavalry lines and had noted the number of corrals and the number of horses to each corral. They had strolled the edge of the town and had seen the barracks where the officers were billeted, and had come up with a total there too. By the time they walked back to their bivouacs by the mahout's hut, they had a reasonably good impression of the enemy's strength.

The following morning, before the dawn came up, they rode back towards Campbell's advancing column. This time they avoided the village which the few rebels were holding, though Raktambar wanted to charge in and take them on. These mutineers had dented the Rajput's honour by forcing him to run and he was desperate to repair the damage. Jack had to remind the Rajput that this was not the priority: that they needed to get the intelligence to General Campbell. Happily his body-guard saw the sense in this, though he had had a fleeting thought that he might ride in alone.

On arrival back at the British camp, Jack made his way to the farmhouse which the general was temporarily occupying. Outside was a knot of cavalry officers talking with staff offi-cers. Jack heard the phrase, 'Old Crawling-camel . . .' which he knew referred to General Campbell.

Too late Jack noticed that Captain Deighnton was one of the knot. The cavalry officer looked up and sneered as Lieutenant Jack Crossman passed by.

'You still around?' he murmured.

'Get used to it, Captain,' replied Jack. 'I'm part of the furniture.'

Deighnton turned back to his brother officers and there was some low talk which fortunately did not reach Jack's ears.

The general admitted him straight away.

General Sir Colin Campbell was now grey-haired and leaner than when Jack had last seen him. He turned an intelligent face on the lieutenant and looked him up and down. Jack remained unmoving, wondering whether he was going to get a dressing down for being in Indian cottons, and prepared his defence. There were so many senior officers who were stick-lers for protocol and would rather lose valuable time than have an officer appear before them out of uniform. Campbell, however, was not one of those.

'I know you,' said the older man. 'I know your face.'

'Perhaps you are mistaking me, sir, for my brother. Both my older brother and father served with the 93rd which you commanded. My brother was a lieutenant, my father a major. The Kirks?'

'Ah, I remember Major Kirk, yes. And the younger one. But – no, now I recall quite clearly – ' a triumphant note entered the general's voice – 'you were in the line, one of those from the hospital, a sergeant at the time if my memory serves me well. The thin red line at Balaclava.' He cackled a little with laughter. 'William Russell made us famous, did he not, with his colourful phrase in *The Times*? *"The thin red streak tipped with a line of steel."*'

Jack was absolutely flabbergasted. Campbell could only have seen him briefly as he stood in that line. To remember his face from such a short acquaintance was truly astonishing. Yet there was a story of Campbell recognizing an NCO's voice during a charge in the Punjab some years earlier, thus turning the battle. It was true then, this fabulous memory.

'If you could see your face,' said Campbell, grinning, then taking a sip of something from a cup. 'Well, laddie, your name is *not* Kirk.'

Jack stiffened. 'No, sir, my army name is Crossman.'

'And the reason you reject your family name?'

'I – I joined the army as a private, not wanting my father to purchase a commission for me. It's – it's family business, sir.'

'Uncomfortable, eh? Domestic strife.' The general waved a hand. 'Dinna fash yersel' laddie, Campbell isn't my name either.'

Jack's eyes opened wider. 'It's not?'

'No, I was born a Macliver and I too have been promoted without purchase in my time, so you see we have two things in common. However, I don't come from a lord's family, so I don't know what goes on with boys growing up inside castles and mansions.'

'My father is not a lord, sir. He's only a lowly baronet.'

'My father, sir,' said Campbell, 'was a Glasgow carpenter.'

Jack did not know what to say to this. Sir Colin had a very distinguished army career; he had been elevated to the peerage and was highly respected. What could one say in response to such a revelation? However, the general let him off the hook, by requesting him to come and look at a map spread across a table, and to divulge what he had learned. Jack was only too willing to do so and went into army business mode.

At the end of the briefing Campbell looked into Jack's eyes and said, 'Well done, Lieutenant. A good job. At least I can go in with my eyes open. The figures I've had so far seem to have been heavily inflated. I think I trust yours more. The plain on the approaches to the town are covered with small streams, you say?'

'Yes, sir, and one of them flows right across the south side of the town, but there are bridges intact.'

'Good. Excellent.' The general nodded hard. 'Well, we'll do what we can. I'd like to get my hands on Khan. That'd be a coup.'

'It would indeed, sir.'

'Off you go then. I'll pass on my high regard of your work to Colonel Hawke. See you on the battlefield.'

A bolt of pleasure went through the lieutenant at these words.

'Indeed, sir. I'll be there.'

Just before he turned to leave, Campbell nodded towards Jack's missing hand.

'Crimea? Or here?'

'The Redan. Siege ladder, sir.'

'Hmm, heavy things. You look as if you've been punctured a few times too. Bayonet or bullet?'

Jack grinned. 'Both, here and there.'

'Me too,' replied the general. 'All right, off you go then.'

Jack left the building. Thankfully Deighnton and his cronies had moved on and the landscape was happily clear of spurred and cockaded cavalry officers. Jack joined some infantry officers in the mess tent. There he had drink or two, before going back to see his own men. He briefed King, ruffled Sajan's hair, commended Wynter on his first operation, and told Gwilliams to go and get himself a brandy or two.

'You know where to find it, if anyone does. Not too much, mind. We'll be fighting soon.'

'You know me, Lieutenant. I always mix milk with mine.'

Jack winced at the thought of this concoction.

'Take Wynter with you. Get him to tell you about his emulation of Xenophon's march of the ten thousand across Asia.'

'Eh?' growled Wynter. 'He's not goin' to come the grand scholar with me again, is he?'

Gwilliams licked his lips and prepared to deliver sermons on Ancient Roman and Greek history. He was stopped by Jack's next statement.

'Wynter came here overland,' explained the lieutenant to his corporal. 'A feat not unlike that of our old Greek general's.'

'This I've got to hear,' said Gwilliams. 'Come on, Wynter, let's go and burn our bellies with some o' that rot gut they call brandy.'

Captain Deighnton had ordered his servant to follow the Crossman group after they had left to spy on Khan. The servant had witnessed the small skirmish in the village where the rebel was shot dead. Deighnton had told his man to gather as much detail as he could on the movements and actions of the group. So, unknown to the lieutenant, Jack and his spies were themselves being spied upon. It was not difficult for the servant to carry out his master's wishes, being an Indian who could melt into the landscape. However, the servant's mind was not altogether in accordance with his master's and when he reported back he chose to include whatever material as he thought fit.

Having nothing incriminating to add to his portfolio on Crossman, Deighnton made it his business to keep a watch on him constantly, even in camp. He knew, for instance, that Crossman and Campbell had hit it off, having served together at a momentous battle in the Crimea. That made it difficult for the captain. He decided to stay his hand until General Campbell was no longer around and some other officer was in command.

The following day they were on the march, across that blistering flat landscape which the Ganges often lovingly covered with the folds of its floodwaters. There were many hawks in the sky, which drew the attention of the soldiers. The raptors fell on prey right before the troopers' eyes. They took it to be a good omen. They were the hawks, the enemy, the quarry in the grasses. So they believed. The truth was that a great column like theirs, marching over the countryside, scattered game and birds alike with their heavy tread. There were trumpeting elephants trundling along with guns and supply wagons, thumping the ground with their large feet. There were oxen, horses, camels and other domestic stock, not to mention the feet of thousands of tramping men, drumming the hollow-sounding earth, shaking the world with their heavy armaments and their big boots.

Jack Crossman and his men rode in the vanguard of the column. Wynter's mount made him feel very important. In the infantry regiments only majors and above rode horses, so he felt he was rather superior to the lowly lieutenants and captains of foot. Every so often he was brought down to earth by the man he called 'that bloody mapper'. Sergeant King did not like this new member of the team. Quite rightly he saw in Wynter a slacker, a waster, a conniving scoundrel, and the sergeant was not going to stand idly by while the army was abused. Once he even clipped Wynter behind the ear with the flat of his hand, when the private dropped back too far behind, which incensed his victim.

'I've been through a war, I have,' cried Wynter, out of earshot of the bloody mapper. 'I'm entitled to respect. I've been a sergeant, oh, yes, I've been there. An' I was tough and fair, but not a bloody bully, like that sod of a sergeant. I treated my men with some respect . . .'

Sajan did not like hearing his father insulted. 'You are a bad man, sahib,' said the youngster, waving a finger in Wynter's face. 'If you were one of my soldiers, I would have you whipped.'

'Oh, you would, would you? An' who the bloody hell are you?' said Wynter, snorting indignantly. 'Bloody kids tellin' me what to do now. What are you doin' up 'ere with us, anyways? You'll be lucky if you don't get my boot up your backside, you little *kaffir*.'

'You are a very ignorant man, sir. It is you who are the *kaffir*, not me. A *kaffir* is a Christian, which is you.'

Wynter tried to rescue his self-esteem with a word he had heard that morning from an Irish corporal. 'I meant to say *khalassi*.'

Sajan laughed. 'That means camp follower. Yes, that is precisely what I am, so it is no insult.'

'Where'd you get that horse from, anyway? You shouldn't be up here with the men. You should be back with the women in the baggage train. You should be in the nursery van.'

'My father gave me this horse. The same man you insulted. It will be necessary for my honour to slit your throat while you are sleeping if you continue to abuse him. I was raised by the *Thagi*. They taught me how to kill a man who is sleeping soundly, as you did last night, when you were full of brandy.' Sajan nodded his sage young head. 'Think about that, sir, while you are snoring like a pig in your bed.'

Wynter eyed the young Indian boy with some alarm. It was true he had to sleep within the vicinity of this child of Satan and he believed that kids out here did not give a damn for their masters and betters. He thought that Sajan would poison the hand that fed him if he felt he could get away with it.

Wynter rode up to Gwilliams. 'What's a *Thagi*?' he asked.

'We call 'em thugs,' replied Gwilliams. 'They're a roadside

cult that prey on travellers. They throttle their victims or cut their throats. You don't want to run into any of those bastards. They've got no respect for the likes of you or me. Cut you off in your prime, they will.'

Wynter went back to Sajan. 'Look, kid, you don't understand. In the army it's right and proper for a private to curse his sergeant. It's accepted. That's the way we let off steam, you see. Sergeants know this and they don't take offence, unless it's to their face, of course, then they call it insolence. I don't mean no harm, really. It's just the British way.'

Sajan was having none of it. 'Sahib, you are a stinking fish.'

Wynter began to get angry. 'Now, look . . .'

'You will stay away from me,' said Sajan, spurring his horse.

The private was left to fume. He felt the whole world was against him. He could not even voice his disgust about sergeants now! That wasn't right. It just wasn't right. It was against tradition. It was almost enough to make a man go back to his regiment and do some proper soldiering. But then, when he thought about it, he liked being a member of a special group. He liked to feel important. And he was good at it. Hadn't he saved the lieutenant's life at least once back there in the Crimea? He was good at this job and he wasn't going to be chased out of it by a ten-year-old punkah wallah. If King got killed, which he well might during this campaign, he would wallop that kid until he begged for mercy. But then Crossman and Gwilliams would have to be out of the way too, and that bloody Rajput, Raktambar. The whole world was against him, that was the fact of the matter.

The combined force reached Faridpur on the fourth of May. Faridpur was only a day's march from Bareilly. Here Campbell paused to take stock. Gwilliams and Jack rode out that evening to inspect the defences of the rather loosely built town. They found that Khan Bahadur Khan had set up solid defences outside the pale of the dwellings. The guns set up on the sandbanks were still in the same neat positions. The cavalry were in their place on the flanks, while the second line of infantry lay back in the protection of the building, within the suburbs of the scattered township. Jack returned to make his report and then prepared his own men for the coming fight.

'This is not going to be easy,' he told King, Gwilliams, Raktambar and Wynter. 'I have General Campbell's permission for us to remain on horseback, but we must stay out of the way of the infantry, and of course the cavalry. This is entirely unprecedented so don't shame me by abusing the privilege. We're to keep watch for any breakaway factions and note which way they run. Pursue them if you feel it necessary, but obviously don't catch up with them or engage them, because you'll be unprotected. We're battlefield observers, there to keep account of any retreat. These rebel leaders have a habit of vanishing once their troops look like being overrun. This time it's hoped that observers like us can monitor the situation and keep track of which way Khan goes, should he try to skip.'

'I will observe too,' said Sajan. 'I have good eyes.'

'You do indeed have excellent eyes,' replied Jack, 'but I'm afraid you will be in the rear with the baggage train, young man. We need no distractions.'

'Sahib,' protested the youngster, 'I am almost a man!'

'Almost, but not quite.' He tried to soften the blow. 'Should your father fall in the coming fight, you must be alive to avenge him.'

'In order to do that I must see who kills him,' argued Sajan. 'I must be there in the front to bear witness.'

King said firmly, 'You will stay at the rear. You have been ordered by your commanding officer. It is not a soldier's duty to argue, but to obey. Isn't that so, Raktambar?'

'It is indeed so. Boy, do as you're told.'

Sajan hung his head in a sulk, but knew he was going to get nowhere in this argument, so dropped it.

Early the following morning, before the heat of the day gripped windpipes in its burning fingers, General Sir Colin Campbell's forces marched on Bareilly. The advance parties encountered cavalry but by six o'clock Campbell's force was formed into two lines ready for the attack. There were of course the Highland regiments at the fore, supported by Punjab Rifles and a Baluch battalion. Horse artillery and cavalry were naturally guarding the flanks, but there was a battery in the centre. The remainder of the force formed the second line, protecting the siege-train and baggage detail, where Sajan was located with other camp followers.

At seven o'clock General Campbell gave the order to advance. He was a general who was highly thought of by his troops. Time and time again he had proved his worth against superior odds and had come out victorious. His men knew his reputation, many had served under him in other battles, and they were entirely confident of victory. His courage was renowned, having stood in front of the 93rd Sutherland Highlanders and issuing that now immortal command when faced by the Russian cavalry at Balaclava: 'There is no retreat from here, men! You must die where you stand!'

Artillery fire answered the advance, the round shot falling amongst the British troops, but not seriously impeding them. On seeing the resolute line still coming towards them, the rebels abandoned their guns and fell back to the edge of the town. The British, Sikh, Baluch and Punjabi skirmishers now splashed through the stream and over the bridges. Artillery began to pound the enemy defences. While this bombardment continued, the whole of the British force crossed the stream and lined up ready to take the town.

Jack was at that moment acting as a courier, having been grabbed by a senior officer on his way past, and asked to carry a message to a colonel in the front line. Just as he reached the colonel, there was a counter-attack by Khan's forces. Almost a thousand matchlock men from within the confines of the dwellings opened fire with a tremendous volley, killing Sikh and British skirmishers. At the same time there was a ferocious charge made by over three hundred Rohilla Ghazis: fanatical holy warriors who cared nothing for death so long as they killed at least one of the enemy, ensuring their entry into heaven. The Ghazis carried small round shields and wielded only tulwar swords, but their attack was made in white-hot fury and was difficult to stop. The 93rd closed ranks and bayoneted many of them. The 42nd were a little slower to react to these fierce warriors in green turbans and cummerbunds, their sacred gold rings bearing Koran texts flashing in the sunlight. The attackers threw themselves full length forward, underneath the line of bayonets, and slashed at the legs of the British soldiers.

Jack was close to the front line when three of the Ghazis broke through, slashing this way and that, cutting at their enemy with their razor-sharp sabres. Soldiers of the Company were harvested like wheatstalks. Some just panicked and ran, and were hacked in the back. Then more Ghazis breached the line. Heads rolled. Skulls were split in two. Legs and arms lopped like sapling trees. The Ghazis were terrifying, with their mad rolling eyes and their high-pitched screams. Their sword strokes came in flurries, slashing this way and that.

'*Bismallah,*' a big Ghazi screamed, leaping from ground level to the back of Jack Crossman's horse. '*Allah! Din! Din!*'

Instinctively, Jack's crippled arm went up to protect his head and he managed to ward off a death blow. The Ghazi grabbed his collar and the lieutenant was wrenched backwards. Jack and his assailant fell from the horse's back on to the hard-baked ground. Jack felt the wind knocked from his body, but he continued to struggle with his attacker, trying to tangle himself with the Ghazi's flailing arms to prevent him from using his weapon. He felt a stinging blow above his eye, rendered by the man's heavy gold ring, and instantly realized the Ghazi had lost his sword in the fall. He punched back with his good hand: a blow which merely glanced off the man's shoulder. They rolled in the dust, the Ghazi frantic to kill him and Jack becoming a punchbag for the blows that rained on his head and body.

The Ghazi was a blizzard of fierce energy, as lithe and as slippery as a cat, impossible to stop or contain except by dealing a mortal blow. He was kicking with bare feet at Jack's groin and thighs, scratching with his long nails. Suddenly there was a knife in the Ghazi's right hand. Jack managed to grip the man's wrist. This left him punching with his stump, rather than with a fist, which was most ineffectual. He was vaguely aware that all around him others were having to deal with Ghazis creating havoc despite their slim numbers. They were frenetic in their attacks, as determined as the ancient berserkers they resembled. Even bullets, unless in the heart or head, only seemed to stun them for a second. On they came, cutting down infantry with their tulwars, dragging officers from their horses.

While Jack was still struggling blindly with his persistent Ghazi, feet were treading all over him and his attacker. Bare feet and booted feet. Above them rifle butts were thudding into bodies. Bayonets were piercing flesh. Swords were chopping away limbs. Blood sprayed on both men. Finally Jack managed to get an armlock on the Ghazi's throat. He tried to throttle his opponent, tried to break his neck. His right arm would have been stronger, would have done the job, but he dare not release his adversary's wrist which wielded the dagger. Finally his own loose horse, whinnying and stamping, terrified out of its mind by the writhing mass of bodies and the noise, trampled upon both of them, causing Jack to loosen his grip. The Ghazi squirmed out from under and was again on top. Now the dagger was poised to plunge into Jack's face. On the Ghazi's features was a twisted expression of utter triumph.

Jack had no idea what happened next. He realized he was being showered with warm sticky blood. The grasp upon his throat had suddenly relaxed and when he looked up his assailant was gone. It seemed the Ghazi had simply vanished into thin air. Jack sat up. The furore was still gushing and foaming around him but many of the Ghazis now lay dead on the ground. There was a headless corpse next to him. Blood was spurting from the neck on to the ground. A short distance from the corpse was a head.

A hand helped him to his feet. It belonged to Raktambar. In the Rajput's other hand was the tulwar dropped by the Ghazi.

'You beheaded him?' said Jack, dazed.

'I did my duty,' replied Raktambar. 'I am your protector. I took his head from his shoulders with his own weapon.' He now tossed the tulwar on to the corpse. 'It is done.'

Jack could tell the deed was tasteless to Raktambar. Yet again the man had saved his life. Once upon a time Jack would have said he needed no one to protect him. But this was a land where men had to watch each other's backs in order to survive at all. They were two soldiers, he and Raktambar, who needed to be a unit in themselves. Each had saved the life of the other half-a-dozen times in this war in which – under normal circumstances – they should be on different sides. But this was a war in a land where the rulers had frequently come from outside: a land continually conquered by foreigners, from Macedonian Greeks to Samerkandian Moguls to clerks from a London-based trading company. A vast land that had known no single ruler, where tribal and religious loyalties were fuel for wars.

As Jack led his horse away from the battle, berating the beast for panicking, Captain Deighnton rode by at a gallop and looked down on him.

This is the last thing I need, thought the dispirited and disconsolate lieutenant, to be seen walking from the field by that man.

Jack felt beaten. The day, as it turned out, was a victory for the British. The enemy had fled inside the town, and with them its leader, Khan. The battle for Bareilly had been won by Jack's side, but the victory was a little hollow in that Khan was still at large. Despite their keenness Jack's men failed in their observations. No one had seen which way the retreating Khan had gone: he had been hidden amongst the thousands of his army who had broken and scattered, and later reformed.

General Campbell moved his own men into empty houses outside the town, telling his officers to be ready for a morning attack.

Lieutenant Jack Crossman washed himself and groomed his horse. He offered it soothing words. His mount had been through almost as much terror as Jack himself and it needed this attention. Jack was not normally one to mollycoddle his steed. Though he would never mistreat an animal, he was not one of those Britons who worshipped horses. Jack preferred machines to living creatures. Horses, he found, sometimes turned right when you asked them to turn left. Machines, on the other hand, almost always did as they were told.

'Good boy,' he said, patting the gelding's neck. 'That wasn't your fault today, it was mine. I should have been more attentive. On the other hand, if you see a lunatic fanatic flying through the air at me again, I would urge you to bolt immediately and take the consequences later. Even should you be severely reprimanded for leaving the field of battle, you'll be much easier in your mind knowing you've done the right thing.'

Raktambar on the other hand treated his horse as if it were a god, and would have laid down his own life to save it from harm. He fussed over it, went out of his way to get the best fodder for it, called it Inesh, which he told Jack meant King of Kings, and generally treated it with huge respect and great reverence. He abhorred Jack's attitude to his own mount.

'You treat your beloved horse as if it was a *Sudra*,' said

Raktambar to Jack. The Rajput was speaking of the lowest Indian caste bar the *Mlecca* untouchables. 'It is a serf to you.'

They were in Jack's quarters in an old camel stable, talking over the day's fighting. Raktambar had not liked the way Jack had berated his mount immediately after the battle, for treading all over him and his assailant while they had been wrestling on the ground.

'I certainly don't treat it like a lord, which is how you treat yours,' agreed Jack. 'Beloved it is not. My horse is merely an animal who carries me because I feed and groom him. A virtually mindless beast. Would you have me endow him with human reasoning? Or emotions? Certainly not. A beast is what he is and I respect that fact. I don't believe in getting emotional over a creature who only obeys me through instinct. I feel the same about pet dogs, which should earn their living, as do hunting and sheep dogs. Inesh earns his keep by being obedient to you on the battlefield and off it, but don't mistake his obedience for anything else. He is not grateful, he is not affectionate, he has no feelings for anyone but himself.'

'Inesh loves me,' protested Raktambar, 'and I him.'

'Then you are both fools to my way of thinking.'

'The horse is a noble creature. You should be ashamed to talk as you do, sahib. It is a high and splendid beast.'

'It is a slave, much as the dog is a slave, and there's an end to it.'

They were becoming heated with one another and beginning to say things neither actually believed, just to score one over on the other. They both realized this so let the subject drop for the time being.

Jack picked up his torn tunic, took a needle and thread, and began sewing up one of the many rips and tears it had sustained that day. He broke the silence.

'How do you think the Sikhs fared today?'

Normally a Rajput might be chary of giving a Sikh any credit in battle, but to give him his due Raktambar was generous to his rival countrymen when it came to fighting, especially when conversing with British officers. It was, understandably, a case of *I am against my cousin, but my cousin and I are against the stranger*. Jack was still the stranger in this land, and a Sikh was for present purposes cousin to the Rajput.

'I believe they did well, sahib.'

'So do I. So do I,' said Jack, with a little reflection. 'I wonder what it is that makes Sikhs so good in battle. I mean, Bengalis are brave – especially the rebel sepoys themselves – but the Sikhs seem to have a passion for battle, much like the Pathans.'

This was a little too much for Raktambar. 'The Rajputs are better than both,' he said testily.

'Oh, that's taken for granted,' replied Jack airily, knowing that wounded pride never made his companion a good conversationalist. 'I take that to be a fundamental truth, but I'm with you all the time so I don't feel I have to mention it. No, no, what I'm after is what's behind the Sikh who wields the sword.'

Raktambar allowed himself to be mollified.

'That, sahib, is not easy to answer. The Sikhs though – as you know – had a big big empire under Maharajah Rangit Singh who led the Khalsa, the army of the faithful, into many winning battles. They are fearsome warriors, when led by good generals. Especially the *Akalis*.'

Jack had met Sikh *Akalis*, religious warriors who always carried an excessive number of weapons on their person – knives, two or three swords, pistols, and even some razor-sharp throwing quoits which they wore around their pointed turbans when they were not in use. The latter they would throw at the enemy at close quarters, amputating limbs and heads (so it was said) and generally causing a great panic in the ranks of the foe.

'Yes, but what's behind the ordinary Sikh soldier, the man who is simply there because he's told to be?'

Raktambar shrugged. 'You know there are five things which a Rajput fights for? I have told you these.'

'Yes, ranging from homeland to cattle. Is it the same with Sikhs?'

'Not the same, but near. They have five things they must keep close to them. They are the five Ks which all Khalsa wear to remind them that they are Sikhs and bound by their faith to their Guru.'

'And those are?'

'*Kesh* – the uncut hair. *Kara* – a steel bracelet on their wrist. *Kanga* – a wooden comb . . .'

'Necessary, of course, because of the long hair,' replied Jack, rather too flippantly.

'Please, sahib,' Raktambar said with a dark look, 'you must not make fun while I am trying to teach you things.'

'Sorry,' said Jack, trying to be contrite. 'Continue with the lesson.'

'Next is *Kaccha*, the cotton undergarments.'

'Cotton underpants, yes,' said Jack with a straight face. 'And the final symbolic item?'

'*Kirpan*, the sword, the most important of all.'

'All right, I'm sorry I was facetious there, Raktambar. One should never make fun of religious symbols and you were right to upbraid me. We British are an unfortunate group of nations, we make fun of all things beyond our understanding to hide the shame of our ignorance. India is so complex and we have a simple love of humour coupled with a natural cheerful disposition. Forgive me?'

'I think so,' said Raktambar suspiciously, still worried that Jack was making fun of him, 'if you are truly ashamed.'

'Well, look at it from our point of view. As if it is not enough to know there are many many religions in India, all of which are immensely difficult for the foreigner to grasp, within those religions there are – I am reliably informed – some three thousand castes and twenty-five thousand sub-castes. How can I, a newcomer, hope to understand even a little of what is India?'

Raktambar smiled now. 'Even I,' he said, 'do not know everything.'

'There you are,' said Jack. 'Now if you don't mind I shall try to sleep; I'm exhausted.'

Jack had wisely used the conversation, artificially inspired by him, in order to try to shed some of the terrors of the day. In fact he had been so close to violent death he could not stop shaking under his blanket and when sleep finally came, it was not blessed rest, but a real torture of the mind. His nightmares were excruciatingly horrible, leaving him in pools of cold sweat and the agony of a brain twisted by horrific events. If ever he and Jane managed an ordinary married life after this, his wife would very lucky, for he carried in his mind visions of hell that would never leave him. When he woke fully in the middle of a terribly hot night he felt as if he had been wrung out by the hands of a giant and left knotted and creased to dry.

It was a little while before he realized it was the lightning and thunder which had woken him. The heat was unbearable. His throat was parched and he felt as if it were crammed with dead, dry insects. His head was hammering and his eyes were being attacked by needles of pain. Groggy, he sat up, hearing chaos around him. Crawling to the stable doorway he looked out at a world that was almost as tortured as his brain.

He had seen this before, but not so bad. An incredible heat storm had broken during the dark hours. There were lightning flashes all around, spooking the horses and other animals, and worrying the men. Clouds of dust whirled within a strong hot choking wind. In the shifting restless moonlight, black clouds raced around the sky, butting each other like rutting beasts. The trees thrashed and lashed the air around them, whipping each other's trunks if they were close. Objects flew across the ground, vanished into it, and then reappeared from wild flailing shrubs and bushes.

'The world has gone mad,' muttered Jack. 'Nature is revolting along with the locals at our presence here.'

But this was fanciful reasoning from an embattled mind. In the early hours of any morning a man with a conscience is attacked by imaginary forces and believes in their power. Jack was as susceptible as anyone to such an onslaught and after getting a drink of water from a canteen, he lay down in the dreadful heat and waited for hell to open and drag him in. It could not be hotter there, he thought. Nowhere could. This was the hottest place on earth or in heaven and hell. This was an oven like no other. Hell would be a cool and blessed relief from this torment of suffocating swelter.

Three

T hat long hot night seemed to last forever. Jack rose in the early dawn and in trousers and shirt walked from the camel stable down to the nearest stream to wash. The water was not as cool as he hoped it would be and there was a faint pinkness to it. Still he washed, and also drank, having little choice. There was a whole army to water and the only source these little brooks. He felt a little ill afterwards, but whether it was the effect of the tainted water, or simply the thought of bodies fouling it upstream, he was not sure.

He was halfway back to his quarters when he heard distant artillery opening up. The blasts appeared to be coming from the far side of the town. General Campbell's own guns then sent out a reply. After a while it became apparent that there were two armies sending shells and shot into the clustered houses of Bareilly, one on either side. General Campbell was not alone in his attempts to subdue and capture Khan Bahadur Khan.

Raktambar met him as he approached the stable.

'Sahib, a rider has just arrived. There is one General Coke on the far side of Bareilly!'

'Coke? He's there?'

'He has come from the other way, with his own column, sahib.'

Two individual friendly forces attacking the same town almost at the same time! That was extraordinary. But what was more extraordinary, and very aggravating – Jack later learned – was that Khan had abandoned the town in the night, taking his army with him. Here were two large British columns and they still let thousands of rebels slip away during the night. Jack found out that General Coke had sent his cavalry after the fleeing rebels, but it was unable to prevent the evacuation. Khan was gone, and most of his men with him. The British had allowed the enemy to get away yet again.

General Campbell had sent a young officer to bring Jack Crossman to his presence.

'Lieutenant,' said the cornet who came to collect Jack and hurry him across the rough ground to the general's quarters, 'I'm told that the general admits to making a mistake. He's very frustrated. He said he knows he should have gone after Khan yesterday. The day was hot and he thought to rest the men before making a concerted attack amongst the houses. Street fighting is a difficult and demoralizing business and one needs every ounce of fortitude for such a task, don't you agree? I don't blame the general.'

Nor should you, thought Jack, being only a seventeen-year-old boy whose chin had barely met a razor. But he didn't say so, for the cornet was clearly almost as frustrated as his general and just giving vent to his feelings. It was a most disappointing business. Coke too had obviously not gone in yesterday, or Khan would now be in chains. Whether this young whipper-snapper scurrying by Jack's side had seen enough street fighting to give this learned opinion was unknown to Jack, but he himself had seen plenty and knew the ugliness and difficulties.

The recapture of Delhi had been a massive exercise in street fighting. The city's alleys and narrow passageways had been boiling with ferocious soldiers and rebels: packed to the doors and walls with pistoleers and swordsmen all struggling to kill one another. At times the melee had been so crowded that Jack's arms had been pinned to his side and all he could do was glare into the face of a foe equally stymied. It had been a terrible and bloody business, ending the lives of many good officers and men, among them the famous warrior-clerk John Nicholson.

General Campbell was indeed frustrated. There was a look of mental agony on his face. He knew he had made a wrong decision and allowed his enemy to live and fight another day.

'Ah, Lieutenant,' he said. 'You survived yesterday?'

'Just about, General. One of those Ghazis . . .' He stopped, realizing the general did not want a full description of his efforts on behalf of queen and country. 'Yes, yes, as you see, I survived.'

'Good.' The general paced the floor, his hands behind his back. Around a wooden table covered in maps were impatient-looking staff officers, silent and grim, waiting for Campbell to brief this one-handed lieutenant about whom they knew almost nothing except that he wore the insignia of the 88th Connaught

Rangers. 'Now, we must track him down again and finish him off. You and your men must find out where he's gone.'

'We'll do our best, sir.'

'That's all, Lieutenant. Send me word as soon as you can.'

Jack having been dismissed, the general and his staff went back to their former deliberations. He heard 'Intelligence' mentioned as he left. Jack hurried across the lumpy ground to the camel stable. Sergeant King was outside watering the horses.

'Where's Raktambar, Wynter and Gwilliams?' asked Jack. 'We have to ride out once I have changed my clothes.'

Once the five men were gathered, Jack split them up into three factions, in order to cover three different compass points.

'Gwilliams and Wynter will go south, to see what they can find in that direction. Raktambar, I'm going to ask you to go out alone. Is that acceptable to you? Good. You will go north-west. Sergeant King and myself will take the north-eastern route. It's very doubtful Khan will have turned back and gone directly west, towards Delhi, where the rest of our forces hold sway, so I'm going to ignore that area. Take water and food with you. See if you can pick up the direction the rebels took, once they were out on the plain, and get word back to the general as quickly as possible.'

King left the boy Sajan in the care of one of the camp followers and joined Jack, setting out north.

'I hear General Coke has arrived,' said King by way of conversation as they rode out. 'When will the two forces join?'

'Tomorrow, I imagine. Now, let's find out where Khan has gone, and finish this bloody business for good.'

Crossman and King drifted about a quarter of a mile apart in order to cover a larger amount of ground. They kept each other in sight. Signs of the evacuation of the town were all round the perimeter, the occupants having scattered every which way in the beginning. What Jack's men were looking for was the rallying point and to then discover where the enemy had headed after that.

The two searchers had only been riding about an hour when Jack saw King's arm go up and wave to him. Jack urged his horse towards the sergeant. When they met up, King pointed to marks in the dust. Clearly a great number of people had gathered in this spot and had headed out towards the north-east. The pair had discovered Khan's direction.

King consulted a map which he opened and rested on the neck of his horse. 'Pilibhit,' he said with satisfaction. 'That's where he's going, unless he veers off.' He looked up and studied the landscape. 'Nothing much beyond Pilibhit except the border of Nepal, and he won't go in there.'

'No. The King of Nepal wouldn't view an incursion of that size very favourably. Khan won't risk incensing the Nepalese. He'd be caught between two armies. I'll wager he intends to rest at Pilibhit and then move on somewhere.' Jack made a decision. 'You must ride back, Sergeant King, and take the news to the general. I'll continue towards Pilibhit to make sure Khan doesn't sheer off somewhere along the road.'

'Wouldn't you be better coming back with me, sir? Khan may leave some units along the road to protect his rear. You're only one man . . .'

'I think I know what I'm doing, Sergeant.'

'Very well, sir,' replied King stiffly. 'I shall inform the general.'

He galloped his horse back the way they had come and Jack continued on at a slow and easy pace, his eyes keenly studying all horizons. It was just over thirty miles from Bareilly to Pilibhit and there was no sense in thundering ahead. A retreating army, dispirited and dull of mind, travels reasonably slowly. Jack didn't actually want to catch up with them. He just wanted to follow at a distance and make sure they didn't change direction.

This he did for the next few hours. When evening came the trail was still heading the same way, towards Pilibhit. Jack decided that in the morning he would turn back towards Bareilly, having established that Khan was not going to tack in another direction. Riding during the dark hours was not impossible, but it was not a sensible option either. It was better to let his mount and himself rest, and ride back refreshed in the morning.

After watering and feeding his horse, Jack did the same for himself, then he lay on a single blanket on the bare ground. He was a little concerned about cobras, but knew that although the cobra is an aggressive snake, mostly men were bitten when they trod on the creatures. If one should come he would be best to leave it to slide over or around his body, without disturbing it. The idea made him shudder with apprehension, but in India snakes, scorpions and huge spiders were a fact of life. You could spend your whole time worrying about encounters with them, if you let yourself. Better to adopt a casual attitude towards wildlife and hope for the best.

He awoke without being molested just as the sun was rising.

The first thing he noticed was the muzzle of a musket which was pointing at his face from about six inches away.

'*Meri samajh men nahin aaya!*' he said.

'No, no – ' a half-uniformed sepoy waved a finger in his face and smiled – 'you are an Englishman – please do not insult my intelligence.'

Jack went up on to his elbows and stared at a ring of men standing round him. Clearly they were rebels. They had hold of his horse – the treacherous beast had simply changed sides in the night – and had removed his weapons from his side.

'You are our prisoner, sir, and will remain so.'

The man who spoke to him was badly scarred about the face: blade cuts by the look of them. But they were old scars, obviously not obtained in the recent uprising. He was a big fellow, not young, with a neat silver-edged haircut. On his tunic were the stripes of a havildar, a sergeant in the Indian Army, now dirty and spotted with black blood. Indeed he did not look at all stupid and Jack was not going to 'insult his intelligence' any further.

'Well, get it over with,' growled Jack testily. He was surprised to find he was not afraid. 'Shoot, damn it.'

The havildar waved a finger again.

'No, no, sir. You are not understanding me. We have no wish to kill you. Not yet. You are our hostage, sir, and will remain so.'

'Hostage?' Jack felt hopeful. It was then he noticed that they had another prisoner, a westerner like himself, in a frill-fronted shirt and tight black pants. The man had his hands tied behind his back and was held by two men who gripped him firmly. Jack ignored the other man and continued speaking to his captor. 'You are taking me to Khan?'

'Not really, sir. By mutual agreement we have left the army of Bahadur Khan and are now free men. But soon the British will begin to hunt us down. We shall go somewhere not to be found. If they catch up with us, then we will offer to kill you unless they leave us alone. That is our plan.'

Deserters, Jack realized, and desperate ones by the look of them. They had first mutinied from the British Army and now had abandoned Bahadur Khan's force. It was obvious they wouldn't be welcomed by anyone, anywhere, and were heading for the gallows. They were a fated group of souls with nothing to lose, being little more than bandits now. Jack and the other prisoner had to be very careful not to set off any panic amongst this forlorn crew of ragged unhopefuls.

'It sounds a good one to me,' said the other captive, speaking for the first time. He was not an Englishman. Jack could hear a clipped accent which sounded Scandinavian to his ears. 'I'd go along with a plan like that, wouldn't you, sir?'

The last remark was addressed to Jack.

Jack nodded. He was forced to his feet by rebels and then, because of his missing hand, his arms were bound at the elbows rather than the wrists. His legs were left free, presumably so that he could walk. And walk he did, for the next few hours, while the rebels took turns to ride his horse. All this time he said nothing to the other captor, who had indeed tried to speak to Jack, but had been struck by a rifle butt for doing so. Jack was also hit for dragging his heels, which of course he did hoping they would be overtaken by his own men. Once he looked back in hope, but saw that no one was following them, not even at a great distance. Only a decrepit old camel, like a walking moth-eaten rug, plodded across the horizon.

It was of some consolation to Jack that the rebels had told him the truth. They obviously were no longer part of the Khan army. They veered away from Pilibhit and seemed happy with open countryside. There were few delights out there. The occasional frangipani tree offered a relief from the boredom and they also passed the carcasses of bloated beasts being tussled over by buzzards, but for the most part the scene was uninteresting. They followed a watercourse towards the foothills of the Himalayas, skirting both Nepal and the various villages on the way. When midday came, with its head-hammering sun, Jack was ready to collapse. Fortunately, so were many of the rebels – Jack counted twenty-three of them – and there was a rest stop.

He was propped against the trunk of an old tamarisk tree and his arms were untied so that he could give himself a drink.

'If you run, we shall be forced to shoot you,' he was told. The speaker had a reflective thought before adding, 'If just one runs away, we will shoot the other one too. We will shoot you both together.'

'Bound together in friendship,' said the other prisoner, 'whether we like it or not.'

'Where are you taking us?' Jack asked one of the more accessible rebels, a small chubby man of about twenty. 'You've got far enough away from any pursuers to be able to let us go now.'

Jack could speak Hindi and Urdu, but he did not want to let his captors know that, as he wanted to secretly follow their conversations. He had already heard one hard-faced character tell his companions that they ought to kill their prisoners before crossing the border into Chinese Tibet. However, another man had argued that they were all in just as much danger from the Chinese Emperor as they were from the British, since it was death for *any* foreigner found inside Chinese Tartary. This individual suggested they keep Jack and the other European alive and use them to bargain with, should the group be discovered by either Tibetans or Chinese. No conclusion had yet been reached and their fate still hung in the air.

'No, no, sir,' replied the man, answering Jack's question. 'You must stay with us until we are very, very safe.' He looked into Jack's eyes. 'No harm will come to you. We wish no blood on our souls. You will be treated like proper sahibs.' The little man grinned at him.

'Thank you,' said Jack, pretending he was relieved. 'I knew we were in the hands of real soldiers.'

The other prisoner laughed out loud. 'You gullible idiot. As soon as they don't need us, they'll blow off our heads. Isn't that right, Fatty?'

The portly sepoy shook his head. 'No, no. No one wishes to kill you.'

'What a lie,' said the other man, still laughing. 'What a big fat fib!' He suddenly switched to becoming passionately angry with his captors. He began struggling with his bonds and kicking out at them with his feet. 'If I could just . . . I'll break your heads for you, you bastards. Call yourself men? I'll take on any one of you! Just take these cords off and I'll show you how *real* men fight. Two of you, no, three of you at once! Knives if you like. No, let's duel like civilized men. Pistols. We'll fight with pistols. Ten of you line up with your weapons. I'll just have my single-shot pistol. I'll put you all in your graves, I will. God give me strength . . .'

He cursed and swore and struggled, telling the rebels he

was going to gut them like fish once he got his hands free. Then, just as suddenly, he burst into tears and began blubbing like a babe. Globules of liquid streamed down his dirty face, leaving white tracks in their wake. He sobbed for at least twenty minutes while one or two tried to reassure him. Fatty repeated the hollow promises that he would *not* be harmed, but the captive shook his head and wept like a widow in mourning, saying he didn't believe it and he knew he would be murdered soon.

When they turned away from him in embarrassment, his face broke into a huge grin and he startled Jack by winking at him and nodding sagely.

Then in a calm voice he called for tea, saying he wanted his afternoon *chai* and how long must a man wait for his refreshments?

'You shall be my *khidmargar* when we get out of here,' he told the man who brought him some tea. 'My butler-waiter. But just for a while though, until I can make you into a *Nazir*, for anyone in my employ gets automatic promotion by the week. If you stay with me long enough we shall be sure to make you into a nawab, ruler of a province. How does that sound? Not bad for a tea-bringer, eh? One moment an abductor, the next a nawab. What, have you no ambition? Seize the day, fellow, make something of yourself! Forget these other ne'er-do-wells and strive for independence. You are your own master.'

The man who gave him the tea smirked at him, as if he were some kind of maniac on a leash, then left him to sup the warm tea. Jack had his arms tied again, and this time his feet too, for good measure. Both he and the other captive were lashed to the tamarisk tree. Then most of the Indians fell asleep, leaving just two of their number awake, to keep watch. Jack and his companion were now able to exchange whispers without being kicked.

'Who are you?' asked Jack, being the first to speak.

'My name is Rudi Hilversum,' came the reply. 'I am originally from Amsterdam. I came to India as a boatswain on a clipper, but jumped ship to make something of myself. Now I deal in firearms. You see that black leather bag one of those fellows is carrying?' He pointed at it with his chin. 'Those are the pistols I have for sale. They were stolen from me and I shall take great pleasure in killing the pig who took them.'

Jack was amused, despite their situation. 'You think you'll get out of this?'

The Dutchman was a handsome dark-haired man of about thirty-five years. He had a two-inch scar on his right cheek-bone. Serious brown eyes regarded Jack. They were the eyes of an actor. They changed expression by the second.

'Of course,' he answered. 'You have to believe that, don't you? If I didn't I would fall into a melancholic state and be good for nothing. Hey, how did you like my performance? What? It keeps them guessing, you see, if you pretend you're half-mad. They don't know what to do with me. It worries them to have this creature whose moods jump back and forth. You don't have a smoke on you, do you? I would kill for a cigar or a pipeful of tobacco. I'll pay you back later, once we've killed this rabble . . .'

Jack shook his head. Perhaps his Dutch companion *was* half-mad. Jack could not help but admire his effervescent nature.

He then asked Hilversum, 'How is it you speak good English?'

The Dutchman snorted. 'English isn't a difficult language. You should try Finnish. Or Cantonese. Do you know each word in Cantonese has nine meanings, all very different? Chinese dialects are tonal languages. You have to say the word in the right tone, or it means something completely different. The word *tong* for instance, when pronounced in a high falling pitch means "soup", but in a low falling pitch means "sugar". On the other hand, in Cantonese there are no tenses, no plurals and no arti-cles. "Me go ship yesterday" is exactly what a Cantonese speaker would say in his own tongue. Who are you, by the way?'

Jack had almost fallen asleep. 'Lieutenant Jack Crossman, of the 88th Foot, a regiment raised in Connaught in Ireland.' He had told the truth, not necessarily the right thing to do in such circumstances, but inventiveness had failed him.

'I thought you Catholic Irish didn't like the Protestant English?'

'I'm not Irish. In any case, you can't blame an entire nation for the actions of a few. There are those in England – and Scotland – who deserve to be hated by the Irish, but not the majority of the population. There are Catholics in England and Protestants in Ireland too.'

'Well,' said the other, 'are you an Honourable East India Company man? Are you one of those warrior-clerks?'

'No, I'm Queen's Army, not Indian Army.'

'You won't get rich that way. It's better to be a John Company man, then you rise quickly, fleece the natives, and build yourself an empire out here. Then you can go home when you're fed up and buy a huge estate in the country, a townhouse in London and live like a king. I know a man who was just a Company writer ten years ago and now he's a resident. Led a few border skirmishes, squeezed revenues from some unwilling tribes, rose from lieutenant to colonel in a few months. That's the sort of career you should be chasing, not this Queen's Army stuff. Have you no ambition?'

Jack gritted his teeth. He was beginning to become exasperated with this Dutchman who ran off at the mouth all the time.

'Not that kind of ambition. I'll have you know I'm a baronet's son and have no need of such an unsavoury career.'

'Younger son, I'll wager.'

'Yes, but . . .'

'Ha, I thought so. Choice of two careers only. Army and Church. Too restless to be a pasty-faced pastor, so the only thing left open was to purchase a commission in the army. Did Daddy put up the money?'

'I'll have you know,' spluttered Jack, 'that I joined as a private and worked my way up through the ranks.'

'And Daddy's peerage rank had nothing to do with it?'

'Not in the slightest. In fact my father tried to block my promotion. He did not approve, you see, of a son with an iron will of his own.'

'I don't blame him. I'd have cut you off without a penny. What nonsense. Who gave you these idiotic principles? A mother, I suppose? They're a woman's work, principles like those.'

'I swear if I ever get out of this,' growled Jack, 'I'll plant you a facer so hard you'll need a new nose.'

'It's no use getting frustrated with me,' protested the indignant Dutchman, 'it's your mother you should be angry with.'

At that moment one of the sepoy sentries came over and demanded that they stop talking. Both captors sat fuming silently until the rest of the rebels woke. Then they were on their way again. Towards the evening they approached a village. The rebels, with one or two badmashes amongst them, were heavily armed. Jack heard them talking in Hindi about raiding the village for supplies. One or two said they ought to kill any men they saw, but leave the women and children alone. The havildar who had first spoken to Jack was against any killing, he said, while he was in charge.

'Why are you the leader?' asked a scruffy-looking fellow with one eye and a hawkish nose. 'There is no rank here now. You are not in the army any more.'

'I am the leader because I am the most senior and also the most intelligent,' replied the havildar, 'which was why I was given my chevrons in the first place.' He took a pistol from his belt. 'Also I will punish you badly if you defy my authority. I have around me men from my regiment who are loyal to me. You are new to our company and I forgive you for not knowing this, but if you speak to me again like that I shall surely shoot out your one good eye and leave you either dead or blind.'

The objector looked around him and saw that several of the sepoys were glaring at him. His head went down and he mumbled that he was sorry for his indiscretion and begged them to pardon his ignorance. However, if they were to eat they would have to raid the village, that much had to be true, and if the village defended itself, they would need to kill.

'Five of us will go down,' said the havildar, 'and the rest stay here.'

He and four others then took their weapons and walked down towards the village. Thankfully, from Jack's point of view, there was no shooting and the group returned a short while later with food and drink. It was survival of the best armed, whether with weapons of war or with the laws of the country.

Once the five had left for the village, the Dutchman had immediately begun working on the badmash who had stood up to the havildar.

'You would be wise to let us go,' he said quietly to the fellow, 'for if you are caught abducting two Europeans, they will hang you for sure.'

'They will hang me anyway, for fighting the *firinghis*.'

'No, for I will speak in your favour. I will tell the authorities how you were forced to join these rebellious sepoys at gunpoint. I saw how that pompous havildar spoke to you. Do you deserve such treatment? No. A man of your fine character must be thoroughly insulted by such words. It must grieve you indeed to put up with this kind of behaviour from a mere havildar in a foreign army. Did you join the English, when they came? No, you stood back, proud of your heritage, and spat at their feet. While that fellow grovelled, took their *annas* and became one of them.'

'Ha!' said the badmash. 'You must speak Hindi?'

'Indeed I do,' replied the Dutchman. 'A little.'

Jack groaned, knowing this advantage had now been thrown to the winds.

The Dutchman was oblivious to his error and continued to try to befriend the one-eyed man. 'I do not need to speak the language to see how arrogantly that havildar spoke to you, and how angry you were at his words. It was written all over your noble face. You are surely the descendant of a rajah, are you not? You have in your features the very image of the Rajah of Jodhpur. Are you sure you're not related to him? He has a nose the very likeness of yours. A very aristocratic nose handed down to him by his early ancestors, conquerors every one of them. I have seen a statue of the great Iskander: your nose copies his to the very curve at the end. How does a royal personage such as yourself, a man with such rich blood in his veins, find himself in these low and uncomfortable circumstances? Surely you have been a most unlucky man?'

All the while the Dutchman was speaking the badmash was running his fingers down the slope of his nose, looking thoughtful.

'Oh, sir,' he said, 'you would be amazed by my poor luck. All my life I have been the victim of bad fortune.' He struck his own head with the heel of his hand. 'The gods have not seen fit to show favour to me. Each time I lift myself up from the dirt, I am thrust back down again. It is a source of great anguish to me, that through no fault of my own, I am reduced to such circumstances as you see me in now.'

Jack sat and watched these exchanges in amazement at the Dutchman's silver tongue. Surely the badmash was not falling for such drivel. The flattery Hilversum was spilling out was so obvious a child could have seen through it. At every moment Jack was expecting the badmash to burst out laughing and tell the Dutchman he knew exactly was he was doing. It was so transparent it was indeed laughable. Yet the fellow was lapping it up like milk.

It was at this point that the five sepoys had arrived back from the village, carrying food and drink, and the conversation between Hilversum and the badmash had ceased.

The exchange between the pair had not gone entirely unnoticed amongst the remaining rebels, though it did not seem as though they had heard exactly what had passed between the Dutchman and the badmash. Jack noticed, while the group was eating, one of the sepoys walk over to the havildar and whisper in his ear. The havildar stared hard at the badmash, who was at that time tearing some bread apart with his filthy fingers. A little later the havildar got up, drifted up behind the badmash, then struck the man a deadly blow with his musket butt while he was eating. The badmash fell forward, a bolt of food dropping from his mouth. One of the other sepoys lifted his head by the hair and looked into his face.

'He is dead,' announced the sepoy. 'You have killed him.'

'This man was betraying us,' said the havildar to the rest of his men, 'with that *firinghi*.' He pointed to Hilversum. 'He was trash. We take these fellows from the sewers and expect them to act like men, but they are nothing but trouble.'

There were, amongst the sepoys and sowars, three more of the kind of man that now lay dead in the dust. They shifted uneasily, looking at each other, then at the rebels. One of them finally spoke.

'We are not like him,' he said. 'He was a Goojur from Dum-Dum, of no account, a worthless individual. He had no honour. We are men of higher regard, with a sense of loyalty to our kind.'

'This I understand,' replied the havildar, no doubt satisfied that he had made his point by executing the badmash. 'We will say no more.'

The three civilians looked relieved. Jack realized they would have stood no chance against the rebel sepoys and sowars, and would have been cut down to a man. However, the havildar would know that he needed all the men he could muster. These were unhappy times which tried men to the limit. Many souls had been thrown into jeopardy.

Unwisely though, the rebels stayed the night where they were, being fatigued by their march. In the early hours they were attacked by angry villagers throwing rocks out of the darkness. No one was seriously hurt but rest was interrupted. Jack himself was struck on the shoulder by a stone, which left his joint sore. In the morning the havildar resisted the impulse to burn the village and moved on before the day became too hot.

On the march Jack spoke to the Dutchman.

'You got a man killed back there.'

Hilversum shrugged. 'What do you care? He was gutter trash. And I might remind you he was the enemy. If I had a gun now I would shoot the lot of them down like dogs.'

'You be careful you don't talk yourself into your grave.'

They spoke no more, since one of the rebels came back and remonstrated with them, telling them to keep up.

If the gods had not been with the dead man, they were not with his murderers either. At noon on the fourth day of the march they came to a narrow pass, a gorge between two sets of high sheer-faced cliffs. There was no other way through into the valley beyond. However, stuck fast in the alley-thin pass was the body of a dead elephant. Someone had tried to lead the elephant through and it had become jammed in the gorge.

One could not climb over the rancid carcass because the pass narrowed above to the width of a man's thigh for at least twenty yards. The only possible answer was to cut the elephant out of the way, an unpleasant and difficult task. Since its death, its body had swollen, bloated with foul gases, which served to wedge it even more solidly into the gap.

The rebels hacked at the corpse with swords and knives, but the work was slow. While the innards of the dead elephant had turned to putrid matter, the skin had dried in the sun and was like armour. All afternoon they chopped and cut at the beast, blunting their swords, cursing and swearing at the man who had thought he could get his animal through such a narrow opening. The sweat rolled from their bodies, even though they were now at a higher elevation and in cooler air. When holes were finally cut, hot fetid gases flared out on the sepoys, causing them to choke in disgust.

The Dutchman was most amused and almost earned himself the same fate as the badmash, when he cried out in Hindi, 'You see, even Ganesh is against you!' What he did get as punishment for the remark, and Jack alongside him, was the pleasure of raking out the stinking rotten guts of the beast with his bare hands once the sepoys had cut a huge hole in the cadaver's hide. He and Jack were forced to crawl inside the creature's backside to scrape out the innards, the rebels hoping that the beast would collapse once it had been partially emptied of flesh. They clawed with their hands at the yellow-grey sludge, slopping it out of the man-sized opening in the elephant's arse, almost fainting with the stench. Jack had a more difficult time of it, being only one handed, but it was a ghastly business for both men.

'Bloody pachyderms,' Hilversum said under his breath in his native Dutch. 'What God made such creatures for is beyond me.'

When evening came they were still no nearer to opening the pass wide enough for a man to squeeze through. The corpse had indeed partially collapsed, but the bones were jammed hard and formed a cage door to keep them out. Men were sent out to find wood to make a bonfire under the remains, to try to burn them out of the way, but there were few trees in the region. Those they found were weak and spindly, offering very little fuel. When the fire was eventually started, just before dawn, the stink was unbelievable and forced them all back to a quarter of a mile from the opening. Finally they decided to approach the spot again and found the bones brittle and blackened but still in place.

What did not help matters any was the lack of water in the area. They could not spare water to wash. It was a dry arid region, mostly bedrock with granite outcrops. Jack and his fellow prisoner stank. They could not even bear their own company and both were sick. In the end they rolled in the dust to try to cover the slime with a layer of dirt to cut down the power of the smell.

In the morning the havildar ordered his men to make some ropes out of various clothes. These were tied to the bones blocking the pass and with the assistance of the whole group the skeleton was finally dislodged. It had been a long and arduous task and even Jack was relieved it was over. Yes, the elephant's carcass had delayed the rebels, but even now he could not be sure he was being followed by his men. Who knew where he was? Sergeant King had no doubt surmised that Jack had been captured by Khan and either killed or taken as a prisoner to that man's camp.

The problem was not yet completely over. Since they were travelling into the high country of the Himalayas, it would soon get very cold and they would need all the clothes they owned. They had to sit and untie all those garments which had been used to make ropes: not an easy task when such force had been put on them. Some of the knots were so tight they had to be undone with men's teeth: an unsavoury piece of work. By mid-morning all was completed and the group continued on their way, squeezing past the remains of the elephant and on to Tibet.

Jack's hair was stiffly spiked with dried slime. It went in every direction. There was filth under his nails, between his fingers and toes, and in every crease of his clothes. His companion had fared no better. They both smelled like sick animals. In truth Lieutenant Crossman had never been so miserable in all his life. His arms had been retied behind him and supplies for the rebels strapped to his back. Reduced to a beast of burden now, he hardly viewed himself as human. Certainly the rebels treated him like some dumb creature, prodding him with their weapons when he went too slowly. Not with any malice; it was just an afterthought to them.

It became colder on the trail. At night Jack huddled against his companion for warmth. He had a constant headache, his bowels were playing the devil with him, and he felt giddy and sick much of the time. Hilversum confessed he too was ill. They were both in dreadful physical condition. However, they were not the worst off. At least both men had been well fed and healthy before their capture. One or two of the sepoys had been on the march or run for over a year and had been half-starved before breaking free of their army. On the first night in the mountains the first of them died. He had complained all day of a pain in his left side, just above his hip, which had him screaming in agony by nightfall. At three in the morning he suddenly stood up, announced that the pain had gone and asked for water. After taking a long drink he keeled over, falling stone dead to the ground.

'What was that?' whispered the Dutchman. 'What took him in the end?'

Jack shrugged. 'I don't know. Kidney failure? Heart? We'll never know.'

'I hope they all die like that,' growled Hilversum. 'Every damn one of them.'

Jack made no reply to this, having some sympathy with the idea, but tongue-tied by a conscience which told him that no man deserved to die in such a dreary depressing place as this. On the battlefield is as good a place as any for those who wished to remain a hero in the memories of family and friends. In bed at home, surrounded by caring folk, was a better one if he cared nothing for glory. Up here in this anonymous forbidding rock land, the men were dirty, dishevelled and wracked by dysentery, and it was not a good place or time for a man to quit the world of the living.

'How are you faring?' asked Jack. 'You think you can make it?'

'Make it to where? We don't even know where we're going. I don't think they know what to do with us. The truth? I feel almost done in. I can't last a great deal longer.'

'Me neither,' agreed Jack. 'We have to try to escape.'

'I'll take my chances with you if you see the opportunity. I'd rather be shot running away than have to endure this stroll through the roof of the world much longer.'

'Well, we can't untie ourselves, but we can untie each other. Tomorrow, when we stop for our first rest break, sit with your back to me. You'll have to undo my arms, because I have no left hand . . .'

'I've been meaning to ask you about that.'

'But once I've got my good hand free, I'll be able to do the same for you. Don't rush off immediately. Wait for my signal. Keep up the pretence that you're still bound by wrapping the cord around your hands. Am I understood?'

'Perfectly. You've done this sort of thing before?'

'I've been a captive once or twice, but actually never managed to escape without outside help.'

'That's very comforting. I'm glad to know I'm in the hands of a professional escapee.'

Jack said, 'There's no need for sarcasm.'

A sepoy jumped up and came over to them.

'You shut up. No talking.'

'We need to talk,' Jack shouted at the man angrily. 'We need the comfort of words.'

'I am not listening to your excuses. You must keep silent.'

The havildar said wearily in Hindi, 'Leave them alone – what can they do?'

The rebel stared at his leader then shrugged and sat down again.

Thus Jack and Hilversum found themselves free to talk in normal voices.

'If we die here, which we may very well do, what will you have left undone that you wished to do?'

Jack, who had been asked the question, replied with some asperity. 'Killing that idiot Deighnton,' he said, then instantly regretted the remark. 'No, no – I didn't mean that. What then? I can hardly think. Oh, yes, I will have left undone a family. I'm newly married and have not yet had the chance to start one.' He thought for a while. 'I haven't even discussed it with my wife. We haven't yet had the luxury of time on our hands to talk over such future plans. I'm one of those, you see, who believe that immortality is leaving part of ourselves on this earth. A child. A grandchild. Perhaps several, if one is lucky. Yet, not only that . . . we influence all those we ever meet, however briefly, and part of us rubs off on them. There is our immortality – in that small influence.'

'I am a God-fearing man, myself,' said the Dutchman, 'but I think I know what you mean. I once gave half a rupee to a beggar in Delhi – a spontaneous action, quite uncharacteristic of me. It was before the mutiny, of course. The upshot was the man blessed me with such fervour I knew he would tell his friends about me and that I would live on in their minds – yes, yes, I can see what you mean, I think. A limited immortality though, if that's not a contradiction in terms, for eventually all who know you will be dead themselves.'

'Not where progeny is concerned. Grandchildren beget grand-children. The likeness will survive *ad infinitum*, will it not?'

They were both quiet for a while, then the Dutchman asked, 'Who is Deighnton?'

'Oh,' replied Jack, 'a man not worthy of further notice.'

'No, please. You've aroused my curiosity.'

Jack sighed. 'A cavalry officer who's taken it into his head to bring about my downfall. I insulted a powerful friend of his – no, I didn't just insult him, I struck him. Captain Deighnton is now determined to make me pay for affronting his friend. We've already duelled once, but the pistols failed us. I'm sure we'll get round to it again if I ever get out of this mess.'

Hilversum suddenly became animated. 'Ah! Now, that's where I can help you, Crossman. This chance meeting was fated by the gods. I'm the very man who can assist you to kill this officer. You know what I am? You see that bag which the sepoy clings to? My bag. You know what's in it?'

'You told me – firearms.'

'Yes, but a particular firearm. Just guess what it is.'

Jack stared at the now battered black leather traveller's bag, quite uninterested in its contents at this moment in time.

'A cannon.'

'Come on, don't be frivolous.'

'This is wearisome.'

'What else have you got to do? Try.'

'You're right, I can hardly stroll down to the mess tent for a glass of Madeira, can I? Um, let me hazard something. Now what does one normally duel with? Single-shot pistols?'

Hilversum first looked disappointed, then brightened. 'How did you guess?'

Jack raised his eyebrows. 'It leapt into my mind.'

'Yes, single-shot pistols. Very accurate and exceptionally well-made pistols. That's what I do, I sell small arms. There is a pistol in there, a beautifully fashioned single-shot pistol, you couldn't miss with it. A five-year-old could knock the pip out of an ace of hearts with it. It's very expensive of course, but how much is your life worth? The balance is perfect, the barrel is made of the finest steel and is as straight as an architect's line. It has been lovingly crafted, that pistol, every part being precision-made over a long period of time, until the whole is a work of art. All you need to do is point and fire and your opponent will cease to breathe.'

Jack was horrified to find himself dreaming of shooting Deighnton through the heart with this miraculous single-shot pistol.

'Well,' he said, composing his thoughts into more acceptable images, 'the chance will probably never come.'

He lay that night staring up at a great expanse of stars, millions of them, which all seemed closer to the earth than they had in Britain. Jack wondered if Jane were staring up at the same skies, seeing the same heavenly bodies. It was possible. It was entirely possible. The moon was in her sphere of vision as much as it was in his. It was comforting to know they were both joined by its light, no matter how far apart they were.

Then he remembered the time difference! It was deep evening to him, but late afternoon for his beloved wife. Perhaps what

Jane was seeing was the setting of the sun, not the rising of a bright golden moon. How easily romance could be shattered by the laws of motion!

He had the vague idea that someone might be responsible for this cold grey state of affairs and derived some satisfaction in cursing him.

'Damn you, Newton!'

The next morning the rebels killed Jack's horse and ate what they could of its flesh, taking some of what was left for the next few days. It was pointless taking the whole carcass: it would be inedible within a week. Jack felt sorry for his nag: it had never known real affection and now it was dead. That was the life of a beast for you. They worked you until you were of no more use to them, then they ate part of you and threw the rest away!

Where they were heading Jack had no idea. Indeed he wondered if the havildar himself knew what lay ahead of them. They seemed to be lost in an endless maze of rock chimneys, gorges and towering slopes. Finally the came to a verdant valley overshadowed by a monastery high up on a pinnacle of rock. There was a village at the far end of the valley. Men and women, poor peasants, Jack concluded from their appearance, were working in the fields as the group entered. These farm hands looked up in shock as the rebels dragged themselves along one of the paths which skirted the fields. The rebels were very wary at this point, though Jack could not see them being challenged by these simple Tibetans. It was doubtful there was any kind of military force in the area and it would take weeks to get word to any Chinese governor of this region. Rescue was not going to come running, that much was certain.

They walked past the villagers, who had all paused to view this motley brigade of armed men. The rebels in their turn looked out of the corners of their eyes at the peasants. Jack knew what the sepoys were thinking: what were the chances of robbing this village of supplies without causing too much havoc? It was doubtful that the Buddhist priests up in their stronghold above – the masters of these field workers – were armed or prepared to use violence. Their religion forbade it. This was a remote region though and one had to be prepared not only for the unusual, but also for the extraordinary. Perhaps they had mercenaries or had armed the ordinary population?

Any foreigners who had been in here in recent times had run the risk of execution, so little news of Tibet had sifted down to India. No one could be sure of anything in these troubled times and caution was the watchword.

During the rest stop Jack and Hilversum had managed to free each other as they had planned. They had been awaiting their chance to bolt ever since. Now the rebels' attention was wholly occupied by the situation. Jack saw a clear opportunity to make a run for it. As it happened an ox wagon was coming towards them. Jack waited for his chance. With heads turned in other directions he slipped away without a sound, ducking down on the far side of the wagon. He then rolled underneath it and swung himself up. He hooked his handless arm around the front axle and, slipping his fingers through the planks of the wagon's base, he held himself off the ground, his boot heels on the back axle. Fortunately the axles of the wagon were turning quite slowly and he did not need to worry about skin burns or injuries.

It was only once he was on his way that he remembered he and Hilversum had agreed on a signal. Jack had slipped away without giving his companion any notice. Still, what could Jack have done? The opportunity had presented itself and had to be taken in a split second. The pair of them could not have escaped in the same way at the same time. They would have been sure to have been seen. Jack acknowledged however that Hilversum's problem was that now that he had gone the sepoys would be especially vigilant, and would probably check their remaining prisoner's bonds. Of course, they might carry out their threat to shoot the other man if one of them escaped, but that threat had slipped Jack's mind.

The Dutchman was just as bewildered by Jack's disappearance as were the sepoys. It was as if the lieutenant had been spirited away. The rebels looked this way and that, staring back at the mountains from which they had descended, wondering at this spiritual landscape they had entered. One even ventured to suggest Jack had been lifted up by the gods, a suggestion which drew scorn from the havildar and others in the party. Yet there was no prisoner there. Indeed the man had vanished from their presence without leaving a trace. Jack's importance at this point in their journey was negligible. The havildar was not going to waste time searching for him. The rebels were ordered on their way.

The wagon went on its journey up into the village. Jack dropped down and lay there until the wagon had passed over him. Then he got to his feet and ran into a nearby hovel. Two women, one very old, one quite young, were sitting over an open fire. They stared at him with wide round eyes.

'Can you help me?' he asked in Hindi, then in Urdu. 'Can you assist me in escaping my foes?'

They continued to stare at him as if he were a madman.

He tried Punjabi to no avail.

In the end he beckoned the young one to the door of the hovel and pointed over her shoulder at the band of rebels moving across the valley. Jack then showed her his arms where the ropes had cut marks into his skin. With sign language he indicated that he had been bound. She was a bright young person and on witnessing the Indians with their remaining prisoner crossing below she understood him. She crooked her finger at him, spoke to the old woman, then led him out of the back of the hovel to a lean-to woodshed. There she covered him with sacking material and then left him to return to the hovel, where he heard what sounded like an argument between the girl and what was probably her grandmother. Finally the quarrel stopped and it was all quiet within. Jack fell asleep under the musty-smelling sacks and dreamed of being chased by a raging bull.

Four

Captain Deighnton had remained behind with Brigadier Walpole, to whom General Campbell had now given command of the forces in Rohilkand. Campbell himself had gone to set up a new headquarters elsewhere, leaving the final suppression of the region to Walpole and Coke. Further south General Rose was finishing off remnants before he marched on Kalpi.

Deighnton was not happy that Lieutenant Crossman had absconded. He had been looking forward to the duel, but the fact remained that his enemy had flown the nest. Crossman's men had gone out looking for him, apparently, and no word had come back from them either. Deighnton felt he had been robbed of satisfaction. It made him all the more determined to grind Crossman's name into the dirt. His interview this morning was with Brigadier Walpole's staff officer, Major O'Hay.

'Sir,' said Deighnton, 'we must do something about the deserters. Would you give me leave to take a few of my troopers in order to track them down?'

O'Hay's eyebrows shot up. The portly major was sitting at a makeshift desk in what used to be a cobbler's workshop. An awl was now being employed as a paperweight. A hammer, likewise. In the corner of the room was a pile of sandals, some of them only half-finished. A box of nails lay by the pile, tipped over and spilled on to the clay floor.

The major regarded the captain with some astonishment for a few moments.

'Deserters? I wasn't aware we had any.' A light came to the major's eyes. 'You mean native infantry?'

'No, sir, I mean British soldiers, Queen's Army.'

The major leaned back in his bamboo chair, making it creak ominously.

'No one has reported any deserters to me.'

'I am doing so now, sir, if you see what I mean.'

The major was distressed. 'I can't believe it. In *these* times, when the whole of the fabric of India is being stretched. Men deserting when their wives and children are being slaughtered? I really have difficulty here, Captain, in comprehending the baseness to which men can stoop. Are you sure?' He leaned forward again. 'Perhaps they were drunk, is that it? Drunk and got lost or something? Irishmen, probably. Or Scots? My own regiment . . .'

'No, sir, the man I am speaking of is an officer, a lieutenant. I use the word officer, but in fact the man is a damned rogue.'

A gasp of horror came from the major.

'A lieutenant? In what regiment?'

'He's in the 88th Foot.' Deighnton waved a hand through the air, disturbing some spiders on the ceiling. 'Oh, he's always been a troublemaker, sir. Not what you'd call a gentleman. His father's something or other, up in Scotland, but the father's disowned him. Cuts him dead, I understand. You know some of these fellows are born rogues, good family or not.'

'Certainly, but . . . *desertion*. While on campaign? Even a gentleman gone astray knows what the penalty is for that. What's the man's name?'

'Lieutenant Crossman.'

'Never heard of any Crossman. Doesn't sound like the name of a gentleman to me.'

'It's an assumed name, so I've been told.' Deighnton leaned on the chubby major's desk and looked directly into his eyes. 'Hiding some dark secret, I imagine. As I say, a rogue officer.'

'In the 88th, you say? Surely they're somewhere much further south?'

'Ah, this fellow doesn't fight with his own regiment. No, this fellow sneaks about picking up gossip and pretending it's valuable information. The fact is the man's a coward. I witnessed an attack on him in the battle the other day. A Ghazi pulled him from his horse. I think the episode unnerved him.'

The major nodded. 'Pretty terrifying fellows, those Ghazis – saw 'em myself. Frightened the life out of me, too.'

'But you didn't run away.'

'And this Crossman fellow did?'

'Hasn't been seen since. There was some talk he'd gone

out after Khan, but does that sound feasible? One man and his sergeant sent out after a whole retreating army?'

The major blinked. 'A sergeant too? Is he missing also?'

'The sergeant returned, saying the lieutenant had sent him back with the news that Khan was in Pilibhit. Well, we knew that, I'm sure. It was hardly startling information. Lieutenant Crossman never returned. It's my belief he kept on riding, his nerve completely shattered by the attack on him by the Ghazi, which I have to say was quite ferocious. It was touch and go who would come out on top.' Deighnton stood up straight. 'At that point I admired the lieutenant. I thought he had regained some of the honour he had lost over the years. I'm told he first joined as a private under this pseudonym of Crossman, in order to escape justice, but redeemed himself somewhat in various battles in the Crimea. However, sir, bad character will out. He's reverted to his old ways, it seems, and has flown the coop. Permission, sir, to chase him down and bring him in for court martial.'

'Well, let's not judge the man too hastily, Captain. He may have some good explanation. But he does sound a frightful fellow, I must admit. Yes, off you go then. Get permission from your colonel, if you please, and then bring this absconder back here.' The major suddenly became very stern. 'We know how to deal with deserters.'

Deighnton left the major with some of his satisfaction restored. He had no intention of bringing Crossman back for trial. They would settle their affairs out there in the wilderness, where there were no interfering authorities. He would take about twenty troopers with him and track the bastard down, then let things take their course. Naturally if Crossman refused to surrender to him, then he would have no choice but to kill him. One could not bring in alive a dog who was determined to remain wild.

Jack now felt very bad about leaving Hilversum. Having himself escaped his conscience was now bothering him. Yes, he *had* given Hilversum the impression that they would escape together. Yet he, Jack, had taken his chance when it came, without considering his companion. He knew himself and he was now totally aware that he could not make good his own escape. It was necessary to go back and assist Hilversum.

'Thank you,' he said in English to the young woman who had helped him. It seemed as good a language as any to be grateful in, since he could not make himself understood in any other tongue. 'I appreciate your help.'

He was now refreshed and feeling better. The elephant slime had been washed from his body and hair, he had been fed and watered, and he had slept the sleep of a babe. The women could not be sorry to see him go, though the young one looked sad. While he remained in their house they were in danger from their own authorities as well as the rebels.

He had no weapon, of course. The havildar had taken his revolver and a Bavarian hunting knife he always carried. All he had were the rags he stood up in, a pair of sandals given him by the young Tibetan girl, and a strong determination to takc his revenge on his captors. He went down from the place on the hill to valley floor below, to find that the rebels had moved on to the far end of the long green river-fed vale between two mountain ranges.

Even before he had begun his walk he heard horns sounding from a monastery which clung precariously to the upper crags like a large black beetle. Cymbals began to clash and a call went up, for what or whom Jack had no idea. He caught a glimpse of figures on a wooden balcony, high above his head, but they did not seem interested in him. Perhaps it was morning prayers? Or the breakfast gong? Or the call to work?

He continued on, following a stream down to a river whose banks separated many fields of rice. The sun was on his face, not hot, but pleasantly warming. A mammal of some kind, perhaps a Tibetan shrew, jumped out from under his foot and leapt into some tall grasses. Here, life was a dreamlike process, which did not seem quite real. The light was intensely bright and the air clear and clean. It was a sharp world, faceted, throwing off blinding glints from white quartz and surface water. Surely he was dead and this was some kind of heaven? Only a breeze to stir things all along the valley, chasing shadows through the tall rice plants.

Then he heard his name. Almost a whisper. He looked around him, seeing no one, yet still hearing the faint cry as if it came from the crevices of the mountains themselves. Was that one of the gods, one of the gods of the mountains? He had been assured by the Indians that they were there, in the gullies and up on the high pinnacles, overseeing strangers.

'Lieutenant Crossman!'

Not only did this god know his name, it knew his army rank as well, which hardly seemed likely.

'Lieutenant! Over here!'

Now he saw them and his heart leapt. Sergeant King, Raktambar, that pest Wynter, and Corporal Gwilliams, making their way by foot down a path on the far side of the valley. Even young Sajan was with them. They kept waving and hailing him. He simply stood there, glad beyond anything to see them, even Wynter. Tears came to his eyes, which he managed to wipe away before they approached.

'You took your time,' he managed to say without a catch in his voice. 'Where the hell have you been?'

Sergeant King grinned at him.

'We've been about a day behind you for a while. Damn, those people with you kept up a pace. You'd think the devil was after them. We could see you climbing up the high paths, like ants, while we were crossing the lower ones. Did you throw them off, then? I take it you were their captive, sir, for you looked to be struggling to keep up with them.'

'Sit down, sir,' said Gwilliams. 'You look a bit shaky.'

Jack did sit down. He realized he was trembling at the knees, but he knew he would be all right in a short while.

'Where are they?' asked Wynter. 'Leave you, did they?'

'No, I escaped,' said Jack. 'They've got another man with them, a Dutchman. We need to free him too.'

Wynter pursed his lips. 'Dutchy, eh? He ain't English then? Do we need to get him? I ain't overfriendly with Dutchies.'

'You're not overfriendly with anyone,' said Jack, 'and yes we do have to get him. Otherwise they'll probably kill him.'

King said, 'Raktambar did most of the tracking. If you owe anyone for the fact that we found you, it's him.'

Jack nodded gravely at his Rajput protector. 'I thank you.'

'You must not get lost again,' replied Raktambar, just as gravely. 'It is a very inconvenient thing.'

Jack looked suspiciously at the Rajput. 'Where did you learn that word, *inconvenient*?'

Raktambar grinned. 'It came from Sergeant King.'

King was blushing furiously.

'Of course it did. Well, I'm sorry to have inconvenienced you, Sergeant King; perhaps in future I'll bear in mind that your time is too precious to be wasting it looking for lost lieutenants.'

'Oh, sir.'

Sajan had so far not spoken. Now he blurted out his one question on being reunited with Lieutenant Crossman.

'Sahib,' he asked excitedly, 'was that your elephant?'

'Which ele—?' He suddenly realized what the boy meant. 'Oh, don't talk to me about *that* beast. No, it was not my elephant and if I ever catch the man who left it jammed in the pass I will not be responsible for my actions. Those damn rebels made me claw out the innards with my own two – well, with my one remaining hand. It was a ghastly business, one I hope never to have to repeat.'

Now that he was back in the company of his men, Jack felt the earlier depression lifting from him. It was imperative now, to catch up with the band of rebels and free Hilversum. They had no horses, of course. It would have been impossible to cross that range of mountains with mounts. But at least the rebels were also on foot. Jack gave orders that they force-march the length of the valley and apprehend the rebels before they got away.

'Sajan?' he said. 'How are your legs?'

'I can walk, sahib,' the boy protested, but in truth he looked done in.

King explained, 'We took him with us at a time when we had no idea we would be crossing mountain ranges. The idea was to meet up with you on the trail and no one knew you'd been abducted at that time.'

Jack made a decision. 'Sergeant, you must head back with the boy. Make your pace slow and easy, so as not to try his strength. We'll catch up with you when our business is done. You can't shoot straight anyway.'

King puffed out his cheeks. 'You always say that.'

'Well, it's true, goddamn it,' offered Gwilliams. 'You couldn't hit a hill if it sat in front of you.'

Jack suddenly changed his mind and sugared the pill. 'Sergeant, I expect you have in that pack of yours the wherewithal to make a survey of the mountains surrounding this village?'

King nodded. 'A good mapmaker is never without his tools.'

'Then you and Sajan remain here and do just that.'

The sergeant's joy was transparent. 'Yes, yes I could do that, couldn't I? No one has mapped this region, it being in the forbidden zone. I would be the first to find the true elevation of those mountains.' He waved an arm at the snow-tipped peaks which hemmed the valley. 'Such a survey would be immensely helpful to the Indian mapmakers, I'm sure.'

'Well, then, you have your work and we have ours,' said the lieutenant. 'On my way down here from a house which sheltered me, I noticed a goatherd's hut, which appears to be empty. You and Sajan stay there. It's just beyond that small orchard. Good luck, Sergeant.'

'And to you, sir. You'll need more luck than me.'

'Don't wager on it. If you're caught in this region, you could be summarily executed. Stay out of sight. Bother no one.'

With that Crossman and his men set out, walking alongside the narrow river, towards the far end of the valley.

Sergeant King and his adopted son went immediately to the goatherd's hut and made themselves at home inside.

Sajan said, as he brought in freshly cut hay for their beds, 'It is very important – our work – is it not, Father?'

'It is indeed,' murmured Farrier King, with some satisfaction.

Until now the lieutenant had suffered the sergeant's desire to make maps with some irritation, not giving the work any priority whatsoever. King however had worked long and hard to become a surveyor. It had not been easy. Though he had been given a short education, it had been a poor one and over with in just three short years. However he counted himself lucky to have had one at all. Then the army had recognized his intelligence and had given him to a mapmaker as an assistant. Farrier King had taken to his new work with a passion that bordered on the religious. When God created the earth, King was certain He did it with his head full of contour lines and trigonometrical points. Sergeant King could not imagine anyone so base as not to be excited by the coloured inks, the pens, the measuring devices, the mathematics, the physics and all the other tools of the mapmaker. His was a skill made in heaven.

King and Sajan stayed in the hut all that day, then under cover of darkness they went out to seek a better viewpoint. After a long climb amongst moonlit crags they came to a stone watchtower on the peak of one of the lesser mountains. Inspecting it, King found some stairs within, which led to a floor above, some thirty feet from the base. Here it was open to the elements. He watched the dawn come up from the far-off Indian plains, creeping up the sides of foothills and spilling over on to each crest below, until it reached the tower. Perfect. This was a perfect observatory for him.

That day they slept, the boy being utterly exhausted. King kept watch for a while, wondering if the tower was used for anything. When no one came he joined Sajan on the stone floor and slept. The boy woke first and made tea on the portable stove. While King was grateful to be woken with a cup of hot beverage, he also felt worried. However, observations from the tower led him to believe no one knew of their existence in this region.

He boiled the water again and checked the temperature with a thermometer to calculate their height above sea level. The lower the water's boiling point, the higher their altitude. It was not a fail-safe or accurate way to read their elevation above sea level, but it was a reasonable guide. His calculations showed they were 9,720 feet above sea level. King intended to check and recheck the altitude using this method.

'Where is the pack, Sajan?' he asked his adopted son.

The boy fetched the heavy haversack in which was carried the precious sextant and chronometer. Together they unwrapped the instruments; Sajan showing almost the same reverence as his father. Once these were ready King filled a small bowl with mercury to use as an artificial horizon in order to measure the altitude of the stars. Thus the sergeant began to calculate the heights of the surrounding mountains and was sometimes astonished by the results. These were indeed giants of earth and stone, tipped with snow, and so exciting were his discoveries that after a few days King's guard relaxed and he spent less and less time watching for intruders.

Crossman, Raktambar, Gwilliams and Wynter pushed on deeper into the Tibetan mountains. They drank from clearwater streams and ate what they could find in the way of vegetables. There was a particular plant with a root similar to an onion which, though so strong-tasting it brought tears to the eyes, none-the-less satisfied a craving for greens. Gwilliams was adept not only at tracking their enemy, but also at snaring game birds and small mammals, which kept them in meat. Gwilliams never tired of boring Wynter with his stories of tracking with Kit Carson in the American West. Wynter was now in the habit of sticking his fingers down his throat whenever the corporal mentioned one of the Wild West heroes he supposedly shaved and gave haircuts to.

'One day you'll swaller them fingers,' Gwilliams told the private, 'and you'll have to keep swallerin' till your hand comes out of your ass and your shoulder jams up your jaws. Then you'll look the dope everyone takes you for anyways. No surprises there.'

One morning, when they were closing on their quarry, Wynter turned the corner at the foot of a mountain path to be confronted by a strange horned beast with a long silky-looking coat.

'Arrrghhh!' he yelled, then recovering quickly called, 'Lieutenant! Here's a hairy bull!'

Crossman joined the private. 'I think it's what they call a yak,' he told Wynter. 'It doesn't look wild. It must have wandered away from its owner.' He looked a bit harder. 'A female with full udders. Wynter, you were a farmhand. Can you milk this creature? Some warm milk would go down well.'

'I weren't no farmhand – I was a bodger.'

'Oh – a forest worker. But still . . .'

Wynter was saved by Gwilliams stepping forward. 'I'll do it.'

The yak, doe-eyed and submissive, subjected itself to this indignity passively, and was then sent on its way. They all had a few mouthfuls of the rich fluid. Crossman, weak from his trials, was especially grateful for the milk which seemed to revive his spirits as well as his physical state. His stump was hurting badly, having been scuffed and grazed. He had lost weight with the heat of the plains and lack of food, and now he was in the cold country his condition was frail. His bones were protruding like sticks through his Indian cottons, which were inadequate for the climate.

'We could've ate that beast,' grumbled Wynter, gulping down the milk. 'Good meat gone to waste.'

Raktambar said, 'That animal belongs to someone. If you kill the yak how will the owner survive?'

'And I'm s'posed to care?' Wynter growled. 'The whole bleedin' lot of 'em could starve and it wun't worry me a jot.'

The four of them pushed on, hopeful to catch up with the rebels before nightfall. However, before they had gone another few yards Jack caught a flash of light on the mountainside. He stopped and peered into the drifting sun-pierced mists above. He saw another glint. Then he heard the unmistakable clink of metal.

'Quickly, behind that outcrop,' he whispered. 'Someone's coming.'

The group scrambled behind several large boulders and waited for the oncomers to emerge from the haze. When they did it felt like stepping back in time for Crossman. A line of Chinese soldiers were filing down the path dressed in padded jackets with medieval armour over the top. They wore large helmets with fly-away rims, chain-mail vests, shoulder epaulettes and greaves. Instead of spears they carried ancient-looking flintlocks. In the centre of the column of about thirty soldiers was a sedan chair carried by four men. Tied to one pole of the sedan chair, and roped to each other by the wrists and ankles, hobbled three prisoners, one of which was Rudi Hilversum. Jack also recognized the other two. They were the rebel havildar and one of his sepoys.

Out of the frying pan into the fire, thought Jack, as he stared at Hilversum. The column passed by without seeing the group. It was moving at a leisurely pace so Jack was not too concerned about catching them up again. He gathered his force around him.

'We'll follow them and wait our chance,' he said. 'Their muskets don't look up to much, but there's thirty or more.'

Gwilliams and Wynter both had Enfield rifles. Jack had King's Enfield. Raktambar had his own weapons, which included two pistols and a tulwar. There was a fair amount of fire power there, but the odds were such that they could not guarantee an easy victory. Jack deemed it wiser to hold back for a decent opportunity to free the prisoners.

He was also more than a little concerned about killing any

Chinese soldiers, however comical their uniforms. So far as he knew Britain was at war with China, but the last he had heard was that the British and French were trying to force a peace by attacking the Dagu forts in Northern China. If that rather dubious strategy had been successful Jack did not want to jeopardize any negotiations by creating an international incident allowing the Chinese to rescind. If he was responsible for something like that he would not only be in trouble with the army, but parliament would want his head, torso and limbs on a platter too.

They trailed the small Chinese column to a tiny village in a mountain valley. At one point Jack's men were surprised by a string of Buddhist monks appearing out of nowhere and trooping silently past them. The monks did not raise an eyebrow and indeed hardly seemed to notice these raggletaggle foreigners standing by the path. One of them was intent on spinning a hand-held prayer wheel, which fascinated Wynter.

'Grown men playin' with toys,' he muttered jealously. 'Give 'im a windmill next.'

The next day the Chinese troops left the village and reached a chasm which had to be crossed by a flimsy-looking bridge of rope and wooden slats. Here Jack saw the officer in charge for the first time when he stepped out of the sedan chair. He was dressed in the rich clothes and had the manner of a mandarin. His ornate robe was covered in golden symbols, on a red background, and had deep hanging sleeves. On his head was a black silk hat with a dangling tassle. In his arms, being fondly stroked, was a strange-looking small dog with a pug nose.

No doubt this man in charge was a local official of a minor region of Chinese Tartary on his way back from Peking or some other major city. Whatever his rank and circumstances he obviously held his own life in the utmost importance, because he sent the sedan chair and prisoners, along with the chair's carriers, over the bridge first, presumably to test its strength. If it held seven men and a heavy chair it would hold the mandarin.

Jack and his men were behind some dwarf trees.

'What we'll do,' he whispered, 'is wait until the prisoners are over the chasm, then rush down firing over the heads of the soldiers and run across the bridge before they recover from their surprise. Then we'll cut the ropes and let the bridge fall into the chasm. How does that sound?'

'Bloody terrible, if you don't mind me sayin',' replied the blunt Corporal Gwilliams without hesitation. 'I reckon your plan's more wobbly than that bridge, which is sayin' somethin'.'

Jack set his jaw. 'Well, that *is* the plan.'

Raktambar shook his head firmly. Jack looked likely to have a mutiny on his hands. However, fortune intervened and overrode such a disaster. The Chinese mandarin was no fool. As soon as his chair was safely on the other side, he sent a contingent of soldiers over the bridge. Then he started out himself over the swaying bridge, alone of course so that weight was at a minimum. He was a clever man when it came to his own precious life, but he had not thought it through thoroughly. He had done the one thing a commander should never do: he had split his forces. On Jack's side of the chasm there were now only six soldiers. He and his men rushed them, taking them completely by surprise. They were felled with blows and disarmed within a minute. One or two shots followed from the other side, but ceased when the mandarin, in the line of fire, screamed at his soldiers.

Raktambar stood with a knife poised over the anchor ropes.

The mandarin stood, white with fear, in the middle of the bridge knowing exactly what was indicated.

Jack stepped on to the bridge and began walking across. He looked down between the slats once or twice and was entirely sympathetic to the mandarin's terror. Far, far below was the twinkling of a thread-narrow stream and on the way down were many a jagged crag and razor rock. Jack himself did not like heights overmuch. He held on with his one good hand and balanced with his left forearm. When he reached the mandarin he stopped and bowed his head politely. The official, who was probably wondering whether he was going to be killed or not, gazed back with relief evident in his eyes. He too lowered his head slightly, knowing Jack was trying to preserve his dignity in front of his troops.

'My apologies, sir,' said Jack, 'for this interlude, but you have one of my men over there. I know you cannot comprehend my words, but you understand the tone and no that no harm will come to you.'

With that, Jack passed on. When he reached the other side some of the Chinese warriors reached out to grab him, but the mandarin screeched again, knowing that he was still in grave peril. They might have a hostage each, but his life was more important than any foreign hostage. Jack was unhanded and left free to cut the bonds of the three prisoners.

'Thank you, sir,' gushed the sepoy, 'you are saving our lives from these barbarians.'

'Oh, I'll hang you later,' Jack replied cheerfully, 'if we ever get out of this mess alive.'

Once free, Rudi Hilversum spoke to Jack.

'Look in the sedan. That swine took my handguns from the Indians.'

Jack pulled back the curtain of the sedan chair and sure enough there was Hilversum's travel bag with the dog asleep across it. He went to pick it up and the pug woke and snapped at Jack's hand. Jack lifted the beast by the scruff of its neck and tossed it back into its corner again. It remained where it was, yapping at him, while he took the bag. There was also a wooden casket on the seat covered in brass studs. The havildar reached for this item but Jack rapped his wrist.

'We are not robbers or bandits,' he murmured.

The havildar's eyes flashed. 'You are not my commanding officer,' he snapped. 'I am not your trooper.'

'No,' replied Jack mildly, 'you are my prisoner.'

The four men filed back across the bridge. Jack could not stop Hilversum from snatching the mandarin's cap off his head and thus destroying his attempt at leaving the man with his dignity intact. Hilversum threw the cap out into the gorge where it floated down on the wind.

'Was that necessary?' he said to the Dutchman.

'Very,' replied Hilversum, 'and not half what the bloody sepoys are going to get once we're clear of this lot. I've been subjected to the meanest treatment by them, and I'm going to get my own back. I was stripped and searched in the most intimate places – still sore from that nasty experience. They laughed while they did it, and him the loudest. That jack-o'-napes was lucky I didn't boot him off the bridge. I was sorely tempted. It was only the fact that one of his soldiers might take a shot at me which stopped me, I can tell you, Lieutenant.'

'Point taken – but the prisoners are mine, not yours.'

Hilversum sighed. 'Meaning you'll take them back to be tried by a court martial which will, without any doubt whatsoever, sentence them to death by the guns or by the rope. What a waste of time . . .'

Hilversum was still complaining when they reached the far side. Jack then sent the disarmed Chinese soldiers over the bridge. On the way they collected their leader. The ropes were then cut and the bridge fell like a flimsy black spider's web on to the far side of the gorge. No one fired a shot. It was doubtful the Chinese muskets were effective over two hundred yards in any case. The Enfields certainly were: they could take a man out at a thousand yards, so the Chinese were wise not to open fire and start a shooting match.

Jack asked Hilversum, 'What happened to the rest of the sepoys? Just the havildar and the fat one left?'

The Dutchman ran a quick finger over his throat in reply.

Sergeant King and Sajan had seen soldiers too. They passed the watchtower in the early dawn, on their way to the village where Jack had first escaped his sepoy abductors. King was still in seventh heaven, calculating the height of mountains, none of which he knew the names of. It wouldn't matter. He could find out their names later. In the meantime he had produced a very creditable map of the area through which he had travelled and had altitude figures enough to please anyone who desired them.

'What have we got left for the pot, son?' he asked Sajan. They were running desperately short on food now. 'Shall I shoot a hare?'

He was being facetious and Sajan knew it. Farrier King had about as much chance of hitting a running mammal as stealing the jewel from the Green Idol of Kathmandu in neighbouring Nepal. They had taken to sneaking down to farms at night and stealing anything that was not locked away. Sajan had even managed to get a cockerel one night, gripping it by the throat before it could call out, and leaving a few feathers strewn around so that its owners would believe a predator got it. The pair of them had feasted on that bird for two days, before having to do another dangerous foray.

It was with some disappointment that King heard English

accents one night, passing below the tower. He went to the parapet and hissed down into the darkness, 'Sir, up here!'

Wynter's voice came back up, 'Who the devil is that?'

Then Crossman's voice said, 'Who do think, you idiot? King, where are you?'

'In the tower, sir. We'll come down.'

Sajan was roused and the pair of them gathered their materials together before joining the group below. There was a reunion, not so much joyous as pleasant. Then the party was on its way again, a forced march heading towards the Indian border. It seemed necessary to Jack to get out of Chinese territory as soon as possible. They reached India skirting the border with Nepal, which was also a dangerous place for foreigners. Once back on the Indian plains they felt a little safer, and camped for two days, where they rested, bathed and took stock of their adventure.

Hilversum was able for the first time to inspect his handguns. Upon opening his bag he was surprised to find an intruder in there.

'What's this? Not one of mine.'

Jack saw it was his five-shot Tranter revolver, with its unusual trigger cocking device. 'No, that belongs to me. It was taken from me when I was captured. The sepoys must have put it in your bag.'

Hilversum nodded, handing it over to the lieutenant.

'Now, let me show you this,' said the Dutchman. 'You spoke about being in a duel recently? And missing your target? This, sir, is a duelling pistol no self-respecting officer should be without.'

He unwrapped a piece of velvet cloth. Inside was a rather plain-looking handgun. But Jack could see that it was a finely crafted weapon, even without fancy embellishments. There was a silver butt cap with a brass ball, either for attaching a lanyard or for balance. But apart from these the walnut stock was free of frivolous decorations. Jack picked it up and felt its balance. It fitted comfortably and snugly in his fist.

'What's so effective about this weapon?' he asked Hilversum, as others crowded round to look at the weapon. 'Does it shoot straight?'

'Not only is it accurate to the thickness of a shadow,' replied the Dutchman, 'it will take a man's arm off. The calibre, sir, is .70. If you take this weapon, for example, or this – also both single-shot pistols – the calibres are .32 and .42 respectively. They are the norm. This beautiful killer was made by Andrew Wurfflein of Philadelphia in the Americas. Plane back action lock, single-set trigger with a guard spur. There is a vacant silver name escutcheon at the wrist. It should bear your name, Lieutenant.'

Jack blinked. 'What do you mean?'

'I mean, this is a gift for saving my life. If you ever have to fight your man again, this weapon will be your saviour. Let me show you . . .' He took the pistol back and proceeded to load it with the rammer. 'This particular model normally has an eight-inch-long barrel, but this one is a twelve-inch – it has a secondary use as a sharpshooter's pistol. It will kill at a distance. There, it's ready. Would you like to fire it?'

'After dinner, thank you. We must eat first. However, I do thank you for such a generous gift.'

Hilversum waved this away. 'My life is worth far more.'

Wynter pushed forward. 'Don't we get no gift neither? We was there too, helping save your life.'

'These are all single-shot pistols, I'm afraid.'

'I an't fussy. What's that little 'un, there?'

Hilversum looked. 'That? That, my lean hungry friend, is the answer to a gentleman's ruin.'

'Meanin'?'

'Meaning if you were a gentleman – Lord Such-and-such or Earl So-and-so – and had gambled away the family estates, that pistol would be your salvation. You would sit at your desk, take infinite pains in loading and priming the weapon under the disapproving gaze of your pater's last portrait, throw back one final glass of the reserve brandy, place the barrel to your temple – and *voilà* – splatter your brains all over the blotter.'

'I'll have that 'un, then.'

An exasperated King said, 'But Wynter, you don't have any estates to lose.'

Wynter was slightly indignant. 'That don't mean I'm no better'n a lord. I'm as good as anybody with this 'ere pistol in me pocket.'

He took it, wrapped it in a filthy handkerchief, and put it

away within the folds of his clothes. In his own eyes Wynter had now raised himself to the level of an upper class gentleman, having in his possession the means to dispose of himself should he bring the family name into disrepute. Thereafter, when he sat down to cards or dice with the lads, he would always place the pistol on the table, ready to do the right thing should he lose all on the turn of a card. Wynter was a proud man, so he told himself. If earls and whatnot could take the noble way out, so could he. No coward, Wynter.

Raktambar declined to choose a weapon, but Gwilliams took the opportunity of owning an Allen and Wheelock .32 single-shot pistol with a spur trigger and chequered hammer.

'There we are then,' said Hilversum. 'All equipped to deal with any emergency duel – or otherwise. Now, have any of you gentlemen the means of a smoke?'

Gwilliams produced a foul-looking cigar which the Dutchman wisely declined, but he borrowed a clay pipe from Sergeant King who carried several. To Jack's delight and contentment, King had also brought with him Jack's long curved-stemmed Turkish chibouque, which he happily stuffed with King's tobacco and sat puffing for a good long half hour. Then came the call to dinner, which King had prepared. They sat on their haunches to eat, having released the two prisoners on oath, so that they could also be fed. Raktambar had prepared chapatis for the two sepoys, stuffed with wild onions. The halvidar and sepoy seemed grateful enough.

Halfway through the meal, a shout went up from King.

'Hey! They've bolted!'

Jack looked up to see his two prisoners several hundred yards away, running hell for leather towards the edge of a forest. He knew that if they ever reached those trees the pair would be lost to him.

'Gwilliams, Wynter.'

'Bloody hell,' cried Wynter, his mouth full of food, but he jumped to his feet and he and the corporal set out after the two runaways.

Nearing the trees, the havildar turned and made a derogatory gesture with his hand, thus incensing Jack.

'Damn his eyes,' he said exasperated. 'We should have hung them.'

It was a meaningless expression of regret. Jack Crossman

was not a hanging man. He felt that though it was cowardly, he preferred such justice to be left to the authorities, not really having the stomach for summary executions. It was one thing to kill a man in the heat of battle: quite another to do so on a cold dawn morning with one's soul lying quiet and peaceful.

The sepoy reached the forest and entered, with the havildar close on his heels.

An explosion by Jack's ear made him jump sideways and clutch his head for a moment. His ears rang with the sound. In the distance the havildar threw out his arms and shot forward, as if kicked in the back by a mule. He fell in the grasses, out of sight, and did not rise. Jack blinked away some gunsmoke as Wynter and Gwilliams reached the fallen man. They looked down, then they looked back. Gwilliams waved his arms, a signal Jack failed to interpret. The lieutenant then turned to stare at the Dutchman.

Hilversum was still maintaining the half-sideways pose of a shooter, feet shoulder-width apart, right arm out straight, weapon an extension of the wrist, one eye still closed, the aiming eye narrowed. In his fist, still smoking, he held Jack's new gift of the single-shot pistol.

Hilversum lowered the weapon slowly to his side and turned to smile at Crossman.

'Accurate? Very. Did you see that? It must be three-hundred yards. Have you ever known a pistol to be so sure at such a distance?'

'Did I order you to kill him?' cried Jack. For some reason unknown even to himself he was angry with the Dutchman.

Hilversum, the smile gone, turned cold grey eyes on Jack. 'I need no order. That pig was ready to kill me without a thought, just as he killed one of his own men. Why do you care? He would have done the same to you. Please get things into perspective, Lieutenant. That man was a rebel and a murderer. I had no other choice but to do what should have been done earlier. As it is, the fat one got away. The heart must have been bursting in his chest . . .'

Before Jack could make an answer Gwilliams and Wynter arrived back. Wynter went straight to the food again and began chomping.

Gwilliams said, 'Hole between his shoulder blades as big as my fist.'

'As I said,' Hilversum remarked, back to his cheery mode again, 'it would take the head off a pi-dog.'

No more was said of the incident. Jack was puzzled by his own outburst. Of course Hilversum had been within his rights to shoot an escaping prisoner, especially a man who might murder again. Jack himself should have grabbed a rifle and carried out the deed. Yet he felt a deep anger about all this killing. He was a soldier, sure, and soldiers are required to kill the enemy, but death should not be the answer to all and every problem encountered by soldiering. There had been butchery enough in this uprising and someone, somewhere, had to call a halt. You could not wade around in blood for ever and blame the other side for atrocities. If it continued in this way the Ganges would flow pink and foul for ever.

Gwilliams came to him as he brooded by the campfire.

'Sir, I know what you're thinkin' – but he asked for it.'

Jack, surprised, said, 'How do you know what I'm thinking?'

'I know the look. But we ain't finished yet, here in this mess. Right or wrong we've got to do our duty.'

Jack nodded. 'I feel some philosophy coming my way.'

Gwilliams, his auburn beard glinting in the firelight, grinned.

'Them Spartans was the ones for battle. Couldn't walk off the field if there was even one enemy warrior left standin'. I recall a story that there was once a battle fought to a standstill and two of 'em left – a Spartan and one of the enemy. They agreed to call it a draw. That Spartan went home and got thunder from his own wife and relations. Shame, they cried. They said he should've died rather'n walk off the field. How's that for duty?'

'I'm a terrible mixture of English, Scottish and probably one or two others, further back, but all I can say is – I'm glad I'm not a Spartan.'

'Me too,' said the corporal with a smile. 'You got to have *some* choice in your own fate, I say. Goddam generals want to preach everythin' to you, but whether a man chooses to stay and die for nuthin' – why, that's up to him.'

Five

The following morning Rudi Hilversum came to Jack and announced he was parting company.

'Are you sure that is wise?' asked Jack. 'The country is still in turmoil, you know. A lone civilian will be prey to every dacoit and badmash on the road. I know you can shoot, I've been witness to that, but one man alone? You'd be better to stick with us for a few more miles – at least until we reach some European outpost, if not a town.'

Hilversum shook his head. 'I'll take my chances, Lieutenant.' He stuck out his hand. 'It just remains for me to thank you again, for coming back. I can't say I'd have done it for you, because I probably wouldn't have. That's me, I'm afraid. If I'd had any honour, I'd be in the army, I suppose. As it is, I just want to make money. I'd as soon sell a gun to a rebel sepoy as to an officer of Her Majesty Queen Victoria, bless her buxom bottom.'

Jack was more shocked by the jibe at his revered monarch than he was by the idea of selling arms to mutineers, but he said nothing, gripping the hand that was proffered and wishing the owner well. They parted at the fork of a dusty road, Hilversum heading west, towards Delhi, Jack and his men continuing south, hoping to hook up with a main column again. At one point they were knee deep in a field of flowers. The blooms brushed against their legs and left pollen marks on skin and clothes. Sajan picked the heads off one or two, until he was admonished by Raktambar.

Wynter surveyed the white-to-purple flowers with distaste.

'What's these 'uns, then? Cattle fodder?'

Gwilliams laughed.

King said, 'What's to laugh at, Corporal?'

Jack intervened. 'These are opium poppies, Sergeant.'

Apart from his fanatical mapmaking, King had very little

interest in much else. An innocent abroad. 'I still don't understand.'

'This is a field of dreams. Opium is a narcotic. You've heard
of opium, surely? It's the basis of such medicines as laudanum.'

Jack spoke hesitantly. In the Crimea he had been wounded
and ill enough to have had to rely on laudanum for a time.
He remembered being addicted to it and even now he was
involuntarily licking his lips. A habit hard to break.

'The Chinese soldiers sometimes smoke it,' said Wynter.
'Lord, you oughta see 'em lying around lookin' like they was
floating on clouds or somethin'.'

'In America too – mostly the workers on the railways,'
confirmed Gwilliams. 'Had a taster myself once, but whiskey
beats it in my opinion. There's nothin' so particular to the
tongue as the amber liquid. I reckon high spirits is superior
to damn funny dreams every time.'

They were heading down to Bareilly now, where they had
left Campbell's column. Sergeant King was amazed how
peaceful and ordinary the countryside looked. It was a stifling
hot day, it was true, and any sun-fearing creature who could
find shade was in it, but there was no sign of the chaos into
which India had been plunged this last year. Blood had flowed,
both men and women of various races had been hacked to
death or blown to bits in their thousands, yet the landscape
showed none of this carnage.

There were women in billowing saris of pastel shades
drifting here and there. Men stood and stared or lay on rattan
beds outside their hovels. Elephants and camels watched the
world through narrow eyes as they chewed whatever was
within reach. Curs slunk by looking hopefully at the group,
only to flop in a shadow when nothing was forthcoming. On
the horizon, above the high trees, cumulous was gathering in
grey towers. There were no running crowds screaming for
revenge, no thunder of the captains urging their troops towards
another slaughter. Just a world of slow-flowing rivers, the
occasional astonishing foliage and sleepy-looking inhabitants.

'What's war for, anyhow?' he said to himself, but unfortunately was heard by Private Wynter.

'Well, it's the proper state of affairs, an't it?' Wynter replied.
'What work for soldiers, without no war?'

King, who envisaged a perfect world full of army

mapmakers – or their equivalent craftsmen – had no answer for this. The army had given him his trade and he was not going to say nay to that.

Raktambar suddenly cried out. 'East!'

Everyone dropped to the ground below the level of the poppies.

'What have you seen?' whispered Jack to his Rajput aide.

'Soldiers on horseback.'

'Ours or theirs?'

'Too far away.'

Jack waited for a while, then lifted his head slowly to peer out. He could see the riders now, in the far distance. They looked like British cavalry but he couldn't be sure. About twenty-five of them. On request King passed him a spy-glass and when he looked again he could see that they consisted of an officer with HM troopers.

Jack stood up and waved his arms. 'Hey!' he yelled. 'Over here! Queen's Army!' A hot wind was blowing from the east, carrying his words towards the west in the opposite direction to the troopers. The officer in charge turned his mount and actually seemed to see Jack waving, but of course then Jack realized he was dressed in rags and looked more like a Gujar than a soldier. No cavalry worth its salt was going to ride half a mile to investigate the waving of a dubious-looking man in filthy cottons.

'Up you get, they've gone,' he said to his men, as the colourful troopers disappeared behind a ridge. 'Sajan, fill the water bottles from that stream and let's be on our way again.'

He was not too upset, since they were only a day or so away from Bareilly now, where he was sure there would be a British post.

They reached Bareilly two days later. The first people to see them walking into camp were Silvia and Delia Flemming. The barefooted girls came running towards Jack, their dresses flying in the breeze. Their faces, framed by curtains of long black hair, were full of delight.

'Oh, my captain,' cried Silvia, her black eyes flashing, 'you have returned safe and sound to me.'

This sentence was repeated word-for-word by her sister, Delia, in the same melodramatic tones. Their yells brought their father to the door of his billet, followed by his Punjabi wife. The corporal, a stocky little man with grizzled hair, stood arms akimbo. His small-stemmed pipe was sticking out of his mouth and he was puffing furiously. Clearly this show of affection from his daughters did not please him. He called them back. They ignored him, clustering around Jack as if there were ten of them, rather than two.

'Oh, your clothes are so dirty,' Silvia said, trying to take off Jack's kurta, presumably in order to wash it.

'So dirty,' repeated Delia, grasping a sleeve.

Jack tried, ineffectively, to wave the pair away. They were such a nuisance to him, these girls – but like many men he could not bring himself to make them hate him. There was that spark of vanity in him which was fanned to a faint glow by their flattery. They were indeed beautiful young women. Forbidden fruit which he would never in a million years dream of picking, and of course he realized it was his reluctance to return their favours which drew them to him. He knew the moment he showed any interest in them he would scare them away. Yet he could not do that either, being at heart a man who could not show false feelings in order to deceive someone.

Gwilliams stepped forward and grasped a slender wrist of each girl, pulling them away. 'Leave the officer be, you vixens – ain't you got no respect for authority?'

'He is our charge,' cried the girls together. 'He is our captain.'

At that moment Corporal Flemming came over, vest collar and coatee unbuttoned, his bare head mussed. The corporal had been an East Anglian rustic before becoming a soldier and Norfolk men like to think their daughters angels. Angels these two may be from appearances, but little demons they were in character. Flemming took the stubby pipe out of his mouth and was indeed about to berate Jack for toying with his girls when Sergeant King beat him to the draw.

'Corporal,' King snapped, 'keep these children of yours under control, if you please. You recognize the officer? Lieutenant Crossman of the 88th Connaught Rangers? These girls are a perfect nuisance and will not leave him alone. I realize there's no harm in them, but it's your responsibility to see they don't bother officers in the performance of their duties.'

The corporal looked indignant and stuck his pipe back in his mouth. He folded his arms and glared defiantly at King.

'And don't give me your country looks, Corporal,' King growled, 'or you'll feel the blunt edge of my fist on your chin.'

The corporal glanced at King's fist and saw a formidable weapon: wisely he kept his peace, though not so his daughters.

'You threaten our father!' exclaimed Silvia. 'He is our protector.'

'Well, let him bloody-well protect you then,' riposted King. 'You're a disgrace, both of you. Any daughter of mine would be brought up to be a polite and well-mannered girl, not a hoyden.'

Mrs Flemming rustled her sari noisily from the doorway of the billet and called out, 'My daughters are respectable ladies.'

All this commotion brought someone to the door of the officers' quarters. After a moment this person strode across the hard-packed earth to where the group were arguing.

'What's all this yelling and shouting?' asked the man, an overweight major who blinked rapidly and a great deal. 'Keep your peace, if you please.' He turned to stare Wynter up and down. 'Who are you people anyway? Are you the remains of Hodson's men?'

Flemming and his daughters had wisely slipped quietly away, back to their billet.

Jack stepped forward. 'Sir, I am Lieutenant Crossman, of the 88th. Could you direct me to a Major Lovelace? I have to report to him immediately.'

The major stared Jack in the eyes. 'Major Lovelace? If he's here I haven't seen him, and I know who you are. You, sir, are under arrest. You're the fellah Deighnton's looking for – the deserter. Look at the state of you! You should be ashamed, sir, to be seen in that garb, in that state of filth. Are these your men? They're under arrest too. You're all under arrest. Guards?' The last word was yelled, though no one answered it. After a moment the major swallowed his pride and said, 'If you will accompany me, I shall take you to some quarters which you will be pleased to consider your prison until I can summon some sentries . . .'

'This is preposterous,' Jack snapped back at the major. 'We are not deserters, sir, we are employed by Colonel Hawke and Major Lovelace – Queen's Army – in the gathering of information. It is our job to go out as agents into the countryside and glean what we can of enemy troop movements, plans, and other vital facts which are no concern of yours. Is General Campbell here? He will vouch for me and my peloton. I might add we are exhausted, hungry and would like to wash. We've been out in the field for a good while.'

'General Campbell has gone,' replied the major, who looked as if he believed not a word of Jack's defence. 'Colonel Boothroyde is in charge here and I am his adjutant. I don't know these people of whom you speak – their names mean nothing to me. Since I know everything that goes on around Bareilly, I would do – if it were the truth.'

'Of course you don't know them,' replied an exasperated Lieutenant Crossman. 'They're concerned with intelligence. They keep a low profile, obviously. Look, is the correspondent William Russell still here? He knows me. Or Rupert Jarrard of the *New York Banner*?' Jack looked towards the seemingly deserted streets of Bareilly, where only a chockra-boy lay asleep in the shade of a bullet-pitted wall. 'There must be *somebody* here who knows me?'

'Oh, there is,' murmured the major, who had now seen a sergeant major and had motioned to him, 'there's Captain Deighnton, who is at this very minute out scouring the landscape for sight of you and your fellow deserters.'

Jack suddenly realized with a chill that the troopers he saw from the poppy field must have been Deighnton's patrol. Having so obviously sown this story about defection Jack suspected the captain would not have taken prisoners. Jack had almost called down his own executioners on the heads of his men. Deighnton would have drilled those troopers – dragoons by the look of them – drilled them in the belief that they were hunting dangerous criminals. Or would he? The man seemed to wallow in the glory of the duel, so perhaps Jack was doing him an injustice? Perhaps it would have been enough to capture Jack and force him to duel? Who knew how the mind of a deviant like Deighnton actually worked.

'Sarn Major,' said O'Hay to the SNCO who was, incredibly, one of a single company of 88th, Jack's regiment left behind when the rest marched out to join General Rose, 'arrest these men.'

'Sir!' bawled the sergeant major, who turned and raised an eyebrow. 'Civilians, are they?'

Soldiers were then summoned by the sergeant major's powerful lungs and Jack and his men, including Sajan and Raktambar, were led away.

'Sarn Major,' Jack asked, as that man posted sentries outside the door of the hut to which they had been confined, 'who's your IC?'

'You British, is it?' asked the sergeant major, peering into the faces of his prisoners.

'Myself, the corporal here, and that private over there – we are all of your regiment.'

The sergeant major cocked his head to one side and after a few moments fired several questions – some of them in Erse, or Irish Gaelic – at Jack and his two rankers, the answers to which would only have been known to a Connaught Ranger. He was surprised when they answered them correctly, then recognized Wynter's name as being one of those who had at some time brought disgrace upon the 88th, though only in the form of whore-house brawls and drunken escapades. Gwilliams' accent threw him a little and he asked where in the world someone got a twisted tongue like his.

'Boone's Lick, Missouri,' replied Gwilliams. 'How about yourn?'

The officer's name, finally dragged out of the sergeant major, was not familiar to Jack, and he began to despair. One could get hung out here in the middle of nowhere, now that law had broken down and death was an everyday occurrence. Men who have witnessed the dismembering of women and children and had seen natives blown from cannons are likely to be slightly hardened to death and to treat it as commonplace. If he managed to convince someone he was indeed an officer in the British Army, he might get them court martialled, but even that was uncertain. Sajan and Raktambar might be set free, but that was unlikely too. Any excuse or none was good enough to execute an Indian after such massacres and fighting. Jack realized they were in deep trouble, though King kept fulminating.

The sergeant said, 'All they've got to do is look in my pack and see I've got mapmaking equipment. People are allowed to go out and make maps for the army's use, aren't they? How do they think maps get made? You can't do it sitting on your backside in a bloody tent.' He grumbled angrily to the sentries who were actually too scared of their sergeant major to reply to these rants.

Jack, as an officer, was removed from the presence of his men, put under open arrest and conveyed to separate quarters, a bungalow that appeared internally untouched by the recent fighting. Outside though was a wide stretch of ground where the rebel sepoys had been camped and the open latrines had still not been filled in. Although there were no human bodies, there were still dead camels and elephants rotting in the sun. Even with the shutters closed the stink hugged every corner of the house.

A subaltern of the 95th came to see him, a reed-thin boy of about twenty years carrying a heavy Roman nose on his sharp face. This was Jack's guard.

'Told to look after you. Comfortable, old chap?'

'Not really,' replied Jack. 'I've a feeling I'm about to be hauled up in front of your colonel. Could you have a basin or two of water sent in so that I can spruce myself up a bit?' A thought came to Jack. 'Listen, as you're aware I'm in a bit of bother. I would feel very inferior going before the colonel in these rags. I wonder if you know any lieutenants in the 88th? There must be a couple of them around, with a whole company here. Any possibility of me borrowing a uniform? I'd feel more army in a uniform. In these cottons I'm very much the poor cousin.'

The young subaltern looked a bit dubious.

'I can get you the water of course – but the uniform . . .'

'I would be most grateful. I can assure you as a brother officer I am not guilty of this charge. I do undercover work and this has all been a frightful mistake, believe me.'

'You mean stuff like Hodson used to do?'

'That's exactly it – just like Hodson. I go out amongst the natives, glean information, and bring it back. I was abducted and made prisoner by some mutineers and simply have to clear myself now.' Jack injected a little persuasive lie. 'I worked for John Nicholson, before the Delhi attack.'

It was true he had provided information helpful to the attack, but had not directly reported to Brigadier-General Nicholson, a hero of the North West Frontier and whose very name worked like magic on Sikhs, Pathans and romantic subalterns with visions of glory in their heads.

'You knew Nicholson?' He breathed the name.

'We were brothers of the blade.'

The subaltern swallowed and nodded. 'I'll do what I can for you – can't promise of course – but I'll do my best.'

'I very much appreciate it.'

The subaltern, whose name Jack had learned was Simon Keenlyside, left the bungalow. Shortly afterwards an Indian bearer brought some hot water for Jack to wash in. He carried out an all-over bathe, standing one foot in the bowl alternately. The water was soon black. More was fetched, now that he had the ear of the bearer. When the subaltern returned triumphant with a full dress uniform, including boots, Jack was indeed 'spruced', having trimmed his beard, nails and hair. Lieutenant Crossman looked almost respectable.

'Lieutenant Cathaway sends these with his compliments,' said the subaltern. 'Though he also said if you're found guilty he'll burn the whole lot and never trust a brother officer again.'

'Does he know who charged me with this crime?'

'Yes – Deighnton – which is why he's loaning you his kit. Cathaway apologizes for the dark patch on the seat of the trousers – camel sweat. The 88th and the Rifles have formed together here to make the Camel Corps and we had a parade the other day. Very hot. Camels sweated like – well, like bloody camels. Devil to get out are camel sweat stains. Can't do it, really. Anyway, he apologizes, and says he hopes you draw Deighnton's cork.'

'Ah, fortunately for me the captain makes enemies amongst the infantry wherever he goes.'

'And Cathaway admires Nicholson as much as I do – you fought with him, you say?'

'In the streets of Delhi . . .' Which was not a lie, and Jack went on to tell the story, because he felt he owed it to this young man, even though he was itching to be at the pen and paper he had found in the desk in the bungalow.

The prisoners remained where they were for the next eighteen hours. Curries and coffee were supplied. Jack considered his position. The charges had been manufactured by

Captain Deighnton, but Jack was at a loss to understand why. Picking a duel with a man because you have reason to believe he has insulted your good friend is one thing. That package came wrapped up in honour. But to deliberately go after that man with lies and deceit – where was the honour and satisfaction in that? Men like Deighnton had a very warped sense of honour it was true, but such men also sought glory. There was absolutely no glory in the dirty business of a trumped-up charge of desertion. Jack was completely flummoxed and decided he did not know Deighnton at all. He thought he had had him pegged but this cavalry officer was more than just a bully. It was a most perplexing puzzle.

In the cool of the following early morning, Jack was sent for. Lieutenant Keenlyside marched him to a palace boasting graceful arches and beautiful latticework windows which was now used by the local commander as his headquarters. On enquiry Jack had learned his name was Colonel Boothroyde, an infantry commander. On the way Jack saw both native and HM troops going about their business around the camp. One or two glanced curiously at him, since he stood out among them in his dress uniform. The heavy stink from the cesspits which had bothered him so much at first was wearing a little thinner as the faeces and urine dried under the sun. The odour from the rotting carcasses did not lessen, however, and he could see some men with perfumed kerchiefs pressed to their noses. In the near distance Jack could see the limp bodies of three hanged men, still on the gibbet, a flock of dark birds hovering around what remained of their heads.

Jack was taken up some marble steps and through a magnificent doorway, the pointed arches of which were decorated with inlaid chips of semi-precious stones: jasper, jade, lapis lazuli, garnet, cornelian, mother-of-pearl, malachite, and several others. The coloured mosaics stood out starkly in the white marble, chipped in many places; Jack suspected by musket balls or grapeshot. He was led around a courtyard of fountains and pools full of lilies hedged with myrtle and cornered with cypress trees to another great five-arched portico where the walls were covered with Sanskrit script which he could not read. Thence up another marble staircase and through yet another doorway supported by slender marble columns into what appeared to be the banqueting hall. Glancing up

Jack could see ceiling paintings on what looked like leather and there were marble lions resting around the edges of the hall, staring at the occupants with steady glazed eyes.

In the middle of the hall, trestle tables had been erected and chairs set out. Behind the tables was a colonel, with Major O'Hay to his left and Deighnton to his right. *The warrior returns*, thought Jack, avoiding Deighnton's direct stare. Jack was certain that Deighnton would have killed him rather than bringing him back for 'justice'. *He must be feeling as sick as a dog*, Jack told himself, *to find me here waiting for him.*

Jack was marched forward, his and Keenlyside's boots echoing in the great hall. A burly sergeant major eyed him disinterestedly. Jack knew the man was there in case he lost his temper and tried to attack any of the 'judges' sitting at the table.

The colonel opened proceedings by introducing himself and informing Jack that this was by the way of a preliminary inquiry.

'. . . into the charge of desertion in the face of the enemy.'

Chilling. A charge that carried the death penalty. Jack had a passing thought about those three hanged men but dismissed it. More likely it would be a firing squad. Live practice for any untried new recruits.

'Have you anything to say at this stage – ' he looked down at a sheet of paper in front of him – 'Lieutenant Kirk?'

'My name, sir, is Lieutenant Crossman.'

Deighnton was smirking.

The colonel shook his head in a puzzled way. 'I understand your name to be Alexander Kirk. Is that incorrect?' The colonel looked sharply up at Keenlyside. 'Have you brought me the wrong man, sir?'

Before the bewildered and flustered subaltern could answer, Deighnton interrupted. 'He calls himself Jack Crossman for some devious reasons of his own.'

'Sir,' replied Jack, standing stiffly to attention, 'I respectfully request that you contact my superior officer, Major Lovelace or his superior, Colonel Hawke, whose orders I was following on this mission.'

'Where did you get that uniform, Lieutenant?' asked Deighnton fiercely. Clearly the captain was suffering a great disappointment, finding his quarry had managed to turn out the very image of a smart soldier. 'The last time I saw you, you were in Pathan's rags.'

Colonel Boothroyde interrupted him. 'That is hardly relevant, Captain. I'm more interested in getting to the truth here, and I'm already very confused.' He stared at Jack. 'Lieutenant, you bear an assumed name?'

Jack sighed, having told the story so many times before.

'I joined the army under a pseudonym in order that my father, a major in the 93rd, should not interfere in my career. Had he known I was in the army he would have wished to purchase me a lieutenancy, which I did not want him to do. In fact I rose to the rank of my own accord from a private soldier. For reasons not the concern of this inquiry, deep domestic reasons which were important at the time but are now irrelevant, I chose to remain Jack Crossman.'

'Most irregular, but a man's private affairs are his own, I suppose,' replied the colonel, shuffling his papers for the third time.

The colonel was a small man, white-haired, with a kindly face. He was withered looking, possibly from too much sun, but his blue eyes shone with an understanding light. Jack felt very much relieved he was not in front of some blustering fool of a colonel whose brains were in the seat of his pants. Jack felt emboldened to offer his defence.

'Sir, may I proffer my report? My escort has it in his case.'

Major O'Hay's eyes widened.

'When did you write that?'

'Last night, sir. It's the report I shall be handing to either Major Lovelace or Colonel Hawke. It tells of my attempt to carry out my mission, my subsequent capture by rebel sepoys and my abduction into the Himalayan mountains by those rebels. My men realized I had gone missing, when I failed to appear at the rendezvous point, and followed my trail. I managed to escape before rescue was needed and when my men finally caught up with me, we continued after the rebels and wiped them out. So far as I am aware only one man unfortunately escaped justice when he ran off.'

Jack took the report from Keenlyside and placed it carefully on the table in front of the colonel, who peered at it myopically.

Deighnton was looking furious, as well he might. Here was

his prey, all snapped out like an officer on parade, not a hair out of place, presenting the inquiry with a detailed account of his escapades. Deighnton had been expecting Jack to be dragged in, filthy and lice-ridden, wearing the same dirt and rags he had been carrying with him for several weeks.

The colonel read just a few lines of the report, then looked up and noticed Jack's missing hand.

'The . . . er . . . deformity – here?'

'No, sir. Crimea.'

'Ah – ' the colonel glanced towards Deighnton – 'and so you two knew each other in the Crimea?'

'No, we did not,' said Jack. 'Until this moment I did not know of Captain Deighnton's presence in the Crimea.'

'Captain Deighnton is a survivor of that dreadful charge the Light Brigade made on Russian cannons, though not with his current regiment.'

He would be, thought Jack. Deighnton was likely to come out of a massacre without a scratch. He was that sort of officer. Damn it, how big did cannonballs have to be to hit a man like Deighnton? He probably rode through a hail of grapeshot and canister with men and horses going down on all sides, and felt only the wind of their passing. If rain were acid, men like Deighnton would walk through it without a drop falling on their shoulders.

'He is a hero, Lieutenant. Were you a hero of the Crimea?'

'He did his part,' muttered Deighnton, without looking up. 'I understand he distinguished himself at the battle for the Redan, which is where he lost his hand.'

'So, two heroes of the Crimea, albeit one of lesser glory.' He sighed deeply. 'What a shame it has to come to this sort of thing, one officer accusing another. One would have thought the pair of you should be toasting each other, rather than be at daggers drawn. Most unfortunate. Now, Lieutenant, please give me an account in your own words . . .'

Jack began his story, noting that the colonel was reading the report in front of him as Jack was telling the tale, presumably to check that the two versions were more or less the same. Jack did vary his oral report slightly, knowing that if he was too exact he could be accused of learning his story by rote and trotting it out verbatim, which would be just as damning as coming out with a tale that differed considerably from the written version.

'My men will verify those parts where they were involved, but of course cannot do so for the part where I was a captive. Nor can they confirm my orders, which were given to me orally by my superior in the presence of no one but ourselves. You will appreciate, sir, that this kind of work requires the utmost secrecy. If anything leaks out, through servants or others, to the general population, the missions would be at risk. My disguises would be useless to me and the whole effort would be compromised.'

The colonel turned to Deighnton. 'Captain?'

Deighnton leaned back in his chair and tapped the table with a coin as he spoke. 'All I know is I saw him run after freeing himself from a Ghazi zealot. The pair of them were brawling in the dust, scratching and kicking like two women. Crossman was fortunate that his Rajput servant was close by to behead the Ghazi, or he would have had his eyes clawed out . . .'

'Those Ghazis are a formidable enemy,' said the colonel. 'Frightful fellows.'

'After which I heard that Crossman had not been seen since. I learned from others that he had ridden north, galloped away from the scene of the fighting, leaving the battle behind him. It's my contention that Crossman – I do not believe him to be a coward, having seen him fight with bravery on other occasions – became overwhelmed and confused by his encounter with the frenzied attack of the Ghazi. His mind disjointed, he took flight.'

Disjointed, mused Jack. Strange choice of word – but exceptionally clever. '*His mind was disjointed.*' He's not accusing me of cowardice, but the result would be the same. If I ran, I ran, whatever the reason. Yet the captain *understands* why I ran, albeit it is no excuse. So very clever. You bloody bastard, he thought. I wish you were dead. Why didn't I shoot straight on that morning? Why didn't I blow your cunning little brains out?

'The captain is right,' said Jack. 'I was *disorientated* after my scrap with the Ghazi, but only very briefly, for a few minutes at the most. I maintain as in the report – I insist – I received an oral order from Major Lovelace to the effect that I had to go out and ascertain the general direction of the retreating enemy army of Khan. This I did, sending back my sergeant to inform General Campbell, while venturing on alone to verify my findings. It was shortly after this that I was ambushed by rebel sepoys and taken prisoner. My men will verify the fact that I was taken prisoner, for though they did not actually witness me being captured, or my escape from the rebels, they did assist me in following my captors and in bringing them to justice.'

The colonel listened to this with care before taking some spectacles out of his top pocket, putting them on, and then peering at some papers on the desk before him.

'I see here Captain Deighnton maintains that the loyalty of your men is such that they will swear black is white if you wished it.'

Jack could not help but let out a hollow laugh which echoed around the walls of the large stone hall.

'Sir, I have a Rajput who would rather be back with his beloved maharaja than trailing about with me; a sergeant who is more interested in mapmaking than doing his job of spying and sabotage; a private who hates all officers and especially those who jumped from sergeant to lieutenant without a by your leave; and an American frontiersman who finds it difficult to show the British Army loyalty, let alone a British aristocrat. I think you'll find that my men are much the same as other ranking soldiers in the British Army – they care nothing for those who lead them.'

The colonel looked over his glasses at Deighnton.

'He's certainly very eloquent,' he said. 'I like a man who puts up a clever and spirited defence.'

The look on the captain's face showed he did not agree.

Throughout the inquiry Major O'Hay had been sitting staring at the tabletop, his bottom lip protruding, a thoughtful expression on his face. He was one of those men who listens with growing indignation and abhorrence to ugly stories about phantom officers, but finds when that officer has a face, a body, a bearing, a manner and a way of addressing others – in short, a character – he can no longer maintain the disgust he felt when that officer could only be imagined. He finds the fellow not at all like he thought he would be: the chap seems somehow more human and credible. Not a monster at all.

The major suddenly came alive. 'May I interject a word here, Colonel?'

'Certainly, Major – what is it?'

'I've been thinking, sir – this lieutenant is not known to us or anyone else in camp – except Captain Deighnton. I have a feeling there is some history between these two men. I've been watching them both very carefully, and there is personal animosity in the way they exchange looks and words. Would the colonel allow me to question both officers?'

Good for you! thought Jack. Unexpectedly insightful. I had you pegged as a lazy Indian Army officer, happy to drift on the tide so long as no effort was required from you.

Deighnton said venomously, 'I object! I'm not being investigated here – the lieutenant is the man before the court.'

Colonel Boothroyde said sharply, 'This is not a court. You, sir, are the accuser – what have you got to hide?'

O'Hay immediately started in on the captain, not giving him time for further protests.

'How is it, Captain Deighnton, that you – a cavalry officer – are familiar with a lieutenant of an infantry regiment? Do your families know one another?'

'No, they do not, sir,' said Deighnton, with some asperity. 'Lieutenant Crossman and I clashed during the siege of Delhi – his Indian servant was in jail there and the lieutenant contrived to free him by devious means which need not concern this inquiry.'

'You quarrelled?'

'Most assuredly.'

'And who won this quarrel – who came out the victor?'

Deighnton almost stood up, but thought better of it and simply twisted in his chair. 'I don't understand the relevance of all this . . .'

'Lieutenant?' continued O'Hay. 'Who came out best?'

Jack said, 'I managed to free my Rajput, who had been wrongly imprisoned in the first instance.'

'So the captain has a cause?'

Deighnton said through even teeth, 'Are you calling me a *liar*, Major? Is there some implication that I'm concocting this story out of nothing?' When he spoke his eyes narrowed and he looked as dangerous as a cobra. The major actually flinched under this attack. But, thought Jack, to give him his due he did not retreat.

'I am not calling you anything, Captain. I, like the colonel here, am trying to get at the core of this rotten apple. You have a grievance against this lieutenant having been bettered by him in a quarrel. One could say you are not entirely without bias.'

Colonel Boothroyde saved the major from another withering look by supporting him. 'The more that comes out here, the less simple the matter appears. You say you had a companion in your captivity – a Dutchman? What was his name?'

'He gave his name as Rudi Hilversum,' Jack said.

There was a sharp intake of breath from Major O'Hay. He leaned across and whispered in the ear of the colonel. Deighnton was suddenly smirking again, victory evident in his expression. The colonel looked severe as he addressed Jack again.

'Are you offering this villain as someone who will corroborate your testimony, Lieutenant?'

'Villain?' Jack's stomach turned over. 'I have no idea of his former activities. Hilversum had already been captive a while when I myself was made prisoner. I had neither met nor heard of the man before that moment. I have to say he showed fortitude and courage in the face of death and I had no reason to doubt his character. May I ask why he is thus branded, sir?'

'Hilversum has been suspected of various crimes from gunrunning to embezzlement,' Major O'Hay stated. 'If you call him as a witness on your behalf you might well regret it.'

'You say *suspected*, sir. Has he ever been convicted?'

'To my knowledge he has not been charged with anything yet, but he has a very undesirable reputation, Lieutenant. I'm surprised you have not heard of him – most have. Perhaps your clandestine activities keep you out of the way of ordinary gossip, which can be no bad thing. Colonel,' Major O'Hay said, turning to his superior, 'may I offer a suggestion here?'

'Certainly, Major,' replied the colonel, seeming only too relieved to have someone make a decision for him. 'What is it?'

'Sir, might I suggest that all witnesses leave the room while we bring this process to a close?'

Since there was only one witness present, that man being Captain Deighnton, the cavalry officer snorted violently.

Colonel Boothroyde stared at the captain with intense dislike in his expression. 'Sir, leave us if you please?'

Without another word the sour-faced captain rose and strode, tall and straight, the length of the hall, his sabre clinking against the metal on his belt. Jack reluctantly admired his adversary's bearing. Deighnton was everything required of a cavalry captain: tall, lean, handsome, and so far as Jack had learned, courageous to a fault. He had breeding. His horsemanship was brilliant. His appearance immaculate. He was also intelligent and articulate: not one of your stuttering Percivals or gormless inbreeds. An aristocrat's son, he was feared and envied for his utter disregard for his own safety. Deighnton had the appearance of a prince and the heart of a despot. Such was the man who had made an enemy of Jack Crossman.

'Now,' said Major O'Hay, bringing everyone's attention back to the table where the colonel sat shuffling papers, 'to the question of what to do with Lieutenant Kirk.' Jack, weary of protest, let this ride. 'My suggestion, Colonel, should you wish to accept it, is that we release the lieutenant for the present time so that he may go about his duties. He is to understand that he is not exonerated from these charges, but at the moment the evidence is too weak to bring court martial against him and his men. At some future date he is to present himself to his commanding officer – the colonel of the 88th – to whom we shall send the details gathered so far. Let his own CO decide whether to press the case or abandon it, according to any new evidence which might be garnered in the meantime.'

Colonel Boothroyde threw a very grateful look at his aide.

'Major, I believe I was coming to the same decision myself. You have put it very neatly into words.' He turned to Jack and wore his severe expression. 'Lieutenant – whatever you call yourself – you are free to go for the moment. But hold yourself ready, sir, to account for your actions. There is a grey mark against your name which has not yet been erased. You, Lieutenant, will bring yourself before your own commanding officer at a future time, once we have this household – ' he meant of course India – 'thoroughly back in the grip of its rightful stewards. Is that understood?'

Although Jack was already at attention, he brought his heels together with a click and saluted the colonel. 'Perfectly, sir. Thank you.'

'Don't thank me,' replied the colonel. 'It is not for you to thank me, sir – I have done my duty, that is all. Dismissed.'

The two senior officers rose and left the room, chatting about some affair to do with the mess, leaving a damp and relieved Jack. Soldiers around the room relaxed. The sergeant major who had been standing just to Jack's right, ready to prevent him from attacking any of the inquiry officers should things have turned nasty, turned and marched briskly towards the hall's exit.

Keenlyside grinned and extended his hand.

Jack shook it, saying, 'Well, I'm not off the hook yet.'

'No, but as good as.'

'I hope so. It's a horrible charge – desertion. My father – well, let's not dwell on such horrors. Can I buy you a *chotapeg*?'

'No thanks. Can't drink. I'm actually still on duty. I should think you could do with some tiffin. Can you leave the uniform in the bungalow? Chap wants it back of course.'

Jack looked down at himself. 'Oh, yes – forgot. It's back to the *choga* for me.'

'I envy you.' The lieutenant ran a finger under his coatee collar. 'I'd prefer Indian cottons to these beastly garments.'

Jack left the hall. He was relieved to find Deighnton was nowhere to be seen. While he still wore the uniform, which had more of an electric effect on soldiers than his Indian garb, he went straight to the billet where his men were confined. As he suspected, no one had bothered to send word to release them. The sentries were still there. Jack dismissed them. They took no notice of him, staring past him at some point on the horizon.

'Who's your sergeant?' he asked one of them.

'Sergeant McKinnon.'

'Well, one of you fetch him – the other can still remain here to guard the prisoners.'

The soldiers looked unsure of themselves.

'NOW!'

One of them left at the double, heading towards the Guard Room. A few minutes later he came out again and whistled, shrilly, between two fingers. The remaining soldier glanced at Jack, saluted him, then trotted off with his rifle in the direction of the whistle. Jack went into the billet and informed Sergeant King that they were leaving.

'Thank God for that,' muttered King. 'I was beginning to feel the rope around my neck.'

'I don't think it would have come to that,' replied Jack, but he said it without much conviction. 'It was a fair hearing.'

Corporal Gwilliams said, 'Well, you're lucky to get one of those – there's not many in the bag, from what I've seen of army justice.'

'Too right,' cried Wynter. 'I've 'ad a good few bad 'uns.'

Raktambar and Sajan said nothing, but Raktambar nodded slowly and seriously in Jack's direction, acknowledging Jack's victory.

The group managed to find some horses and prepared to ride south to join General Rose's advance into Central India. Before they left, Jack went to see the young subaltern, Lieutenant Keenlyside, who urged Jack to find his superiors as soon as it was possible.

'Captain Deighnton has left camp,' said Keenlyside, 'and is far from satisfied with the outcome of the inquiry.'

'I can understand that,' Jack said. 'He wanted me found guilty.'

'The word is that once you were out of Boothroyde's sight the colonel began having second thoughts. He's anything but convinced of your innocence, but is constrained by the lack of evidence both for and against your case. I believe if you stayed around here too long, you might end up back on arrest again. My advice is to scoot before the Old Man changes his mind. He's apt to that. Not a constant man, our commander. He can be influenced. Fortunately for you, O'Hay turned against Deighnton, but the commander listens to whoever has his ear at the time. Deighnton may very well return with some officer of senior rank and you'll be back in the pot.'

'Thanks for the advice. I was of the same mind.'

'Off you go then, old chap,' said Keenlyside, grinning. 'Scoot on down to Rose and see if you can't find your Loveladle or whatever his name is – you need some big guns behind you.'

Six

J ack had learned from the young Lieutenant Keenlyside that
General Rose had defeated Tantia Tope at Kunch and had
later captured Kalpi. Having completed operations in
Rohilkand, Rose's force had moved on towards Gwalior. The
rebel armies had now fragmented into guerrilla groups which
ranged the countryside, creating mayhem on a smaller scale
than before, but with irritating effect. They were now harder
to find, less easy to pin down, yet still as ferocious as before.
These were men who had nothing to lose. They had made a
bid to cast off their British rulers and had failed, but they were
not simply going to lie down.

Gwalior lay nearly two hundred miles south of Bareilly and
the going was through some thickly forested regions. Any
clump of trees or bushes could contain rebel guerrillas, as
could any group of village huts, any gully or dip in the landscape. Jack's men had to be wary of substance and shadow
alike. Twice they stumbled upon small groups of rebels and
engaged in brief skirmishes which both ended in the rebels
slipping away. Jack did not doubt that their own appearance
– that of a dirty, weathered bunch of men – had saved them
from other attacks. From a distance they did not look like
British soldiers and only when they actually came face-to-
face with guerrilla forces did their disguise let them down.

Jack was now full of optimism regarding the containment
of the uprising. Delhi, Lucknow and Cawnpore had all been
taken. Other towns previously in rebel hands had been prised
away from them. At Bareilly Campbell had defeated a rebel
force of 36,000, a force which had been able to put forty guns
into the field. Jhansi, held by 11,000 rebels with Tantia Tope's
20,000 reinforcements on the way, had been overrun. In the
war as a whole at least half of the total 123 Native Regular
and Irregular units had mutinied against British rule. They

had been defeated by a seventh of their number, though it was not the fighting man at fault in the rebel army but the lack of leadership and command structure. On the contrary the rebel sepoys had fought with the same immense courage and resilience that they had showed when fighting *for* the British. Jack dreaded to think what would have happened if the whole native contingent of the Indian Army had risen up: the British would be but a memory, wiped clean from the landscape of this vast land.

The night before they caught up with General Rose's army, Jack's men camped on the banks of a fast-flowing river. They had been sleeping in the open for the most part, but occasionally built bivouacs from staves and palm leaves. This was one of those nights, when the day sky had massive columns of black cloud which climbed up to enormous heights. However, as often happens in tropical regions, the sky cleared magically as the evening swept in. The smell of threatened rain disappeared, to be replaced by softer floral fragrances overlain with whiffs of river-mud odour. Jack left his bivouac to see the night sky covered with stars like silver nails in a black door.

He breathed deeply, feeling something close to contentment, and walked to the edge of the encampment.

'Stop there! Who's that?' cried a gruff voice. 'Make yourself known, or be shot to bits on a purpose.'

'It's me, Wynter – Lieutenant Crossman.'

The rifle pointing at Jack's belly was slowly removed from its present aim.

'Just doin' me diligent sentry duty, sir,' sniffed Wynter. 'No offence to the officer.'

'None taken, Wynter.' He thought for a bit, then added, 'That march you did, from the Crimea. That was a very great feat.'

'Din't get no medals for it though, did we, sir?'

'I don't know, didn't you? Anyway, Wynter, you always sell any medals the army gives to you for gin. It's a pointless exercise. Haven't you thought about keeping them for your grandchildren?'

'An't got none of those, not so's I know. Anyways,' the soldier acknowledged, 'when I gets a thirst on I'd sell a grandchild for a drink, let alone a medal. You can't trust me, sir, with anythin' really. I'd sell the balls out of the barrel of me rifle for a woman or a bottle, even though they might save me life in the next minute. I mean, what're we here for, if not to get the best of it?'

'Some think a family *is* the best of it.'

Wynter laughed hollowly. 'Not me. That's for the likes of 'im over there . . .' He nodded in the direction of square, thickset Sergeant King, who was at that moment poring over the maps he had drawn of the mountains of Chinese Tartary. He was speaking to Sajan in a low voice, the son and the father learning together. Raktambar was sitting on a log not far away from the two, looking on indulgently, just as an uncle might observe with satisfaction the education of a nephew.

It was a pleasant scene. Jack knew that the father and adopted son had become quite close after their time together in the Tibetan tower. His feelings were in a way tinged with jealousy. An instant family was something to envy. Would he and Jane have a child soon? It seemed unlikely unless it could be done by post. He had not seen Jane now for over a year, though letters had flowed between them thick and fast. Lately he had not seen a letter, of course. They were around somewhere, in India, chasing him no doubt – but there had been none at Bareilly.

'You did very well, boy – very well.' King's voice came to Jack on the breeze. Jack saw the sergeant ruffle Sajan's hair and noticed the smile on the child's face, grateful for the praise and attention.

'Thank you, Father.'

At one time Jack had been suspicious about the sergeant's reasons for his strong interest in an Indian child, but that was before he had learned of King's activities during an earlier visit to India. The sergeant had made a village girl pregnant then lost contact with her. Jack now realized King had wanted a surrogate son. Sajan was certainly not King's real son, but the hope of finding the latter was so faint as to be almost negligible. King's conscience had troubled him initially, and that guilt had translated itself into some idea that in Sajan he had found his lost son and heir, blood of his blood. Jack had tried to dispel this false conception without success and had finally accepted that though King might fool himself for the rest of his life, no real harm could come of it. Sajan was an orphan and useful to the group in certain given circumstances. If Jack had ever felt any twinge of guilt himself at using the boy, it was quickly gone: there were British drummer boys of Sajan's age who had marched into the thick of battles for the sake of usefulness.

Jack needed to go to the toilet, so he now left the camp for a clump of trees nearby. Completely out of step with the rest of British soldiery in India, Jack was often constipated. He was dreadfully embarrassed by this affliction and had once said unthinkingly to Gwilliams that he would have given his right hand to be rid of it, which allowed Gwilliams a guffaw of amusement and to point out that he had given his left hand and got bugger all in return for it.

Always wary of snakes, which seemed to come out at night with the bats and other nocturnal creatures, Jack trod carefully to find some privacy amongst the trees. He could have gone out in the open, but coupled with his bowels problem was another affliction – his class. An ordinary soldier might drop his pants where he pleased, but a lieutenant from an aristocratic family might not. Jack would rather be bitten by a deadly cobra than show his backside to the troops. How could he hold up his head if caught in such a position? It would have been impossible for him. An officer who leads from the front must never show his rear without it being covered by cloth.

Jack found a dark spot and felt safe from prying eyes. He went about his business. Squatting there, straining for a few moments, he suddenly became aware that the crickets and other jungle noises had ceased. Was that because of his presence? He did not think so. Crickets did not normally bother about animals of any kind, even humans, unless they were within inches. Then, as he listened hard in the deep silence, he heard the sound of breathing coming from close by. Still squatting, with his trousers round his ankles, he reached carefully for the Tranter revolver in his waistband.

The regular breathing made Jack think that whoever it was, was asleep under a bush. He peered hard, searching for a shape amongst the bushes. How humiliating – and dangerous – to be caught in such a position at such a time! He could hear no stirring: just the slow in-and-out motion of breath. At that moment, as if in order to assist him in his search, the moon came out from behind a cloud. Now Jack was able to look around the glade he was occupying, to find the owner of that breath.

The first thing he saw were the eyes. They stared at him from about ten yards away: gold-flecked almond-shaped eyes. Unblinking. A beam of moonlight had caught them full on and they gazed at Jack with an unvarying languid intensity, almost curious in their aspect: the eyes of one who has woken from a long sleep and sees a stranger squatting before him, and is possibly thinking, 'Oh, hello – what are you up to?'

From the eyes Jack travelled down and gradually, gradually made out the rest of the shape. It was a huge, lolling beast that had flopped to the ground for a rest or sleep. As Jack's eyes became accustomed to the barred moonlit forest he could see the stripes like black bent bars on the lighter coat. An ear flicked. A tail swished.

Tiger.

Having spent all this time in India, he had previously congratulated himself on never really encountering a tiger. There had been that hunt with the rajah, but then he had been surrounded by muskets, blasting away at every twitch of grass or leaf, the only danger being from an over-eager matchlock man swinging his weapon in the wrong direction. Now here he was, a fully grown feline monster just yards away, regarding him with a schoolmaster's solemn interest. His revolver felt like a peashooter in his hand.

What could stop this ton of muscle and bone if it decided to come at him? Only a bloody field gun, he thought to himself, his heart drumming rapidly. Only a regiment of heavy-bore sharpshooters. Only a forest of bayonets and sabres with no inch to spare between their points.

For a long time the pair just remained where they were, hardly a movement coming from either of them. Jack tried looking away, thinking that his stare might be upsetting the beast, but when he looked back again yellow eyes were holding him in a steady gaze. Cramps began to set in his legs. He was not as used to squatting as the Indians, who did it all the time, whether they were at toilet or not. Pretty soon his calves knotted and he wanted to scream out in pain. Then his right foot and toes followed suit, bringing tears to his eyes. He wanted to yell, jump and run about, to rid himself of the bunched, locked muscles that twisted into ropes of agony. But any such move on his part he was sure would bring the tiger leaping forward, teeth bared, ready to rip open his belly.

How do I get myself into these situations? thought Jack, miserably. All I wanted was to perform my rightful ablutions in peace. Is that too much to ask? Have I offended God so much that He has decided not only to end my life, but to do it in such a fashion as will leave men sniggering at the manner of it? Jack could not bear the thought of being found mangled, fettered in the act of running by his own pants, caught as it were, *in flagrante delicto*. How desperately humiliating. Could one's family history survive such a death? Jack imagined his descendants attempting to suppress the story, yet the sordid tale living on for ever as a bar-room joke.

The cramps finally subsided, but Jack was ringing with perspiration, flies sticking to his skin.

He started to get slowly to his feet, but at the movement the tiger suddenly sat up: a big cat preparing to rise. Its eyes had narrowed to slits. Huge paws flattened on the hard-packed earth.

Jack froze, the fear coursing through his body. The obvious happened and his constipation was cured at a stroke.

In a moment the glade was filled with a horrible stench.

The tiger stared at him. Then after a few moments it got to its feet and padded away, obviously disgusted by the smell. Jack remained squatting, the sweat dripping from him. He had come so close to an inglorious, ignominious death it was not true. He began to think that perhaps he should fling himself at death in the very next battle, to ensure that his descendants would have nothing to be ashamed about.

On his way back into camp he decided to say nothing to anyone about the incident. Gwilliams looked at him curiously as he washed his hands in stream water.

'You all right, lootenant?'

'I'm fine,' Jack replied, not looking at the corporal. 'Why do you ask?'

'You look kinda pale – you ain't sick'ning?'

'It's the firelight,' muttered Jack. 'It throws out all sorts of . . . of light. I'm perfectly well, thank you.'

'Have a good one in there, then?' Gwilliams nodded towards the forest.

'Corporal, I do not discuss my ablutions with *anyone*, let alone my troops.'

'Just askin'.'

'Your concern in this area is not appreciated.'

'Jeez!'

Sergeant Farrier King came into the firelight.

'What's going on?' he asked.

Gwilliams shrugged. 'I was just enquiring after the lootenant's crap. You know he gets problems.' A grave nod followed.

'Oh? Have you still a difficulty, sir?' asked King politely. 'Can't be easy one-handed either. I myself . . .'

Jack hissed, 'I'm not interested in your condition, Sergeant – and I don't wish to discuss my own. I wish to be left in peace, if you please. Can a human being not be entitled to carry out his private acts without half the world wanting to know the details? Good God, there are so few secrets amongst us. Please leave me with *some* degree of dignity.'

'Keep it down over there,' growled the voice of Wynter out of the darkness. 'The officer's out there in the woods tryin' to have a shit. You know what he's like – he needs to concentrate, bein' as his gut is usually stuffed up tighter than a turkey at Christmas. He gets crabby if he don't make a good showing of it.'

Jack gave up and went to bed.

The group caught up with General Rose's column as it made a forced march south towards Gwalior. Jack learned that Tantia Tope had escaped his previous battle with Rose and had regrouped. With him were two strong allies, Rao Sahib and the Rani of Jhansi.

Despite the fact that she was their enemy, the Rani had captured the admiration of many a British officer, Jack included. He could not but help compare her with Boadicea, the British warrior queen. In fact their general careers had followed similar paths. Both had lost their ruler husbands and had been robbed of their rightful inheritance by occupying armies. They both rose up in defence of their claims, to become serious threats to those armies. The Rani, whose name was Manikarnika, began to recruit an army even before the uprising, which included women like herself. She had already defeated two neighbouring rajas – of Datia and Orchha – who had invaded Jhansi on the back of the sepoy rebellion.

Jack had heard that the thirty-year-old Rani dressed like an Indian fighting man and wore a turban. Her horsemanship was superb. There were those who said she had lovely eyes and a beautiful figure, but others remarked that her face was pockmarked with the ravages of smallpox. Whatever her physical appearance she fought with a ferocity unmatched by many men and was a good tactician. When the revolt had broken out Jhansi had become a centre of the rebellion. A group of British officers had taken refuge in its fort and were promised safe passage to leave, only to be slaughtered by waiting rebels. Manikarnika was held by the British to be responsible for this massacre and this left her no choice but to turn her energies to ridding India of the 'Honourable' Company.

Now here was the honourable Jack Crossman, going to war against women. He wondered if he could kill a female in hand-to-hand combat. He supposed he would have to, but the thought made him sick to his stomach. Battling with a fanatical Ghazi warrior in the dust was one thing, but to have to do the same to a female? Could he really plunge a blade into one of the Rani's girls, even if she was trying to kill him? Could he really shoot out a pair of liquid brown eyes set in the face of a beautiful woman? He felt nothing but disgust with this war now, with all its unforgivable atrocities.

'Dollar for those thoughts, Jack?'

Jack Crossman whirled round at the sound of this voice and he felt nothing but delight on seeing his old friend Rupert Jarrard.

'Rupert! You devil. Where have you been? I heard you were here in India.'

They shook hands warmly, smiling into each other's faces.

Jarrard was a tall, handsome, evenly sized man, neither too lean nor too heavy. He was one of those men who look good in any sort of clothing, be it smart or casual wear. In a uniform he would have caused women to swoon away, but as he often told Jack, he would be sooner dead than join the military. He liked danger, but he liked it on his own terms. Like his British counterpart, William Russell, he was a war correspondent. His paper was the *New York Banner* and he and Jack had become fast friends when both realized the other was enthusiastic about new machines. New inventions quickened their pulses.

Jack led his friend to a space away from the hubbub of the Bombay Native Infantry, where he had been having a peaceful pipe. If he could not escape noise he preferred the chatter of Hindi and Urdu to that of his native tongue. It appeared to be less intrusive on his thoughts, since he understood it less well.

'Well, Rupert? Still carrying that Colt?'

Jarrard smiled. 'You bet.' He patted his jacket just in front of his left armpit. 'Had to use it once or twice over here, too. How are you faring, Jack? Hand giving you any trouble?'

Jack waved his stump. 'No, not really. I had a couple of false hands – one of them mechanical. You should have seen it, Rupert. I could crush rocks with it.' He sighed, flapping the empty cuff of his left sleeve. 'But it's gone. Ripped off in a battle – there's been so many I've forgotten which. Had a nice wooden one as well – the one I hit Hadrow with – but that's gone too.' He paused, realizing he had not answered Jarrard's main question. 'Otherwise, I'm fine.'

'You don't look fine – you're ragged and worn out. Been through the wringer lately, eh?'

Jack smiled wryly. 'One way or another.' He looked down at himself, past his black beard to the filthy cottons. When he had last looked in a mirror his face had been tanned the colour of his boots and his skin had looked dried and lined. He had lost weight too, so that his cotton shirt hung on him like a limp rag. 'I wouldn't get into White's, that's for certain,' he said, speaking of the London gentlemen's club. 'They'd throw me out with the rubbish, I'm sure.'

'Who the hell is Hadrow?' Rupert asked, lighting up one of his cheroots.

'Oh, a chap I had some personal business with.'

'He's not the fellah who jilted Jane?'

Jack's head went back with a snap. Even close and respected friends like Rupert Jarrard were not supposed to be privy to that sort of information.

Rupert had obviously noticed Jack's astonished reaction to his words and felt he ought to explain. 'I met with Jane when I was in London, before embarking for India. She's had a letter from a man called Deighnton, telling her you've been unfaithful. Didn't believe it, of course. She wondered if it had something to do with you flooring the man who – in her words – shamed her family name. Now, Jack, what the hell did you do a thing like that for? You know men like that aren't worth the dirt under your boots. As I told Jane, he's shamed his own name, not hers.'

'I know what Deighnton's trying to do,' snarled Jack. He almost bit through the stem of his chibouque in his anger. 'He's trying to force this damn duel.' Something then suddenly struck Jack. The time element. He looked at Rupert with wide eyes. 'But he must have written that letter months ago! We've fought since then. Is he so base he's trying to turn my own wife against me? I can't believe this has all come from my striking Hadrow in London over a year ago. It doesn't make sense.'

'Jack, the man is clearly mad. The only way to treat madmen is to let them burn themselves out. You are best to ignore him.'

Jack Crossman was aghast at these developments. 'To write to a man's wife? Good God! It's difficult to believe.'

'Mad, completely crazy. The letter spoke of two Eurasian girls – not long out of the schoolroom.'

'Silvia and Delia,' murmured Jack.

It was Jarrard's turn to open his eyes wide.

'You know these girls?'

Jack sighed. 'Deighnton is too clever for words. There is a grain of truth in what he's written, but he's turned it into a mountain. Silvia and Delia are the daughters of a corporal. These two young ladies have nothing better to do but daydream while this war drags on and they follow their father here, there and everywhere. Their heads are full of romantic nonsense. It's their age and circumstances I suppose. They've decided they have formed an attachment to me. It's all of a piece. They're a blasted nuisance – Gwilliams will tell you. I chase them away, but they keep coming back and . . .'

'They're besotted with you.' Jarrard puffed on his cheroot.

'They're besotted with the *idea* that they're in love with me. As you say, it's all schoolgirl stuff. A pair of hoydens, both of them. The younger one simply follows the older girl in everything she does. Oh, good God, what will Jane think? There's no smoke without a fire?'

Jarrard shook his head. 'You should give your wife more

credit for good sense than that. What she thinks is that there's a maniac here who's doing his best to destroy your reputation.'

Jack said, 'I don't deserve her.'

'Well, as to that,' said the American, 'you're the best judge. Take my advice, Jack, and steer clear of this Deighnton. If he persists, then shoot the damn cur.'

'I will have to do that in the end.' Jack did not add that Deighnton was a crack-shot, who had already killed three men in duels, and would likely shoot Jack first. 'If his sole intention in writing to my wife was to ensure I fight this damn duel with him, then he's been successful.'

Outwardly, Jack was calm, as a gentleman should be when discussing his wife. Inwardly he was boiling over with rage. How *dare* this excuse for an officer of Her Majesty's Army be so crass as to write to the wife of another man accusing him of infidelity? It was beyond credulity. Jack wanted to stamp the man's face into the dust, there and then. If Deighnton had been around he would certainly have gone to him this instant and fought with him.

'Let's talk of better things,' Jarrard said, crushing his cheroot butt under the heel of his boot. 'How is this mess faring?'

Somehow Jack managed to snap himself back to the attention of his friend, whom he had not seen in a long age. Seething with hatred though his brain was, he knew there was nothing he could do about it for the moment. The very next time he saw Deighnton though, there would have to be a reckoning.

'Oh, this? Damn East India Company. There were some good men amongst 'em, but they were few and far between, Rupert. Lazy officers, rotten decisions. Men in high places trying to force through policies using John Company's Army that were clearly going to inflame the locals.'

'You mean the greased bullets?'

'No, not that so much. That was just a little fuel on the flames – the fire was already burning. It was – oh, I don't know – forcing the Indian troops to travel overseas, appearing to interfere with their religious beliefs and giving the impression that we were trying to convert them to Christianity – all that sort of thing. The pot was simmering by the time the greasy bullets came along. And European company officers had got out of touch with their men and failed to notice that it was boiling over. You must have heard all this – the incompetence?'

Rupert nodded. 'Sure. There's talk in your parliament of abolishing the East India Company's Army. Your Queen's Army will take over their duties.'

'Sounds like a sensible plan to me.'

'All this trouble,' Rupert said with a sigh. 'It comes of living under a monarchy, you know – you Brits should think about changing to a republic.'

Jack smiled wryly. 'Like you Americans, I suppose?'

'Us and . . . well, look at the French.'

'Yes,' replied Jack, 'just look at them. They can't decide whether they want to be a republic or a monarchy. They chop off the heads of royals and nobles, then along comes a dwarf who calls himself an Emperor and what do they do? They listen to him, go through a few wars with him, and once he's been dealt with by us, they bring back their monarchy, on and off, until only ten years ago.'

'Well, yes – they should have followed our example,' said Jarrard. 'Get rid of kings once and for all. Decisive, that's us.'

'Not so decisive as all that,' argued Jack. 'A good half of your countrymen remained loyal to King George when you made the break. You always make it sound as if it were a unanimous decision to break with the United Kingdom. A lot of those loyalists fled to Canada after your independence, heavily assisted by those dithering Frenchies I might add, and are still waiting for the day when we march back in and take Washington.'

'Just damn well try it, that's all,' said Jarrard with a mock snarl. 'We'll kick your asses back across the Atlantic again.'

The pair then got on to their favourite subject: new inventions. Although in the back of Jack's mind was the smouldering feud he was engaged in with Captain Deighnton, he had been through too much blood and terror to allow it to obsess him. Outwardly he chattered happily about the latest agricultural invention to come along, the advances in medicine, the newest advances in transport. There was a friendly rivalry between him and Jarrard regarding which nation had the best inventors, the most innovative scientists, the most imaginative builders of machines.

Jarrard was unusually generous in telling Jack of an Englishman who was making great strides in a certain field.

'You remember the analytical engine, your guy Babbage built at – where was it? – Oxford University?'

'Cambridge,' replied Jack. 'A machine enabling arithmetical operations with decisions based on its own calculations. I believe Countess Lovelace, my superior's aunt, wrote some tables to enable the machine to perform?'

'Major Lovelace's aunt, eh? Well, hell – we ought to have a word with him. Anyway, I'm not sure the machine ever did what it was supposed to be able to do, but there's another fellah's come along – George Boole. He reckons he's invented a whole new way of mathematics, called *binary logic*, based on using the numbers nought and one, which would make it possible to really mechanize logic.'

Jack frowned. 'Nought and one? That doesn't make sense. How can you have mathematics with just two numbers – and one of them zero?'

'Search me, Jack,' said Jarrard laughing. 'They threw me out of the Royal Society when they found I was as dumb as a mule.'

Jack laughed too, at the idea that either of them should ever have pretensions to the Royal Society.

As Jack refilled his chibouque, Jarrard looked around him and asked, 'Talking of mules, where is that jackass, Gwilliams, anyway?'

Jarrard and Gwilliams were the only two North Americans Jack knew and he was bemused by the fact that they seemed to dislike each other intensely.

'Oh, he's found some fellow Canadians – the 109th Foot. He's busy boring them with tales of his prowess.'

'Huh! Prowess . . .' However Jarrard was unable to finish what he was saying due to a bugle call cutting him short. Drums began beating in various parts of the camp. 'I'll see you later, Jack,' yelled the correspondent. 'If we're both still alive.'

Jack and his men were ordered to ride out to meet another British column heading to join General Rose. They stayed with this force, which came out of Rajputana and met the rebels at Kotah-ki-Serai, intending to drive them towards Gwalior. Their ranks had been swelled by the young Maharajah Sindhia's army, who had been induced to join the cause. The maharajah himself had fled with his personal bodyguard to Agra, unwilling to sacrifice himself, convinced that the British would never be defeated.

This time Jack and his men fought on foot, having offered themselves as skirmishers. When the battle was at its height he saw the Rani herself, tulwar in both hands, reins in her white teeth, slashing her way through her enemies. Then later, a shout went up in Hindi, 'The Rani is down! The Rani is down!' and to Jack's astonishment the rebel infantry began to attack their own cavalry, screaming curses at them for allowing the Rani to be killed.

The Rani was indeed dead: shot and then run through by the sabre of a trooper of the 8th Hussars. She had flung her jewellery amongst her troops and then was taken to a mango grove where she expired, along with one of her two maids of honour, who had also been mortally wounded. A truly magnificent woman, Jack was not alone in admiring her. With her death, it seemed, the real heart of the rebellion died too. There was much work for the British to do, but it was piecemeal work: the elimination of armed guerrilla bands, badmashes and dacoits.

With an exhausted army General Rose took the fortress at Gwalior which was high up on a ridge and surrounded on three sides by steep cliffs. Jack was again in the thick of the fighting, the stink of battle-smoke in his nostrils.

When it was all over, the only casualty amongst Jack's men was Raktambar, who had lost a finger to a stray ball. Overall British casualties were very light and the rebels had been defeated yet again. Many fled the field, escaping on foot and horseback. Their commanders, Tantia Tope and Rao Sahib, also ran: it was believed they had crossed the Chambal River into Raktambar's home of Rajputana.

Later, Jack was thanked personally by one of General Rose's aides for his part in the battles. He and his men had distinguished themselves. Even Wynter had flung himself into the fighting without too much whining and grumbling. Jack asked if anything had been heard of either Major Lovelace or Colonel Hawke. He received a shake of the head in reply.

'Where will I get my orders, then?' he asked.

'You are to be given licence to hunt down stray groups of rebels, Lieutenant Crossman,' came the reply. 'Keep in contact, from time to time, with the authorities in this region – otherwise you and your men are on your own.'

Jack went to say his goodbyes to Rupert Jarrard.

Jarrard was in a large house converted to messes, talking with an infantry sergeant from the 95th. The sergeant, like the rest of his regiment, was heavily bearded and currently wearing a white smock, tattered blue trousers and Indian slippers. On his head he had a Kilmarnock forage cap with a white cover, a red-white cotton towel wrapped around the brim. There were officers going up the stairs to the upper rooms, where the commissioned ranks drank and ate, dressed in grey frocks. One of them who passed Jack wore a stove-pipe hat with a lady's muslin scarf fluttering from it. Any dress code had temporarily been put aside and officers and men enjoyed eccentricities for a while.

'Rupert, we're off again.'

He had to shout. The hubbub in the room was tremendous, being full of NCOs from various regiments, including his own 88th, who along with two companies of the Rifles had been formed into a Camel Corps. He had that day seen soldiers having terrible trouble trying to control their dromedaries using – having no other information at their disposal – the same commands they might use on the old farm horses back in Connaught, Ireland. He had watched them sway and slide on the unfamiliar humps, yelling obscenities at their mounts. The camels themselves, naturally nasty-tempered to begin with, were angry at having to cope with some lump of an Irishman on their backs, a rider who had no idea what he was supposed to be doing and terrified by the height at which he did it.

Jarrard beckoned with a hand, waving Jack to his side.

Jack weaved his way through a bunch of 72nd in their faded tartan trews to reach Jarrard and his companion.

Jarrard roared, 'Ah, the brave Lieutenant Crossman. Jack, shake hands with George here – he's from Nottingham.'

The sergeant, a tall, red-faced man, saluted Jack a little apologetically.

'Sergeant Stone, sir.'

Jarrard frowned, then twisted his face into a grimace. 'Oh, yeah – I forgot. It's this British class thing.'

'Nothing to do with *class*, Rupert. This is an army thing – yours as well as ours, I'm willing to wager. I'm afraid I can't drink in here, Rupert, any more than George here can drink upstairs. Happy to have you join me when you're ready.' He turned to face Stone. 'You understand, Sergeant?'

'Of course, sir,' the man said nodding.

'A year or two ago it would have been fine – I had the same stripes on my arm – but now . . .'

'You're not even in uniform, Jack. Who the hell can tell what you are in that get-up?'

Jack adjusted his kurta self-consciously.

'There are people in this room who know me, Rupert. You might have noticed the place is crawling with Connaught Rangers. I'm already in enough trouble. I've been accused of desertion in the face of the enemy, a military crime punishable by death. I'm trying to make as few waves as possible until it's all been cleared up. It's best I remain as inconspicuous as possible for the time being.'

'Right – inconspicuous – in a red turban.'

'Don't labour it, Rupert.'

Jarrard joined Jack in the officers' mess just ten minutes later. Jack was enjoying a warm gin.

'Sorry about that down there, but you know . . .'

'So, you're off into the jungle again?' Jarrard asked.

'How did you know?' asked Jack, surprised.

'No secrets amongst this lot.' Jarrard waved his whisky glass around. 'Even George knew about you. Your bunch of spies and saboteurs are becoming famous, Lieutenant Crossman. Someone will write a story about you one day, turning fact into legend.' Jarrard grinned. 'It might even be me.'

'I thought you'd already tried that – in your column.'

'Yeah, you're right – it wasn't all that successful, because you're a damn Englishman. If you were an American backwoodsman, a grisly nobody from nowhere, and had opened up the Oregon Trail, I could have made you famous by now – but who the hell is interested in a British aristocrat in a red coat who goes into battle looking as if he's entering a drawing room full of aunts and uncles? If you could just stoop a little when you walk, shamble into rooms carrying a battered old musket with worm-eaten stock, then we'd get somewhere.'

Jack grinned. 'Listen, Rupert, I've got to go. You look after yourself – the mutiny is contained, but not yet over.'

'What's the rush?'

'Horses. I have to be up early tomorrow to get to the horse bazaar.'

Jarrard raised his eyebrows. 'There's a horse bazaar?'

'Six miles out from Gwalior – life goes on, Rupert, mutiny or no mutiny.'

'I guess so. Well, good luck, Jack.' They shook hands. 'If they hang you, I'll be sure to report it as an injustice in the *Banner*. We Americans love to read about European injustice. It makes us feel we did the right thing in leaving. I'll create such a furore they'll have to reopen the case and you'll end up getting a posthumous pardon.'

'Thank you,' replied Jack drily, 'I appreciate your concern.'

Jack went back to his quarters, which were in a dingy corner of Gwalior Fort, near the kitchens. It was the small narrow holding room where they used to keep prisoners before taking them to the cells. It was just wide enough for a biscuit-thin horsehair mattress. The room was crawling with lice and he woke after being bitten viciously in several places. Deciding that outside was preferable to this stone coffin, Jack dragged his mattress out under the stars. He went to sleep suffering the smell of boiled vegetables which wafted over from the cookhouse.

Raktambar woke him just before dawn and the pair of them set off on their horses in the direction of the bazaar. The mounts Jack and his men had at present were heavy beasts previously owned by dragoons. Jack knew that if they were to be successful in hunting down guerrillas they would need small, fast creatures, used to the terrain and the climate, comfortable in their environment. It made sense that in India one should ride Indian ponies who were happy with the Indian climate and terrain.

When they arrived, Jack was at first stunned by the sight and sound of the bazaar. There were sellers and buyers from all over the region, and beyond. Tents were everywhere: tall and elegant, squat and dull. Most men were dressed soberly but some were in flamboyant colours and costumes denoting their nationality or local tribe. There was yelling and shouting from every corner, as men argued over prices, emphasizing their disgust at high suggestions and low counter-offers with wild gestures. Dozens of breeds of animal were on show, being trotted back and forth, limbs being inspected by expert hands, jaws being held open for the teeth to be studied, tails swishing, manes flying. A few – very few – horses had been dyed red or yellow ochre. And hanging heavy over the whole scene, the stink of horse manure and sweat.

Here no one was interested in mutiny – the only concern was in the qualities of four-legged beasts: their speed, their character, their style, their action. These, and whether the animals were hale and strong, not too advanced in years, and worth their salt. No buyer wanted to be swindled by a crook horse. Every vendor wanted more than the creature they were selling was actually worth.

Jack had been to Tattersalls in England, of course, but this bazaar had far more zest and colour.

Raktambar, on whom Jack was relying to get them properly mounted, did not purchase Indian horses for them. The Rajput chose Mongolians instead. He told Jack they were Karashahr animals from the Northern edge of the Takla Makan Desert.

'They will suit our purposes, these animals,' Raktambar told Jack, as the Rajput stroked the flank of a sturdy looking creature of about twelve or thirteen hands. These Karashahrs had powerful chests and necks, and large hook-shaped heads. Their legs looked strong and well-built. But they were not especially good-looking beasts, not to the classic English taste in any case, and Jack was rather disappointed in them.

'What about those big ones over there?' he suggested to Raktambar. 'When I sit on a horse I want to feel I'm a bit above the world.'

The horses Jack pointed out were about sixteen or seventeen hands high. They had long black tails that swept to the ground and silken manes which fell to the point of the shoulder, rather like the Moroccan horses Jack had known. Their noble-looking heads were large and well-shaped, their eyes bulged slightly – though not in an unbecoming fashion – and they had long sleek necks with high pointed ears. With their short backs and round barrel chests they appeared always to be moving. Jack liked the idea that they had so much energy they could not stand still for a moment.

'No, no, they are useless,' replied Raktambar irritably. 'You see they are shod with iron.'

'And?' remarked Jack, who would not have thought of riding a horse which was not shod. 'Ours are not?'

'No, of course not. This makes them more sure-footed. We

will not be riding them on hard ground, so their hooves will not wear. 'See, ours are well-ribbed, straight in the pastern!'

Jack stared at his mount's leg, the point between the fetlock and the hoof, and wondered how this straightness benefited him as a rider. He was just as exasperated with Raktambar as the Indian appeared to be with him. Get any two men together, whatever their knowledge and background, and they will have different opinions on breeds of horse. Men will often cluster around the same woman hoping to make her their wife, while other ladies just as beautiful are ignored, but they will privately and even openly scorn each other's choice of steed.

'Well, what about those beautiful creatures over there – ours are rather drab, don't you think?'

'White is for royal personages,' muttered Raktambar, 'not for war – do you want your enemy to see you coming from miles away?'

'Well, one of the chestnuts then?'

'Very bad luck.'

'That black beast?'

'You will be riding your own shroud!'

Jack gave up. It seemed they were going to have the Karashahrs.

'You'd better be right about these hairy beasts – they look a bit wild to me.'

'They are like milk-fed lambs if you use them right.'

Raktambar also insisted they bought the right saddles before they left the noisy marketplace. The Karashahrs had been raised with padded wooden saddles on their backs and would not take to European saddles, the Rajput informed his leader. Everything had to be right or they would not perform in the proper manner.

'I expect we shall have to feed them caviar,' Jack said sarcastically, 'washed down with champagne.'

'No – butter balls and flour bricks.'

'What?' cried Jack, but Raktambar rode off leading a string of the Karashahrs, leaving Jack to follow with two of his own.

Jack very soon found his mount had an unusual gait, one he had never encountered before. The two offside legs went forward and backward at the same time – and the nearside legs did the same. It was rather as if the creature were walking on stilts, but Jack found to his surprise that it was a very

smooth ride over the uneven ground. The padded saddle with
its definite high back and front (creating a kind of slot for the
rider) was certainly the right equipment, for Jack could tell
that an English saddle would have him sliding this way and
that, and his balance on the mount would be highly suspect.
It was comfortable and the little horse moved with some style
and pace.

When they got back to the barracks, where the other
members of the team were waiting, Wynter was disparaging.

'What the 'ell're them nags for?'

'To ride, Wynter, to ride,' said Jack.

King said, 'I've told you before, Wynter – you do not address
remarks to the officer directly. You speak to *me* first and I
decide whether or not to pass on the information.'

The sergeant then stared at the mounts, which were indeed
only ponies to Europeans used to tall horses. They were
reasonably hairy beasts. One could tell that King was not
over-enamoured with them either, but he refrained from criticism in front of the troops.

Jack was warming to the Karashahrs. He had cut one out
for himself already. It was a dun-coloured gelding with a
bright intelligent expression. He felt it was weighing him up
as a rider, just as he was judging the creature as a mount.
Jack liked the look of the animal, as horses went.

Raktambar asked, 'What will you call him?'

'Oh, I don't name my horses,' replied Jack airily. 'They're
just transport, after all.'

The Rajput looked dreadfully shocked. 'But, sahib, you *must*
give your horse a name. How will he know who he is if you
do not? Do you *never* name your horses?'

Jack felt uncomfortable. 'No – not often. That is, if the
horse is already named I don't take it from him – but to my
knowledge I don't recall ever – oh, yes, once – but . . .'

'Sahib, *this* horse you must give a name.'

'Oh, yes,' piped in the boy Sajan. 'It is very bad luck not
to give a horse a name. It would be like you not having a
name, sahib. How would people know who you were?'

'I am not a horse. Horses do not actually need names.'

'But they do, they do,' cried Raktambar. 'Demons will enter
his soul if he has no name to protect himself. A name is like
a shield to ward off evil. If you do not name him,' he continued

darkly, 'he will throw you over the edge of a cliff – or trample you when you turn your back. Now, what name will you give him?'

Jack was beaten. He looked at the horse. The horse stared back at him with enquiring eyes. Jack shrugged. 'I don't know – Jane?'

'Jane is the name of your wife,' remarked King. 'You can't call your horse after your wife. Anyway, the horse is male.'

A flash of genius saved Jack.

'In that case, I shall call him Cadiz – my uncle went there once and described the place to me. I was enthralled.'

'Cadiz,' murmured Raktambar. 'Yes, that sounds very well. Very magical. Cadiz. He will like that name.'

'He's a horse. He will not even know he has a name.'

'Of course he will, sahib,' said Sajan, firmly on the side of his countryman even though he knew nothing about horses. 'You will tell him his name and he will come to you when you call him.'

Jack sighed. 'If you say so.' He became briskly authoritative, partly in order to cover his chagrin, and partly because it was necessary. 'Now, listen up, everyone. We have a task to do. We are to assist in clearing central India of guerrilla bands. Naturally we're a small group, so if we come across a large band of rebels I will send a rider back here to inform the commander and dragoons will be dispatched to deal with the enemy. Or for a really large force, infantry will be sent. But our task is to seek out and inform. You're well-used to this work and it doesn't need me to tell you that we have to remain as anonymous as possible. It's dangerous work, of course. If the guerrillas realize that someone is marking them, they'll send out their own squads to deal with us, so if we're discovered for what we are we cannot afford to let any individual escape. We are going back to our old foxhunts, from Crimea days.'

'We kill them all?' said Gwilliams, dispassionately. 'Wipe 'em out? No prisoners?'

'Unpalatable, but necessary,' Jack confirmed. 'Oh, if it's one or even two men, we can take them prisoner and send them back with an escort, but we are few and they are many – we have to preserve the integrity of our group. Any more questions?'

There were one or two, especially from Wynter. As ordinary soldiers of the rank and file they did not have a history of being consulted by their commanders or being asked for an opinion, but Jack ran his group a little differently from the normal army way. It was necessary that he did so. From time to time strong initiative was required of his men – individual inventive decision-making and action – and he needed to encourage his soldiers to use what resources were at their command. It had been necessary to help them awaken and nurture original thinking in brains that were, in the past, expected to do nothing but listen to orders and to follow them. Initiative usually lay dormant and was in any case discouraged as being dangerous. But Jack allowed his men to act on their own, something the army considered unhealthy.

Who did he have for this type of work?

Corporal Gwilliams, a North American barber, who used a razor for tasks more nefarious than just shaving a man's face. Gwilliams was a backwoodsman of sorts who knew how to think for himself and act upon his decisions. A very good man to have in such circumstances. Lacking in discipline it was true, but Fancy Jack's group had only use for discipline when they were not out in the field engaged in espionage and sabotage.

Sergeant King, who was an engineer and mapmaker. Slightly resentful of anything that impinged on his career, King too was capable of original thinking. A little insubordinate at times. As could be expected of a man who knew about topography he was a good navigator and could pinpoint positions with magical accuracy. Moreover, he kept Private Harry Wynter in check in a way that Fancy Jack Crossman could never do. Farrier King had fists of iron but unfortunately could not hit the side of a mountain with a rifle.

Private Harry Wynter was a reprobate. Capable of great acts of bravery and also of base cowardice, he was an enigma to Jack who as a child had been shielded from such characters. Crafty, sly creatures like Wynter had been outside his experience. He did not know how Wynter thought or what processes the man used when making decisions. Certainly Wynter had initiative but it was a fox-like, rat-like, snake-like intuition. He was a drunkard when he had the means, a whore-chaser, complained about everything and everyone, hated manual work, yet had saved Jack's life on many occasions. He was a puzzle.

Raktambar was a reluctant bodyguard given to Jack by a maharajah for the duration of his stay in India. He was a good solid soldier, whose loyalties were split between Jack and the cause for independence of his country. He claimed to have no feelings for the British, yet remained by Jack's side nonetheless. Jack admired the man for his strong sense of honour and his capabilities as a warrior.

Sajan was merely a boy, but very useful in certain circumstances, and like the rest of the group, Jack was very fond of the child.

Then there was himself, Lieutenant Fancy Jack Crossman, a man in the army under an assumed name. A father-hater who had learned that he was a bastard son of an English maid whom his aristocratic Scottish father had seduced. Jack thought he knew who he was until that duel with Captain Deighnton, when he deliberately injured himself to prevent a re-duel from taking place. Was he then a coward like Wynter, capable of courage but basically bearing a yellow heart in his breast? Had he thrown away his honour to save his miserable life?

Perhaps.

Seven

The clean-up operations began reasonably successfully. The group acted as spotters for a squadron of dragoons, who swept on past them and dealt with the guerrillas with a firm and sometimes not-so-just hand. There were murderers and rapists out there and it was difficult to tell them from those who were merely mutineers with noble aspirations. So the army tended not to discriminate and to treat them all as if they were as bad as each other. The less culpable were hanged along with the worst of brigands. It was a sorry time for all, but the British needed to stamp out the last vestiges of flames and prepare for a new beginning. Jack was not sentimental enough to disapprove of what they were doing, though he was often left wondering whether his soul was destined for hell.

When the guerrilla bands were small enough his own group dealt with them. Usually it resulted in a pitched battle and the rebels were shot before they could be captured. On such a day King and Gwilliams were riding ahead of the others and they saw three armed men strolling from some mud huts towards a gorge. The men were wearing remnants of Indian Army uniform. King gave a yelp, drew a large horse pistol that he carried, and fired before Gwilliams could stop him. He missed his target, who turned and after a second returned the shot.

Gwilliams cried, 'Come on, we'll have to finish 'em now.'

He spurred his mount forward.

King drew his sabre and was not far behind him. The runners began racing for the edge of a gorge. One tripped and went sprawling, his weapon flying from his grasp. The others left him to his fate, which he soon met at the edge of King's sabre. He was still on his knees, trying to get up, when King sliced down to where the man's neck met his shoulder. Blood pumped out on to the dusty ground as the man fell with a final groan.

The other two reached the gorge and disappeared beyond its edge. King and Gwilliams rode to the lip and looked down.

'Oh, Jesus and Mary,' cried Gwilliams.

On a shelf just below the gorge were about twenty or so more rebels, around a dozen of them on mounts. Some immediately fired up at the two soldiers, but the excitement caused by the jabbering of their two recently arrived companions caused them to be inaccurate. Gwilliams fired down into the gorge and then turned his mount to race away. King instantly followed him. Within a minute they were being chased by rebel cavalry with fleet-footed infantry not far behind. There was a race across a dusty dry lake on the other side of which was rocky scrubland. There the other members of Crossman's group had stopped to rest their horses. It was Sajan who gave a shout.

'Sahib – my father comes, with men after him!'

'What?' exclaimed Jack, looking up.

Indeed, through the curtains of heatwaves he could see King and Gwilliams riding for their lives.

'Find some cover,' Jack shouted to Wynter and Raktambar. 'Try to pick off a couple of the leaders.'

Raktambar grabbed Sajan and was soon behind a boulder but Wynter ignored his orders. He threw himself up on to his mount. What he intended to do – run or fight – was never known. His horse shied at the unexpectedness of his rider's actions and attempted to bolt. Wynter first pulled it up short with the reins. The Karashahrs had very hard mouths and the bit had little effect, so Wynter smacked the horse around the head with the flat of his hand. The animal kicked out his back legs, then bucked, sending Wynter flying through the air.

Wynter landed deep in the middle of a huge thorn bush. The bush carried three-inch thorns as protection against birds and goats. Wynter screamed like a broken woman. At first he struggled, but just sank deeper into the heart of a bush several yards in diameter. Those terrible spikes penetrated his cheeks, arms, legs and torso. His left eye had been spiked clean through the pupil: he would be blind on that side if he lived out the action. Another of nature's stilettos had entered under his jaw and was gradually working its way up through his throat towards the underside of his tongue. Two more had struck him in the genitals. Wynter moaned loud and long while he still could: while his tongue was still unpinned.

Blood began running down the thorns into the middle of the bush, staining it bright red.

'Help me! Help me!'

Jack and the others could do nothing. Gwilliams and King arrived and threw themselves off their mounts, to find cover. There were around a dozen horsemen bearing down on them. All four opened fire and emptied three enemy saddles between them. Shots were now coming from the guerrillas on foot, as they caught up with the riders. The cavalry decided one charge was enough and retreated out of range, to tether their mounts and then to join their comrades who had the British surrounded. There were twenty-odd rebels circling Jack and he realized it was a bad place in which to be caught. There was no real shade to be had, the temperature was well over a hundred and the water source out of reach.

'Oh, gawd! Please get me out. Lieutenant, don't leave me.'

'We're not going to leave you, Wynter – stop whining. It's only a few prickles. You've been blackberrying before, surely.'

This was hardly fair. The thorns were as long as a sailor's needles and probably twice as sharp. Small birds had been known to accidentally impale themselves on these long green spikes. But Jack had little time for Wynter's complaints. He had three other men and a boy to consider. Bullets were zinging off the rocks now. Wynter was actually a sitting target and it seemed likely that his problems would not last a great deal longer. It seemed probable that he would soon be hit. Certainly some of the shots from the rebels zipped through the bush. But he was now low enough in his personal vegetation to be out of sight of the shooters.

'Ahhhhhhhhhhh,' came a long low sigh of despair. 'I'm still goin' down and now it's got me in the ammunition pouch – ' Wynter's euphemism for his scrotum – 'I'm done for. I'll never have brats now . . .'

'Thank heaven for that,' muttered King.

Wynter was forgotten as the battle continued, with shots going back and forth without any material change in the situation. Then the guerrillas ceased firing and very soon it fell quiet again.

'Have they gone?' King whispered.

'Nah,' growled Gwilliams. 'They know they've got us pinned. They'll wait now for our water to run out. They don't need to kill us. We'll die of thirst. I got to do somethin' for that poor bastard Wynter.'

King was horrified as Gwilliams raised his rifle and took careful aim at the middle of the thorn bush, about ten yards away.

'You can't just kill him . . .'

But Gwilliams had fired and was reloading. Wynter had renewed his screams now, the sound echoing around the rocks. Gwilliams fired three more times in Wynter's direction. Finally there was a crashing sound as the centre of the bush collapsed. King now saw that Gwilliams had been shooting at the main woody stem of the shrub and had finally weakened it enough for it to break under Wynter's weight. The private was still under the attack of stabbing thorns, but at least he would not sink lower into them. He now lay a whimpering heap in the very middle of the vicious vegetation. However, a new cry came up from him.

'There's a snake.'

'Well, ignore it,' snapped King. 'Try not to bother it.'

Sajan asked, 'Is it a cobra?'

'How the bloody hell should I know,' shouted Wynter. 'I've only got one good eye an' the other's full o' blood. I can hear it slitherin'.'

Jack had not been listening to any of this. He had been making plans in his head.

'We'll hold them off until dark – then one of us will have to ride out of here, break through their lines, and get help.'

'I'll do it,' growled Gwilliams.

'No,' called Raktambar from behind his boulder. 'It shall be me.'

'Sergeant King?' asked Jack.

'I don't want to go,' came the firm reply.

'Well, I'm afraid you *are* going. You're the worst shot. I need men with me who can hit things with their Enfields. You are not a great deal of good to us here. You must ride and fetch the dragoons.'

'They're all round us,' King said reasonably. 'I'm certain to get shot.'

'There's no moon tonight,' Jack argued, 'and if you stay here it'll be even more certain that you'll be killed. I've no choice but to send you.'

'Why can't we all go?'

'There's a man who can't.'

King might have said, 'It's only Private Harry Wynter,' but to his credit he remained silent.

Jack called, 'Gwilliams?'

'Sir?'

'You know what I'm going to ask of you?'

'Do some work with the knife, to cause a diversion?'

'Exactly.'

'Leave it to me, lootenant.'

Every once in a while one of the rebels would take a shot in the hope of hitting something. Every so often one of the British group would also try to flush out one of the enemy. There were no casualties on either side the whole day. In the defenders' camp the water had to be eked out. It was a very hot day, even at the going down of the sun. A scarlet sunset seemed an ominous sign, if not for its colour then for the fact that the following day would be just as hot as the one they had just made it through. Slaked lips and dry throats seem that much worse when water is scarce.

The psychology of the situation was entirely against the defending group. Loud clicking insects seemed to mock them. During the day, birds had come and gone, freely and without hindrance. Bats replaced them in the twilight, gathering the massed insects above their heads. Other creatures could eat and drink with impunity, while they were denied sustenance. Flies drank their sweat and mosquitoes their blood. They were still able to give, but not to receive. Even their own horses, left to graze by the rebels to whom they were valuable beasts, were allowed to amble down to a pool not far away and drink their fill. Time crawled.

When darkness fell, the rebels lit fires all around. The nearest of the Karashahrs had been Jack's horse. He was encouraged by others to call to it softly. The Karashahrs lived on a diet of wheaten flour and butter balls which they took in the evening, and a measure of chickpeas in the morning. On occasion they would be given a treat of sugar cane. Jack had no sugar cane to give it, but he had saved a ball of wheaten flour and butter.

'Cadiz, Cadiz . . .' Eventually he felt it nuzzle his hand.

'You see,' said Raktambar, 'if you had not named your horse . . . ?'

The other Karashahrs followed Cadiz, including of course King's mount.

'Gwilliams?' Jack said.

No one heard the corporal leave the camp. Jack gave him thirty minutes then told King to mount up. Another short while, then a horrible scream went up from the direction of the enemy, followed by shots flaring the darkness. King spurred the horse, heading straight for a gap between the fires. He had picked out a path earlier in the evening, when there was light, and knew there were no boulders on it. Jack and Raktambar let rip with their rifles at the fires, not trying to hit any figures for the sole reason that one of them might possibly be the returning corporal.

Then all went quiet again.

Gwilliams crawled into camp, a bloody dagger in his hand.

'Did he get away?' he asked.

Jack said, 'I hope so.'

Then peace settled once again, except for the occasional soft groan from a nearby thorn bush where a man was gradually bleeding to death.

It began to rain.

King rode hard and fast out into the night, but soon reined in his mount. The skies had opened up, but the rain did not last very long. He hoped the lieutenant and the men had managed to collect some of the water. Out here on the plain it was as dark as the inside of a cave and, sure-footed though the animal was, there was a good possibility of it stumbling and perhaps breaking a bone. It was a credit to the beast that it charged on blindly, naïvely trusting that its master had the night eyes between them. Farrier King had called his mount Samarkand, a place he had vaguely heard of which sounded exotic to his ears. He was already growing fond of the creature, which was strange since, like his lieutenant, he was not sentimental when it came to horses. His father was a blacksmith and horses to King were simply machines that came to his father's forge to be mended and sent on their way.

King dismounted and began walking, leading Samarkand by the rein. He waved his sabre in front of him, having learned a lesson from Wynter regarding thorn bushes. He also trod warily, cautiously, in case of drops. He had no idea in which direction he was heading, but he hoped if he kept on the move he would eventually see a light somewhere out in the night. Three or four times he tripped over in the dark, grazing his knees. He did not curse. King had been raised as a strict Presbyterian and very rarely used oaths. He always felt his father looking over his shoulder at him. King's father was what local villagers called a good man. He was quietly reliable, honest and religious. He made no comment about the failings of others, but you could feel his censure if you behaved ill. King certainly worried about his father's unspoken criticism and tried to live his life in the same right manner.

'Oh, blessed light!' King suddenly said to his horse. 'Do you see it?'

Samarkand whinnied at the sound of his master's voice after so long a silence.

In the distance was a twinkling star on the ground. As he headed cautiously towards it, it grew in size and luminosity. It was a lamp, not a fire, which encouraged him. He did not wish to stumble back into the guerrilla camp: how stupid that would have been.

When he reached the house he saw that it was a hunting lodge, probably of some rich nawab or rajah.

These had been uncertain times but the mutiny had been broken: any local ruler would have to be extremely foolish to side with rebels now that the British were back in control. In India if you had something – and most did not – you protected it by any means available to you. This land had had many foreign rulers. The wise amongst them waited patiently for a time when the invader either infused with those already there and became Indian themselves – as with the moghuls from the north – or they left.

So King hammered on the brass-studded doors with the pommel of his sabre.

'Open up, in there! A traveller out here!'

After a short while a small door twelve inches square opened just in front of his face and a voice inquired in Hindi.

'I'm a soldier,' King said to a woman's dark eyes which stared at him. 'A soldier of her Majesty, Queen Victoria.'

'What you want?' asked the woman in heavily accented English.

'I want to come in, of course. I'm lost. I need help.'

A male voice called from somewhere and the woman finally opened the doors. King led Samarkand into a courtyard. Lights were being lit all around. King could smell water and lemon trees. Eventually a tall lean man in an embroidered robe and a turban came out of the house. It took him only half a minute to assess Sergeant King before he held open his arms in a gesture of friendship.

'Welcome to my house,' he said in perfect English. 'Do you have companions out there?'

King thought about this for a brief moment, but decided not to lie.

'My companions are being held prisoner by guerrillas – I managed to escape.'

'You are very fortunate. Come – ' the man gestured towards an open doorway – 'take some refreshments while you tell me of your troubles. My servants will take care of the horse. Does it need to be fed?'

'Yes, if you don't mind.'

King was led into a room where the walls were covered with tapestries and the floors richly carpeted. A hookah lay with its pipe curled around its brass belly in the corner. There was a writing desk in the middle of the room, with paper, quill and ink looking as if they had been abandoned in haste. Clearly the man had been working when King had seen the light. The sergeant thanked God for a diligent man, one whose duties carried him late into the evening.

'I'm grateful for your hospitality,' King said. He suddenly felt very weary. 'May I sit down?'

'By all means.'

There were no chairs, other than the scribe's chair at the desk, so King flopped back on some large cushions.

'My friends are in dire peril,' he said.

'Nothing can be done until the morning,' replied his host. 'I am Abdul Kashmar – and you, sir?'

'King. Sergeant King. Engineers.'

'Ah, an engineer. I have always admired engineers. You build bridges and roads?'

'I'm a mapmaker.'

'Even more interesting.' Kashmar had very fine chiselled features and eyes that bore into King with a strange intensity. He was about fifty years of age and had an intelligent air about him. King could not decide whether he was a warrior or a clerk. His manner and bearing seemed to possess the ability to hold both qualities. He certainly did not seem to be one of those dissolute rulers one found so often in India, who were interested only in the pleasures of life. He looked too healthy to be a hedonist. 'Will you take some food and drink?'

'Most gratefully.'

Servants entered the room a short while later with trays of meat, bread, fruit and – blessedly – cups of tea and beakers of wine. King ignored the wine and gulped down both cups of tea, suddenly realizing how thirsty he actually was. Then he apologized, knowing he had swallowed his host's tea as well as his own. He was told it was not a matter for concern and that Kashmar understood perfectly how it was. Then the pair settled down to eat together, though his host merely picked at the food, probably just to be polite. There were no utensils and King remembered to use his right hand, as Sajan had taught him, knowing the left was unclean.

As for his state of spirit and mind, he was elated to have come across such a friendly household but he also could not help feeling ashamed of himself, feeling horribly guilty, that he was here, safe and satisfying his needs, while his companions were still in great trouble. Wynter was slowly being drained of blood in that devilish thorn bush and maybe one of the others had been shot by now.

But Kashmar was right: there was nothing to be done during the dark hours.

'Would you like to sleep now?' he was asked.

'I should, but I don't think I could. Can you point the way to the nearest British settlement when dawn comes? I should like to be away as soon as possible.'

'No need, mapmaker. I and my men will accompany you. How many bandits surround your officer and his men?'

'Over twenty – perhaps twenty-five.'

Kashmar nodded. 'I will gather some warriors tonight. They will be ready to ride at first light.' He looked at the window. 'It is fortunate that it rained. Your trail will be easy to follow.'

King blinked. 'I hadn't thought of that – how to find my way back.'

Kashmar smiled. 'Hopefully all will be well.'

'Do you have enough men amongst your servants?'

'There is a village just three hundred yards away. You did not see it in the dark. I have men who sleep there. Men who are used to fighting.'

King thought about that then decided it was time to be very blunt with his host. 'Which side were you on?'

Kashmar knew exactly what was being asked of him.

'Mapmaker, you are speaking of history.'

King nodded. He believed his question had been answered. He felt he could trust this nawab as much as anyone could trust any man in these peculiar times. It had been better to discover the truth than to worry. It did not matter that they had been enemies: they were now, if not friends, allies. They might be enemies again one day, but not today. Today the strength was with the British and always in India when two men of honour met and liked each other, as King felt Kashmar did, then they suspended any feelings of hatred for this or that nation. His troubles were now Kashmar's troubles. King knew he would be in safe hands.

'If you cannot sleep, then tell me about maps,' Kashmar requested. 'I am very interested in your profession.'

Profession? Now *there* was a word which made King swell with pride. He had never heard his job called that before. It added huge prestige to a work which King had always regarded as something special, but believed he was one among few who did so. Profession! He would have to slip that into the conversation when next he spoke with Lieutenant Crossman. Right at this moment he would have given his soul to Kashmar, had that man asked to borrow it. 'Be my guest,' he would have said, 'do as you will with it.'

Instead, he began to explain the system of triangulation to the nawab, telling him about the Great Arc, the tale of how India was mapped from one coast to the other, from South to North. He spoke of the terrible trials and tribulations, the deaths while travelling through perilous country, the early graves for those who caught some disease or other in swamps or rainforests or unhealthy estuaries. Kashmar's obvious interest encouraged him and he spoke of measuring chains, Lampton's huge theodolite (which weighed half a ton) and how it had to be transported across India by ox-wagon, the building of survey towers throughout the land, perambulators, and all the other tools and objects required by an artificer. His delight, now that he had an enthralled audience, was unbounded. He felt it a great shame that it had to be an Indian aristocrat who was prepared to listen to his enthusiasms, rather than a European gentleman, but not because he felt the man before him was any less intelligent or discerning – quite the opposite – he just felt it was a shame that his own countrymen were not able to appreciate this wonderful *profession* in which he – Sergeant Farrier King – was skilled.

'How I wish,' murmured the nawab, when King ran dry, 'I had some obsession on which to fix my interest. Men like yourself must view the world through very different eyes, Sergeant King. I see nothing but bitterness and strife, whereas you see landscapes unfolding and draw maps which are works of art . . .'

'You have experienced many tragedies?'

'I have had a wife die in my arms and my only son fall in battle – those two terrible events are enough to crush any man.'

'Ah. I'm sorry. But,' said King, 'forgive me for saying this – you are a Mussulman – you must have other wives? Not, I hasten to say, that you did not love the wife who died, but you must have other children, surely? Are they then all female children?'

'No, I have never had another wife. My first and only wife was an Englishwoman.'

Despite himself Sergeant King was shocked. It was one thing for men to come to India and marry Indian women, though these days even that was frowned upon, but for an Englishwoman to marry a Mussulman? His shock must have shown in his expression, for Kashmar explained, 'We met in England – when I was sent to the court of your queen as an emissary.'

Inexplicably, King felt ashamed of himself, and lied.

'Oh, I wasn't thinking of that – I just remembered I haven't looked at my horse since I arrived.'

Kashmar was quiet for a minute, then his dark eyes bore through Sergeant Farrier King again, as if he could see spectres beyond this substantial soldier. 'Naturally my own people disapproved of my marrying an Englishwoman, a *Mlecca*. My father refused to speak to me until the day he died, when he cursed me for bringing dishonour to the family. My mother was kinder, but brothers and cousins were less so. For a time I was an outlaw in my own land. However,' he said, lifting his chin, 'I am a ferocious man when it comes to my own. I fought for my inheritance and wrested it from those who would keep it from me. I made them regret their treachery.'

King was bewildered. Surely it was the Englishwoman's family who should have been shocked by the marriage, not the Indian household? After all, an Englishwoman was a great prize, or so the sergeant thought. How strange that there should be this double-edged sword opposing the love match.

'I – I'm sure you did. But my horse?'

'He will be well looked after,' Kashmar reassured his guest, knowing full well the sergeant had not been thinking of his steed. 'Now, you must think how very ill-mannered it is of me, to be heaping private information on a relative stranger, but from the first moment I saw you I knew we were brothers under the skin. I felt we knew each other well, that our destinies were tied. Did you feel that, mapmaker?'

King was embarrassed by this remark. It was the kind of thing he heard when walking through every bazaar in India. Carpet sellers said it all the time. Purveyors of articles made of brass, or soapstone, used it with cheap regularity. *You are my very good friend, my brother. Come, just look. No need to buy. I will give you special price because we are brothers.* And so on, and so forth. But here was a nawab, a king, telling him this and he had to receive it in a different manner.

This local monarch did not need anything from him, by way of money or favours. He ruled a land. The sergeant was inferior in rank and breeding. The sergeant was also a Christian, an untouchable. Yet Kashmar was an Indian, and therefore (it followed from King's education in the narrow lanes of England) he should feel he was his inferior in the club of human beings. In short, though King felt different and strangely flattered, he also felt very uncomfortable. It was a complex creation, his growing relationship with this man, and he had not the learning to handle it. He had not yet mixed socially with Englishmen of deeper understanding, as his lieutenant had, and his impressions had been garnered mostly from men of lower intellect. In the villages and small towns, and even in the cities of England, a foreigner with a dark skin might be prince of a continent, but under it all he remained a heathen savage.

King suddenly realized something. 'You had an English wife,' he said, 'and I had an Indian wife. I have a son, with a skin . . .'

'As dark as mine?' finished Kashmar, who then smiled. 'There, I knew we were brothers.'

Once again, King felt a mixture of pride, shame and embarrassment and was puzzled as to the reason for these intermingled feelings.

But shortly after this he must have saved himself by falling asleep, for when he was roused it was morning. A dull grey light was penetrating the room. It had been the scent of hot tea which woke him. He sat up and rubbed his face with his hands, running his fingers through hair stiff with dust. He found a bowl of water, washed his face, and then drank some of the tea before going out into the courtyard. There he found Kashmar and around a hundred armed men on camels and horses, ready to ride. A saddled Samarkand was also waiting. A woman thrust a roll of bread in his hand, full of crushed banana. Kashmar nodded at him and then signalled for the gates to be opened.

Eight

The band rode out, following King's trail now hardened into solid impressions under the morning sun. The sergeant did not recognize the country through which they passed, it having been in darkness when he travelled it the previous night. They covered ground quickly and easily, now that obstacles were visible and could be circumnavigated. King felt a little guilty that he might have overslept and therefore had failed to ride out at the earliest opportunity, but he was not going to say anything to the lieutenant. He just hoped Wynter did not bleed to death in the last hour before his saviours arrived.

Two thirds of the way back they saw a dust cloud coming towards them. King wondered if Lieutenant Crossman and the others had escaped. But he soon realized there were too many riders for that to have happened. In a short while he recognized British light cavalry. Another rescue party or simply a coincidence? Quite soon the two groups came up against each other, the captain of the cavalry lifting his arm to halt the nawab's men. King's heart sank when he saw who led the around a score of Queen's Army troopers. Was there only one captain in Central India? He seemed to be everywhere – or at least, everywhere Crossman was. He also seemed to have a command of his own, uncontrolled by senior officers.

Deighnton kept his troops a little way off, to the front, eyeing the numbers of the nawab's force. Then he noticed King. He frowned.

'What's this, Sergeant?' he called. 'Up to your old tricks?'

'We are a rescue party, sir,' cried King, unwilling to leave the nawab's side in case it caused an attack. 'My lieutenant is trapped by insurgents and we are on our way to save him and his men.'

'Insurgents? You are riding with insurgents, Sergeant.'

'I think not, sir. The nawab . . .'

'Don't argue with me, man. I tell you they are rebels. I know the family.'

Abdul Kashmar stood up in his stirrups. 'Captain, my son was a rebel, but I myself, though not loyal to the British, refrained from joining against them. My son, the nazir, died in battle. He has paid for his zealous feelings. Now there are men who are in great peril. They will also die if they are not reinforced by superior numbers. Someone needs to assist them – if not us, then yourselves – or both? Time is of the essence.'

'Don't lecture me, you damned impudent dog!' roared Deighnton, shocking King to the core. 'I'll cut you down where you stand.'

King boiled over with uncontrolled anger and spluttered, 'How dare you speak to . . . to the nawab in that fashion?'

Deighnton smiled. 'You heard that, Lieutenant?' he called over his shoulder to a cavalry officer. 'Insolence.'

This same lieutenant spurred his horse to the captain's side. He spoke in undertones but because the wind was from that direction, King heard the words distinctly.

'Sir, I do think we should investigate this claim of trapped men.'

Deighnton completely ignored his subordinate.

Instead he bawled, 'Nawab, you will accompany me back to Gwalior – I order you to disperse your men.'

Kashmar was silent for a moment, then he called back. 'Please do not try to prevent us, Captain. We outnumber you five to one. I am aware how well the British Army cavalry fights – only too well, having heard how my son was killed – but be aware that many, perhaps all of you, will die. My own men will fight to the death. They have their grievances too and scores to settle. Please stand aside.'

'Are you mad?' roared Deighnton. 'Are you threatening *me*?'

The young lieutenant spoke in a clear firm voice. 'Captain Deighnton, sir – we must investigate this claim. I will not be a part of your personal vendetta. I have had enough of these escapades.'

Deighnton drew a pistol and levelled it at the lieutenant's chest. The lieutenant was startled but not cowed.

He said, 'Have you lost your reason?'

'You are refusing to obey an order, Lieutenant. I am within my rights to shoot you dead, sir.'

A rough-rider sergeant called out, 'No you an't, Captain. Beggin' your pardon, we are all witnesses here. There has bin no order given yet.'

Deighnton spun in his saddle, red-faced and full of fury. Then, as he saw the mounted troopers behind him, staring at him, he seemed to calm a little. Clearly the captain was not a popular man. He was not one of those leaders beloved of his soldiers. In fact King could see the hate blazing in their eyes. These cavalry troopers were just looking for an excuse to destroy their captain. Only his Indian servant, riding just behind and to the left of him, retained a neutral expression. The servant looked as if he were a million miles away, on the mountains of the moon. He was a wise man, whose placid expression had saved him from many beatings.

'There are a hundred warriors here, sir,' continued the lieutenant in an even tone, 'and we are twenty. I put it to you that to attack the nawab, who to my knowledge is not on the wanted roster, would be to sacrifice your patrol. At any subsequent inquiry I would have to proffer my opinion that I considered such a course of action unwise in the extreme, and what's more, quite unnecessary. We can accompany the nawab and assist in the rescue.'

'Rescue? Damn any rescue. What about a trap?'

'Sir, there is a British sergeant over there, who has given us the reason for this armed band being abroad. Is he part of a plot to ambush us? Sergeant,' called the lieutenant, 'are you being coerced?'

King rode forward to confront the captain and lieutenant.

'As you see, sir, I am not. Last night I escaped from an outcrop of boulders where my officer was trapped with three men and a boy. One of the men is bleeding to death and may well have passed on by now. I found the nawab in the dark and he agreed to help me. On my mother's grave, he is not an insurgent, I swear it.'

'You would, would you, you damned idiot? You have an insight into this man's black heart I suppose. You can read his mind? You have his history in a little notebook, I suppose?' said Deighnton, but it was in the tone of a defeated man. 'A mother you might have had, but not the name of your father.'

Before the sergeant could protest, Captain Deighnton ordered his men to wheel about, and follow the rebels.

King and Kashmar led the way, followed by the nawab's army, with the British light cavalry taking up the rear. When they reached Crossman's camp the situation seemed not to have changed from the previous evening. The British were still surrounded by guerrillas who were determined to break them. The guerrillas were soon routed by the combined forces of the nawab's men and the British cavalry. Those that did not get away stood their ground and fought to the death, knowing they would be hanged, or worse, if they allowed themselves to be captured.

Captain Deighnton fought as bravely as any man on the field, but afterwards led his troop away before Jack had knowledge of his presence. Deighnton did not realize it, but Jack would have duelled with him on the spot if he had realized. Strangely, the cavalry captain no longer seemed interested in arresting the nawab any more. King could only surmise that there was no longer any profit in it for him. His main goal seemed to be, as ever, the destruction of Lieutenant Crossman. Now that had failed he showed his back to those he had helped rescue. King did not doubt they had not seen the last of this dogged captain. Even the sergeant was now convinced that there was more to this obsession that just an insult. Deighnton was hunting Fancy Jack Crossman down. He was waiting his chance to destroy him. Why else would he always be in the same area as his quarry?

Water was given to the thirsty men who had spent the night fending off guerrilla attacks. Apart from a terrible thirst, Crossman, Gwilliams, Raktambar and Sajan seemed to be hale and without wounds. Wynter, however, was still in the clutches of the thorn bush, buoyed up by the spiked branches.

Kashmar quickly arranged the building of a derrick. Two men were sent out to cut staves. When these were brought back they were lashed together with ropes. A makeshift crane was fashioned. With this tool they lowered a lightweight man down to within arm's reach of Wynter's body. The dangling man tied a rope to one of the trapped man's wrists. Then a horse was used to winch the pale limp body of Private Harry Wynter from the centre of the thorn bush. Once he was clear an expert amongst the men removed the thorns that were embedded in his flesh. Some of the spikes were more than two inches deep. Wynter's body had been almost drained. He was so weak he could not open his eyes nor manage more than a whimper. Several times he passed out and it seemed he would not regain consciousness again. On top of his present hurts those places where the thorns had penetrated began to swell into lumps the size of a man's fist. It appeared there was a mild poison on the tips of the spines.

'I've never seen a man look whiter than bread flour,' said Gwilliams. 'He's a goner, for sure. He's got no chance, that man.'

Jack said, 'I wouldn't write off Wynter if I were you.'

'I'll wager a quid of baccy, lootenant,' said Gwilliams.

'I'll take that wager, Corporal.'

A shocked King said, 'How can you gamble on a man's life?'

'We jest did,' said Gwilliams, 'as easy as you like.'

King stared at Wynter, lying naked and pale while one of the nawab's men swabbed him down with ointment. One of Wynter's eyes was protruding like an oversized ball from its socket, stretching the lids aside. The other was closed, though puffed. The tongue was swollen and stuck out between his lips like the stem of some succulent plant. Some of the lumps had burst and were oozing fluid down his legs, his back, his shoulders. It was only then the sergeant realized why Wynter looked so white: his hair had lost all its colour and was the hue of fresh snow. He looked like a ghost. He would soon *be* a ghost if he was not saved. Yet for all these disfigurements there was something very dramatic about the change this condition had wrought in Wynter. For the first time in his life the private looked contented. Strange. So very strange. A lifetime of whinging and whining, misery and self-hate, and now that Wynter was close to death he seemed happy. How odd was that?

'Not a pretty sight,' came a murmur close to his ear.

King turned to face his lieutenant.

'Well done, Sergeant,' said Crossman. 'I shall commend you to our superiors for last night's action. You did exactly right.'

King, unsettled by the praise, said, 'You've never really had a high opinion of me, have you, sir? Of my abilities as a soldier, I mean?'

Crossman looked disturbed by this question.

'I have not yet formed an opinion. You do not shoot well, it's true, and that's the first requisite of an infantryman. You are also more interested in maps than real soldiering – I think you'll give me that too. But these days there's more to the army than just drilling and killing. A man – even one of the rank and file such as I was and you are now – needs to use initiative. The time has gone when all a soldier had to do was obey orders. The army needs men to think for themselves. The fog at Inkerman took care of that. Regiments were broken up by the mist and groups of men had to decide for themselves the best course of action, often led by ranks as low as corporals who did just as good a job, if not better, than their generals were doing.

'Last night you had the courage to make decisions – decisions that in the end proved to be the right ones. You placed your trust in a stranger about whom you knew nothing. You did not panic. You stood your ground before a captain of the light cavalry – one of the crème-de-la-crème who can do no wrong in the eyes of our generals – and did not back down. I am proud of you, Sergeant – proud to have you serve under my command.'

King blinked. This from the lieutenant? He had no words to reply, and before they came, Crossman had turned away. Next to come to him was Abdul Kashmar, the stranger in whom he had placed his trust.

'Well, mapmaker?' Kashmar smiled, his lean features forming a thousand creases in his weathered complexion. 'You have saved the day.'

'Not without your help, sir.'

'Do not call me "sir" – we are now friends. More than friends. We have fought together and triumphed. There is a bond.'

The sergeant let out a short cynical laugh. 'I fight together with generals and I would not dare to call them friends, for that they are not.'

'We are not in the same army, mapmaker. It is permissible.'

King smiled. 'I appreciate the honour . . . sir. Lord, I have to give you some title. You're a sultan. I can't just leave the words without a proper end.'

'As you wish,' laughed Kashmar. 'Now, your lieutenant has

agreed that we should take your man with us and care for him. I have given him my word of honour that this injured soldier will receive the best of attention. I hope you and I may meet again, mapmaker. You must tell me more about your science, and the art that accompanies it. I am fascinated. Perhaps you could map my kingdom, one day?'

'I would be honoured,' said King, delighted. 'Most honoured, sir.'

'Until then?' A hand was proffered. King took it warmly and shook it.

'And thank you, sir, for all your assistance.'

Kashmar waved a hand to say that it was nothing.

'Please,' King said, 'please come and meet my son, before you go. He is a bright child. I think he'll make something of himself . . .'

Later, when the group had organized themselves once more and they were riding out, Corporal Gwilliams said, 'Mighty chummy with the locals, Sergeant?'

King frowned. 'You have some objection to that?'

'Nope. None at all. Just mentioned it, that's all. Shakin' hands and the like. Appeared you was the best of friends.'

'Corporal,' protested King, 'he's a nawab.'

'Nawabs ain't of great account at this point in time. Wouldn't be surprised if John Company toppled 'em over. Anyways, had a lot to say for hisself, I expect. Not that I disfavour that. Him and his men saved my bacon, that's certain.'

King stroked the neck of Samarkand. 'Yes, he did.' He went quiet for a few minutes, when all that could be heard was the clopping of hooves on stony ground, before he said, 'You know his son was half-English? The nazir? The prince who would have succeeded him. His son and heir?'

'Nope, I didn't know that – why would I?'

'No, of course you wouldn't. But why I bring it up, is – he fought with the mutineers.'

'Who, the nawab?'

'No, the nazir. He was killed in one of the recent battles. Half-English. You would have thought he would have fought with his mother's people. But he chose to fight with the half of him that was Indian. I find that very strange. After all, we're Christians.' King struggled with this anomaly. It was not personal arrogance that made him believe his race was superior, but the teaching of his fathers. 'I mean, if I was half and half, I know which side I would be on.'

'That ain't strange. That's normal.'

'What do you know about such matters?'

'Why, in America those that are half and half almost always fight on the side that's been put down, trod on, pushed aside. What's the real word . . .?' Gwilliams screwed up his face and searched his brain. '*Oppressed*. That's it, they usually fight against who they think are the terrible oppressors. In America it's the white man who's crushing the Indians. Here's the same, only different Indians. Most men are lookin' for a cause. A just cause, they think. So they fall on the side of the victim, thinking themselves victims, and liking to think that because it gives 'em a way to get rid of all that anger inside 'em, not realizing everyone's got it, whether they're victims or oppressors. Nah, that ain't so strange. It's normal.'

King digested this, not completely understanding it.

Gwilliams chuckled. 'Back home we have Southern gals who're married to Northern men and their offspring don't fit in either society. Neither Yankee nor Southerner. You'll have 'em too. Commoners married to aristocrats. Yep, life's full of half 'n' halfers. One meself. Half-idiot, half-genius.' He roared with laughter at his own joke and startled his horse, Champlain.

Later that day the patrol entered a vast jungle and a difficult life became an almost impossible one, with mosquitoes, snakes and impenetrable foliage to contend with, as well as guerrillas who knew the area better than Crossman.

At the time Crossman and his men were entering the jungles of Central India, continuing their mission of rooting out guerrillas, Major Nathan Lovelace was setting up an intelligence network which would, his superiors hoped, ensure that any further uprisings would not surprise the British command in India. There would always be discontent, there would always be those who treated the native population with arrogance and contempt and thereby aroused their fury, but it was Lovelace's job to see that this fury was recognized in time to stamp on it. This was being done at the express wish of Lord Canning. Lovelace was required to recruit Indians, whose loyalty could be trusted, to act as spies. He called them his Watchmen.

Lovelace was ambitious and utterly ruthless in his work.

He was one of a new breed of men who had read Niccoló Machiavelli's *The Prince* and thought the ideas in there were damn good ones. There was too much talk of gentlemanly conduct; too many leaders like the late Lord Raglan, who had called spies 'skulkers' and would have nothing to do with them.

If men like Lovelace had been in charge of the Indian Army there would have been no mutiny in the first place. He was unsentimental, cold-hearted, and genuinely patriotic. Had Lovelace not been a man who kept his innermost beliefs private, Jack would not have courted his company for a minute. Fortunately, neither man knew each other well enough to understand what it was that separated them. Jack was as private a man as was his superior officer. Each thought the other a conscientious officer of the Queen, which indeed they both were. Lovelace believed he could turn the raw material that was Lieutenant Fancy Jack Crossman into a man as uncompromising as himself.

Lovelace had now formed the core of his Watchmen and a certain amount of training had taken place. He had sent some of them out into the field to test their abilities. Amongst them were Hindus, Mussulmans, Jains and Sikhs. They came from across all five of the main castes, including the Untouchables. They spoke several different languages. Finally – an entirely revolutionary idea – some were even women. Lovelace had thought long and hard about including this last group, but he reminded himself that women could be present yet entirely unnoticed when men gathered to plot and plan their activities. At this moment in time he was not concerned with any further uprisings: they would come later, if at all, for the country had been bloodied and no one was in any mood to rise up out of the gore and begin a new civil war. No, he had another task in mind for his spies: a private venture of his own. He had sent them out to gather information regarding the growing of flowers. How they performed on this training exercise, as individuals, would determine whether they would be retained for the more hazardous government missions of the future.

In the meantime, Major Lovelace went in search of a certain Captain Deighnton, whom he found based at Gwalior. Lovelace had his horse stabled, took a bath and shave, then stepped into a fresh clean uniform held out at arm's length for him, item by item, by his Indian batman. He always carried his silver-mounted brushes and combs, without which any gentleman would feel naked and exposed. Using these essential implements his barber combed his blond hair into a style which suited the shape of his face. Lovelace was an extremely handsome man, but was not greatly interested in women. He enjoyed their company, but found it frivolous for the most part.

Lovelace discovered Deighnton in the mess, drinking and playing cards with a group of cavalry officers. At first the major remained by one of the huge black marble pillars, which stood on a white marble floor supporting a ceiling painted with scenes of hunting in mythical-looking forests full of tiger, deer and birds bearing fantastic plumage. After a while he moved over to the card tables, where he smoked a cigar and affected to be interested in the run of play until someone addressed Deighnton by name. Then he raised his eyebrows and stared at the cavalry officer.

Deighnton did not look up, but seemed to know there were eyes on him.

'Something bothering you, Major?' he said, as he dealt.

'I do beg your pardon, Captain,' replied Lovelace. 'Awfully ill-mannered of me to gaze like that – but I have heard your name before.'

Deighnton snorted softly. 'Famous, am I?'

'No, nothing like that – well, you may be for all I know. No, I've heard it from one of my subordinates, a Lieutenant Crossman. He complains about you. Says you're chasing him over hill and dale. I'm Lovelace, by the by.'

Now Deighnton looked up, a dangerous glint in his eyes.

'Oh, yes, he's spoken of you, Major. Pulls your name out as if you're his trump card. That man is a menace. What do you want?'

'Here,' said a captain in the uniform of the 14th Light Dragoons, 'are you playing cards or holding a conversation?'

'I'm talking,' replied Deighnton, throwing the pack on the table. 'And I'll thank you, Willoughby, not to interrupt.'

With that the captain left the table and motioned Lovelace to join him at another table, where Deighnton signalled to a mess waiter, resplendent in scarlet puggree turban and *jodh-puri* suit, gliding between the potted plants.

'Whisky?' Deighnton asked.

'Certainly, thank you. My tipple exactly.'

The waiter was given his orders.

'Now,' said Deighnton, 'are you going to warn me off seeking a duel with your Lieutenant Crossman – it won't wash, you know. Fellah's a menace.'

'So you said before,' replied Lovelace coolly. 'In what way?'

'He insults gentlemen and then expects to get away with it.'

'I understood you and he have already fought your duel.'

Deighnton's eyes narrowed. 'There was some trickery. My own weapon misfired.'

'And the lieutenant eloped?'

'No, he had already discharged his weapon – he missed.'

'Ah. And so you want a second go?'

'He refused a second attempt on the spot. There was some nonsense about a wound to his hand. Listen, Major, I have no argument with you. If you have something to tell me, please say it and leave . . .'

Lovelace said, 'Duelling is illegal, of course.'

'This is India, not England. Here a gentleman needs to protect his honour or what is he?'

'Indeed,' agreed Lovelace, wondering what possible honour there was in killing a callow youth like Ensign Faulks. 'I'm entirely with you on that. You and I know that nothing is more precious than a man's honour. I understand you've had to protect yours three times in the last five years?'

Deighnton sat back and observed Lovelace, then lit up a pipe.

'Do you wish to make further comment on the subject?' he asked eventually.

Lovelace feigned surprise. 'No, no. A man must look to his family name, however many duels, but – ' he leaned closer to Deighnton and affected to glance around the room before speaking – 'what of the authorities? As you say, this is India – but the army doesn't sanction duels. An officer might get away with it once, but three times? Bit excessive, what? How is it they haven't come down on you? I have no problem with duelling, you understand – just intrigued, old boy.'

A smile hovered around Deighnton's lips. 'Ah – well, that's a bit of a secret, Major. Here's the whisky . . .'

The waiter with the tray placed the whiskies carefully on

the table, then said to the captain in a quiet tone, 'Your servant is outside, sahib. He wishes to know if he's to stay there or return to your quarters to prepare your bedding?'

'Tell the damn fool he's to wait where he is,' replied Deighnton irritably. 'I'd have sent a message if I wanted him back at the bungalow.'

'Yes, sahib.'

The turbaned waiter melted away as they always did. There and gone, like a flickering shadow. Lovelace had always admired this skill at being shadow. It was exactly what was required of a spy, to be there but to be unnoticed, and to leave like a grey cat in a grey dawn, without a sound, without being seen to leave. He was expecting great things from his newly formed team of Watchmen.

Deighnton threw a look back at the table where the card game was in progress.

Lovelace said, 'So, Captain, what brings you to India?'

'My regiment, of course.'

'Yes, yes,' said Lovelace, smiling, 'but you didn't need to come here. You have a choice. You could have bought out, or transferred. This land is pretty hostile to us, is it not? Ridden with disease and lately with hostility. We're all lucky to be alive, you know – it was a close run thing, this uprising. If the mutiny had spread further than Bengal, we'd all be corpses by now. India is not a place an HM soldier comes to get rich either – we're not like the Company men, are we? We're not given much chance to line our pockets.'

Lovelace made it sound as if only an idealistic fool or someone with no choice in the matter would come to such a bedevilled land for no profit. He had gauged Deighnton correctly, for he could see from the man's face that he agreed with every word. Lovelace sensed that Deighnton despised India. And although the major knew Deighnton was a second son, he also knew the cavalry captain was not a poor man. Deighnton certainly had the means to leave or change his regiment, if he had wished to remain in Britain or obtain a posting to a much more tranquil clime.

Deighnton felt the need to protect himself from this accusation of being gullible. 'Oh, I don't know. One can find opportunities here, if one looks for them.'

'Such as?'

He laughed. 'Major, I'm hardly likely to tell you, am I? My own close friends are not privy to such information. Otherwise I'd have competition. Let's just say I know some people who need the kind of skills I have to offer.' He suddenly realized the whisky was making him indiscreet. 'But you, Major. You're here too.'

'You know what I do for a living. Oh, I know you think it ungentlemanly – but it's something I'm good at. Probably the only thing I'm good at. Where else in the world at this point in time would I get the opportunity to practise my art? India is ideal, being rife with intrigue and murder at the moment. I couldn't wish for a better stage at this point in my career. At this rate I'll be a colonel within the year, perhaps even a general within two. There's not a lot of competition in my game either.'

'Lieutenant Crossman?'

'Fancy Jack? He's hasn't the callousness to progress too far. Too many principles. Too much integrity. He's not a ruthlessly ambitious man, like me. He's happy to progress slowly, by keeping in touch with my coat tails. I do not think less of his character for that: one way is as good as another. We each of us have our skills, Captain, and this was actually not his chosen profession. I brought him into it kicking and screaming. That's not to say he's not good at the kind of work I need him for – he's assiduous and dogged when it comes to a task. That's the kind of man I need working under me – officers who do the job and do it well.'

Deighnton looked down into his whisky glass. 'I have learned to dislike the man intensely . . .'

'Not from the beginning?'

'No – but he's as slippery as an eel.' Again, Deighnton felt he had said too much, for he added, 'Not that I wouldn't be the same in his position. I'm a very good shot, though I say it myself.'

'It takes more than being a good shot to kill a man in a duel,' replied Lovelace, finishing his glass.

'That's true. I've got that too. Whatever it is.'

Deighnton looked back at the card table, then said, 'Was there anything else you wished to talk about, Major?'

'Oh, no – nothing in particular. I hoped to persuade you to leave my man alone, but obviously that's not on.'

'This thing between me and Crossman, there's no stopping it now, I'm afraid. It's gone too far for that. I couldn't hold my head up if I pulled out.'

'An apology from him?'

'Sorry, Major, won't do.'

Lovelace sighed. 'No, I suppose not. And what's more I don't think he'd do it. He doesn't want the duel, but he'd never kowtow to avoid it. Well, it's between the two of you. I'm sure I would do the same in your place. I admire a man who's prepared to put his life on the line for the sake of his honour,' said the major, intending to fence verbally with Deighnton over this matter. 'My God, there have been some glorious duels in the past, eh? What about the one between Cardigan and – now who was it? – oh yes, Harvey Tuckett. Captain Tuckett was badly wounded, wasn't he? And Cardigan was arrested and tried in the House of Lords.'

'Acquitted though,' added Deighnton quickly, who knew exactly what Lovelace was doing and he sought to lighten the tone. 'But what about the petticoat duel? Lady Almeria Braddock and Mrs Elphinstone?'

Lovelace chortled and slapped his knee. 'Oh, *that* one – over Lady Almeria's true age, I believe?'

'In the first exchange of pistol fire, Lady Almeria's hat was damaged!'

The two men roared out laughing.

'Then,' continued Lovelace, wiping away a non-existent tear, 'when they took to the swords, one of them was pinked and the other apologized.'

They roared again.

'Women!' said Deighnton, nodding. His eyes narrowed and Lovelace knew something more significant than a petticoat duel was coming. 'But my favourite is the duel between the Marquis of Londonderry and an ensign in the marquis's regiment, a boy named Battier. Battier's pistol misfired, but he declined to reload and shoot again. Battier walked, much like our Lieutenant Fancy Jack Crossman, and was later horse-whipped for it by Sir Henry Hardinge, one of the marquis's seconds.'

Lovelace murmured, 'I'm sure he deserved it,' then slipped into a casual mode of conversation in which he subtly explored Deighnton's likes and dislikes. Lovelace was a great believer

in 'know thy enemy'. He cleverly explored Deighnton's background and preferences without appearing too inquisitive. They
had more whiskies, more cigars and pipe-fills, and the evening
mellowed on, card games forgotten in the pleasure of stories
of watching barefist fights, female conquests at masquerades,
tales of wagers which had made fortunes for some gentlemen
and wagers which had ruined aristocrats – all those tales in
which two like-minded officers indulge, on Lovelace's part
mostly fictitious.

'I expect you hunt of course, when at home?' Lovelace
asked.

Deighnton nodded, saying that pig-sticking in India was
not a patch on chasing a fox or deer back in England. 'But
one makes do with what's available. Tigers. Now there's a
sport . . .'

And so it went on. Lovelace himself did not hunt or shoot
wild animals for sport. It was not something he found any
entertainment in. He could kill a man, if it was expedient and
absolutely necessary to do so, without compunction. But
Lovelace was not a person who did such things simply for
the pleasure of letting blood. He saw no good reason to spend
a day tracking down a perfectly harmless stag and shooting
it for the sake of its antlers. He saw such sport as a waste of
good time. However, he did enjoy fly-fishing. He found it
relaxing and it gave him time to think over those many knotty
problems which beset assassins and spies like himself.

'Do you like angling?' he asked Deighnton, thinking that
such a slow sport would not interest the captain. 'I am fond
of it, myself.'

Deighnton laughed. 'Do I like it? I adore it. I'm a member
of the Houghton.'

For the first time that evening Lovelace was taken aback.
In fact he was stunned. Astonishment was quickly followed
by a feeling of monstrous envy. He could hardly believe his
ears. The Houghton Fishing Club (along with its sister club,
the Amwell Magma) was the oldest and most exclusive fishing
club in the United Kingdom. It had only twenty-four members,
all immensely wealthy men, and it owned something like a
ten-mile stretch of the River Test and its leaders – a length
of water which boasted the best trout fishing in the whole of
Great Britain. There were thirteen wardens who looked after

the Houghton's interests along the Test, tending this prime piece of fly-fishing heaven. How in God's name, thought Lovelace, did a man like Deighnton become a member of such an exclusive club?

'I would sell my mother into slavery to be a member of the Houghton,' he said, aware that jealousy laced his every word. 'How did you do it? Prime Ministers, Field Marshals, members of the Royal Family – they've tried and failed to enter the portals of the Houghton. I myself once went to the Boot Inn in Stockbridge just to catch a glimpse of the men who do belong.'

'I know,' said Deighnton in a self-satisfied tone, 'it's delightful, is it not?' He frowned a little, as if in thought. 'Perhaps I could take you along as a guest sometime? We seem to like the same things. Get on well together, I would say. Yes, I'm sure that could be arranged, once we're both back on home soil.'

'Well, that's mighty handsome of you. I would like that above all things,' said Lovelace. He glanced at the mess clock. 'Now, I have to go. I think you're needed back at the table. Thanks for the chat.' They shook hands.

Outside in the cool evening air, Lovelace drew deep breaths. What a loathsome creature was Captain Deighnton. A slug. Yet a member of the Houghton! He was very valuable to someone, that much was certain. You only got into the Houghton when a member keeled over and died. Who had purchased Deighnton the unobtainable? And why, for God's sake? It was a mystery which needed unravelling and Lovelace was determined to do it. Clearly Deighnton must be involved in some scheme which made other people a lot of money, and was well paid for it, and therefore made it worthwhile for the captain to put up with being in a land he hated, full of people he loathed. Lovelace had seen the way the captain had looked at the Hindu waiter, and had heard the way he spoke of his servant. It was quite obvious Deighnton despised the local population, perhaps even more than he did the country.

'Yet he remains here,' Lovelace said to himself, 'which speaks volumes.'

Nine

At the same time Lovelace was chatting to his mortal enemy, Jack was hacking his way through jungle. He and his men had been tracking a group of guerrillas for several days. It was no use calling in the cavalry, or any other outside help. The jungle was too dense for ordinary troops. Only a small unit with experience of rugged travel could penetrate that foliage. And since they were actually already there, Jack realized his group might as well finish the job. He had left Sajan with the horses in a friendly village and taken Raktambar, King and Gwilliams into Hell.

Not that his men liked Hell very much. Raktambar and King in particular were disgusted with the place. Both had 'Yellapuram fever', an illness named after the village where the first British soldiers in India caught the disease. Jack Crossman believed they had picked it up in the miasma of the swampy areas through which they had passed. Raktambar said he knew how to deal with the sickness and found a vetch which he called *moong*, a cure for the fever. Certainly the vetch was helping, though clearly not banishing outright all the symptoms.

Both invalids had a great fear of snakes, of which there were many and various. Both did not like being in enclosed spaces, especially dark green ones full of spiders and large savage insects.

'You'll be telling me you're worried about tigers next,' muttered Jack to Raktambar, 'and wild elephants.'

'No tiger with brains would come in here,' replied Raktambar, slicing through a thick vine with his blade. 'No elephant would fit in here.'

He had learned to use British humour from Gwilliams, who though he was a North American was as dry with his mirth as any Yorkshireman.

'Well, we'll soon be out of it.'

'All we have to do is kill a dozen men and then be on our way, sir,' added a disillusioned Sergeant King.

Jack said, 'This is new country for you, King. I would have thought you'd have taken the chance to do one of those linear maps of yours.'

King's face, ravaged by insect bites, covered in sweat and the muck of a humid jungle, raised what was left of his eyebrows. 'Map? Sir, I can't see more than two feet in front of me. It's always night in here. How do I make a map? What's more, the birds make a racket enough to wake the dead, clattering around in the tops of trees we never get to see. I get frogs in my bedding, leeches in my leggings, and ants in my food . . .'

The complaints went on. Jack did not try to stop them. They were better out than in, festering away.

Gwilliams was the only man who took such places in his stride.

'You shoulda bin with me in the swamps of Louisiana. Indians – our kind – tracking you down, dogged as you like. Moccasin snakes and copperheads fillin' your boots of a morning. Mosquitoes the size of your thumb. This is a walk in the park compared to Louisiana, Sergeant, I can tell you.'

'And you frequently do,' retorted King.

'We'll rest here,' said Jack, his arm almost dropping off with the effort of cutting through the undergrowth. 'Make camp.'

They were in a clearing the size of a small drawing room. Exposed tree roots snaked over the whole area forming a lumpy network. It was impossible to lie down with any comfort. Between the roots was spongy moss, but these small pockets would not have offered space enough for a mouse to sleep. There were insect-eating pitcher plants dangling from the canopy, for which King should have been grateful, except that he was a clumsy soul and continually knocked against them, spilling foul fly-rotten liquid down his clothes. The air was close, hot and very humid. Headaches and diarrhoea were almost universal complaints amongst the group.

'I will die in here,' said Raktambar miserably, 'and never know the sweetness of the marriage bed.'

They all made themselves as comfortable as their environment would allow, using dirty blankets and spare clothes.

Gwilliams and King were 'leech partners' as were Jack and Raktambar. They each performed the act of burning off the day's collection of bloodsuckers with a red-hot twig, much in the manner of monkeys grooming each other. No sooner had one set of leeches been cremated however, than a new set began their insidious journey to find flesh. They would not be long without their constant companions, the parasites of the dank quarter.

Jack held up a sock sodden with blood, wondering whether it was worth keeping. Silk socks such as he owned were a luxury and he was reluctant to throw one away if it could be avoided. But there was not water to wash it in and the blood would soon dry to a crispy scratching crust which irritated the skin. He tossed it into the jungle, then wondered whether some predator might smell the blood and come to investigate. It would have been better to burn the sock on the fire for safety reasons!

Gwilliams was cleaning his rifle.

Jack said, 'Best follow the corporal in his task – weapons foul up easily in this atmosphere.'

'Powder's damp in any event,' grumbled King. 'I'll wager they won't fire, clean or not.'

'Won't concern you,' Gwilliams grunted. 'You can't shoot for . . .'

'Yes, yes, we've heard it all before, Corporal. I think the fact that I can't hit anything with a rifle is probably engraved on the Taj Mahal. Thank you very much for reminding everyone though. I'm sure it had gone completely out of their minds.'

At that moment Raktambar leapt spectacularly to his feet and rushed in an attempt to climb a tree, failing when he could not keep a good hold on the mossy branches. What had made him jump was a huge python that glided past his elbow as he worked. The monster was as thick as his thigh and probably of great length, except that at first the tail was hidden in the undergrowth on one side of the glade, then when it entered the foliage on the other side, the head was not visible either. It bothered no one, this giant reptile, and expected bother from no one.

Gwilliams laughed, as he rammed his cleaning rod down the barrel of his Enfield, twisting and turning it.

'Now there's a big critter.'

King said, 'This isn't funny, Corporal – that monster nearly bit Raktambar.'

'They don't bite, they squeeze. I admit, that one would have hugged an elephant to pulp. Big bastard, wasn't he? Ate a few cows in his time, eh? Still, you gotta respect him. Saw a bunch of us and thought, not today, Alphonse – too many of 'em. While I'm crushing one, the others will knock me on the head.'

'You can't give wild creatures like that rational thought,' said King, 'any more than you can give a soul to a heathen.'

'I can do what I damn well like, so long as it ain't against army regulations,' replied the laconic corporal. 'Snakes have thoughts, same as any other critter. Might even have souls as well.'

King drew a sharp breath. 'I suppose you're one of those who follow the blasphemies of that madman Darwin?'

'Never heard of him. What'd he do?'

'Only said we were monkeys.'

Jack interrupted. 'I don't think Charles Darwin said we *were* monkeys – I believe he said we were descended from the same stock.'

'And what's the difference, sir?' cried King. 'If you come from monkey stock, you *are* a monkey, surely?'

Everyone fell into silence after this, contemplating their unhallowed position in the new chain of being that Mr Darwin had presented them with. Right at that moment King would have actually given his eye teeth to be a monkey. He could have shinned up one of those cathedral-tall trees and scuttled along the canopy.

'Can't get any worse than this,' he grumbled.

But it did.

At midnight it started raining. As was often the case in the tropics, it was a deluge. The noise of the continuous heavy rain hitting the wide waxy leaves of the foliage was deafening. And of course, everything was soaked through within a few seconds. The men huddled together around the trunk of a tree, but if they expected the canopy to keep them dry, they were wrong. Water poured down the trunk as if it were a drainpipe, washing over their equipment. They remained, miserably trying to breathe in the torrent that fell from the heavens on their heads. Then their misery turned to alarm. The ground was beginning to swim with water. It rose rapidly and soon they realized the glade was in danger of becoming flooded.

'We must move to higher ground,' said Jack. 'Pack up and leave, men.'

They gathered together their sodden belongings, much heavier now that they were soaking wet. Off they trudged, battling their way through thorny bushes, slimy succulent plants, entangling creepers and vines. It was hard going, through this waterfall of the gods. Eventually they reached a place which seemed to be higher than the rest of the land around them and they fell in an exhausted heap. Some slept, others could not.

It rained all the next day, and the next, during which it was impossible to see more than a foot in front of a face. Those that tried to eat found the food washed from their hand before it reached their mouth. King's fever reached a pitch whereby he was shaking from head to toe, sometimes gently, sometimes violently. When he was thrashing they pinned him down at the corners. Jack, Raktambar and Gwilliams managed to make a bivouac out of foliage which kept some of the rain off the sergeant's face, but it was not greatly effective. Since Raktambar was not well either and Jack was more concerned about King, Gwilliams spent much of his time forcibly diverting the snakes that fought to reach the high ground too. Serpents, he found, were not overly fond of floods either, and though they arrived exhausted he needed to get a stick under them and flip them back out from whence they came. He whipped the same snakes up and out several times, before they were deterred from returning.

On the third day the rain stopped as suddenly as it had started.

King had got over the height of his fever and had returned to the land of the living. He found he was hungry, but there was not a lot left to eat. The group were saved by a small deer which had got bogged down in the flood. Since no fire could be started Gwilliams skinned the creature and they gnawed the meat raw off the bone. Raktambar said it was fortunate that Wynter was not with them for he had only two teeth in his jaw and could only manage stew.'

Once they felt ready, Jack called for King.

'I think we can say we've lost the rebels,' Jack said. 'Find us the quickest way out of this unholy forest, Sergeant.'

King said nothing in reply and when Jack looked at his NCO he saw something in the man's expression he did not like.

'What is it?' he said. 'Are you still sick?'

'No, sir,' replied King, miserably. 'Not sick – lost.'

Jack instinctively glanced around him. 'What do you mean, lost? Look, we know we came in here from the east – retrace our journey.'

'I – I've lost the compass. It must have fallen out when we were in that storm, sir. I have no means of finding the direction.'

'Lost the . . . ? Well – ' Jack fumbled with his still wet pockets – 'use mine then.'

After a few minutes it was obvious he did not have his compass either.

'I don't understand it,' muttered Jack. 'It was here a few days ago. I remember taking it out . . . What is it, Sergeant King?'

The other man was looking even more devastated.

'I – I borrowed yours. You were not around, having gone off to shoot a meal with Gwilliams. You left your waistcoat hanging on a tent pole. I took the spare compass from your pocket, sir.'

Jack was thunderstruck. 'For what purpose, Sergeant? Have you not got it with you still?'

'I gave it to Sajan. He . . . the boy wanted to copy me, as I took our position. He still has it, I'm sure. It's not lost.'

Jack raised his voice. 'It's not lost, but we don't have it here – where we damn well need it. Sergeant, I could kill you. Did you not think? Did you not for one moment stop to think?'

Raktambar and Gwilliams looked across at the pair.

King hung his head. 'I'm very sorry, sir. I will do my best to take us out of here – only . . .'

'Only what? We can't see where the sun is in the sky, below this bloody canopy. Raktambar has his brass astrolabe but we can't see the stars either and an astrolabe is useless without the stars. We could roam around in here for days, weeks, perhaps months before finding a way out. Do you realize what you've done, Sergeant?'

'Yes, I do, and I'm very sorry.' King lifted his head and his face suddenly became very fierce. 'But I said I'd find a way out, sir, and I will. We must just stop and think.'

Jack suddenly realized his shouting was doing no good whatsoever. In fact it was making matters worse. King was right.
They had to pause to think. About what, he could not be sure,
but certainly shouting was not the way out.

Jack stared around him. They had left tall tree country and
were in an area of high shrubbery. Some of the bushes around
them were over thirty feet tall, but they were flimsy plants.
King tried to climb one but the slim branches would not hold
him and the thickness of the growth prevented him from getting
more than a few feet off the ground. There were trees there,
certainly, but they were weak saplings and no easier to climb
than the tall shrubs which robbed them of their light.

Gwilliams was pursing his lips, a sure sign his brain was
working.

'Sir,' he said, 'this here is new growth, these young trees.'

Jack nodded, hooking on to the corporal's train of thought.
Jack kicked around some of the lumps in the moss. Sure enough
he found rotten stumps beneath.

'Someone cut the trees down,' King said. 'Sir, why would
they cut timber this far into the jungle? Firewood? Canoes?
Do you think there's a village in here?'

'It doesn't seem possible, does it?' replied his lieutenant.
'The atmosphere here is foul and unhealthy, not to say
poisonous. The insects are numerous and highly carnivorous.
There appears to be no fresh water, only stagnant pools. It's
the worst location for a village I've ever seen. There's no agricultural ground to be seen anywhere. The hunting is not that
good. Where there's a village there are usually worn pathways
through the jungle. We've seen nothing.'

'No village then – but I know who would clear trees,' King
said, inspecting the stump that Jack had uncovered beneath the
carpet of moss and creepers. 'Yes, I know for certain.'

'Who?'

'Engineers, sir. British engineers. These trees have not been
chopped down with an axe – you'll agree the locals would use
axes? These trees have been *sawn* down. Look how clean the
cuts are. Good steel saws made in British workshops and
wielded by men with experience in tree felling. Army engineers, for certain. A railway, perhaps? Do you think they were
building a railway?'

'Can you see a damn railroad?' muttered Gwilliams. 'Wait!'

He cupped his hand to his ear. 'I hear a toot-toot in the distance. Train's comin' this way, I guess, to pick us up and carry us to paradise.'

'Shut up, Gwilliams,' ordered Jack. 'King, why else would engineers clear the jungle?'

'A road? But no road here. No road, no railway, no bridge needed, no township. A building of some sort? A building?' He stroked his beard, then cried, 'Wait?' Then he let out a laugh. 'I think I have it, sir. Could we make a star search, each going off in a different direction, but staying in touch by calling to each other? I suggest we don't go *too* far – and make a trail as you go, of broken branches, so that you can find your way back again to this spot.'

'What are we looking for, King?' Jack was aware they were all weak and not likely to have the energy to search for long.

'You'll know it, sir – when you find it.'

'King, you're not over the ague yet – are you sure you can walk?'

'This is my fault, sir,' replied the ravaged sergeant, swaying on his feet, 'if I don't help, I shall be forever ashamed.'

They all went off in different directions, shouting to maintain contact the whole while. It was not King that found it, but Raktambar. The Rajput soldier let out a whoop which stopped the others in their tracks. Jack called out to meet back at the spot they had left from. When he arrived back himself he found Gwilliams and Raktambar, but no Sergeant King. They followed his trail and found him face down near an ants' nest. He had passed out and had suffered bites on all the exposed parts of his body, but was still alive. They carried him back to their gathering place and bathed his face with water. After twenty minutes King opened his eyes.

'Did you find it?' he croaked. 'Is it there?'

Raktambar said, 'I found it, Sergeant – what is it?'

King smiled, weakly. 'It's a survey tower.'

'Why did they build it here? In the bloody wilderness?' asked Gwilliams, reasonably. 'Rak here says it's covered in creepers now – moss and such, and plants growin' out of the cracks. Why build somethin' like that and leave it to rot?'

'That tower was probably built by the Surveyor-General George Everest,' explained King, 'who would have used it once and then left it to nature. Everest would have needed it to take measurements from one point to another – there's probably a line of towers through this countryside. We were lucky to be near one.'

'So, one of your mapmakers left a tool behind,' said Jack, 'which we can use to see our way out.'

'A very tall *tool*,' said King, managing to sit up and drink some water Gwilliams was offering him. 'I think this is the area where Everest was set upon by the natives. They didn't like him messing around with their temples – he used them for survey towers too, which saved him building them – and they didn't believe he was a mapmaker. They had seen mapmakers before, simply walking the roads and drawing pictures on paper and that wasn't what this man was doing. This man even had to ask directions to the next village. If he was a great mapmaker he would surely know where he was and where he was heading for.' King laughed and coughed, almost in the same breath. 'So they came at him with matchlocks . . .'

'Was he killed?' asked Gwilliams.

'No – he survived. Some of his men were shot, I believe.'

Later, when King had recovered enough to totter along with them, assisted by Gwilliams, they set out for the tower. It was indeed in a dilapidated condition. However, Jack managed to haul King to the top, despite the rotten timbers, and from there one could see over the tops of the tall shrubs. King gauged their compass direction from the position of the sun, but that way lay a large expanse of forest. He could not be sure, but in the far distance westwards, he could see a faint line running through the trees, like the shadow of a long snake.

'Sir,' he said, 'that could be a river. That line out there. Do you see it?'

Jack stared. Indeed, he could make out a fine wriggle in the pattern of the trees about a half a mile west.

'Are you sure? That it's a river?'

'No, sir – not certain – but I can't think what else it could be.'

'Any idea which river?'

'No, sir,' replied the sergeant truthfully.

'Well, rivers often have settlements along them – looking the other way . . .' He sighed. 'I just don't like it.'

Jack and his men left the tower behind and struck west-

ward. They were soon back in the dense forest. Somehow
they managed to keep a fairly straight line and at noon they
reached a fast-flowing, dangerous-looking river. King had
recovered somewhat from his fever, but Raktambar was now
looking the worse for wear. He had to be supported between
Jack and Gwilliams as they first tried to make progress along
the east bank. However, there was too much debris – drift-
wood tangled on the banks – which impeded their progress.
Finally Jack ordered a raft to be built. They used vines and
some of their clothes as ropes to bind together bamboo poles
to make a rickety vessel. The only way to stay afloat was to
lie full length on the raft. If one tried to stand the poles parted
and feet and legs went through. Spreading bodyweight was
the only answer.

They passed at least two villages at such a rate they could
not paddle the raft to the shore. Then there came a point when
the river widened and turned, and they were able to get nearer
to the bank. When they next rounded a meander they crashed
into a loosely built jetty which broke up the raft. Gwilliams
immediately grabbed Raktambar and dragged him to the shore,
while King was left clutching at one of the support poles from
the jetty. Jack struggled through the current, his legs thrashing
away madly to counteract the fact that he had only one hand
for swimming. However, since his disability his right arm had
grown in strength – and his left forearm was not completely
without power. Still, it was all he could do to save himself,
without concerning himself with others.

'Help! Sir!' King cried, as Jack struggled past him in the
foaming torrent. 'I can't hold on!'

The sergeant's eyes were full of panic and terror as he reached
out and tried to grip at Jack's clothing.

Jack reached the shallows but was spent, having had to swim
with only one good hand. Gwilliams got to his feet and tried
to totter towards the jetty pole, but his legs gave out under
him. Fortunately by now villagers were appearing. Two men
ran down and risked their own lives to wade out far enough
to reach King. With the current ripping at all three men, the
rescue pair pulled him to the safety of the shore. More villagers
arrived and a great chatter began as they surveyed the wondrous
flotsam that the river had tossed up on their banks. Three white
men and a tall aristocratic-looking Indian. It was true they did

not look much in their present condition, but the villagers knew well that all white men were rich and rewards would be forthcoming.

Raktambar was in no state to talk, but Jack's Hindi had improved with every month in India. He soon sorted out who was the headman, asked that they might be given food and water, for which he promised to pay in coin. The headman, a Hindu, said that payment for the basic needs of life would not be necessary. He explained that his village was not a poor one, since many of the village youths were matchlock men for a British plantation owner who grew opium poppies.

'Not in the jungle, surely?' said Jack in Hindi.

'No, no, sahib,' said the headman, bobbing and smiling, 'in fields to the west.'

However, Jack insisted the headman take a gift on behalf of his people. The silver coinage was gratefully received.

By the time evening came round the four men were in semi-comfort, on bamboo and rattan beds, having been given fish soup, vegetables and bread. They wore dry clothes for the first time in a week.

King asked to see the two villagers who had saved his life. At first they refused to attend, but the headman was asked for and King insisted he *had* to meet his saviours. When the men came they seemed very shy. Jack noticed they were taller than the rest of the villagers: from their features and bearing they seemed of different stock. Raktambar confirmed that their accents indicated they came from the north, rather than from Central India.

'What do you think that means?' asked Jack.

'Perhaps, sahib,' Raktambar stated, 'they are two of the men we have been seeking?'

'Guerrillas?'

'I am sure of it.'

This left Jack with a huge dilemma. All but Gwilliams had lost their Enfields in the river. Gwilliams had strapped his rifle to his back and so had managed to retain it. Jack still had his five-shot Tranter revolver, but his ammunition was wet and useless. There were hunting knives on most of the four and Jack was sure Raktambar would have weapons secreted about his person. However, there was no saying King's two saviours were not alone. There might be others with them. They would certainly be armed. Arresting the two men could be very dangerous. Then there was the fact that they had saved King's life at risk of their own. If Jack did manage to arrest the two, they would at best be hanged or shot, at worst they'd be strapped to a cannon and blown to pieces. Certainly they would be executed.

Yet Jack was an officer of Her Majesty Queen Victoria and was expected to put duty before feelings. He was the law in India. Allowing rebels to escape was, he did not doubt, punishable by death. In these violent and passionate times no court martial would take into account an act of bravery on the part of the prisoners. It would indeed be a foolhardy officer who would not harden his heart and bring the rebels to justice, especially when there were other ranks as witnesses.

If Wynter had been there, Jack would not have contemplated letting the men go. King was dead to the world and so would know nothing about it. Gwilliams? Who knew the mind of this wild man from the Western frontiers, with his squared copper beard and his brain full of ancient history. Nevertheless, Jack trusted Gwilliams' loyalty to him. The North American certainly did not think a great deal of the British Army as an entity and Jack doubted he would betray him to authority, even if he suspected Jack of what he was about to do.

'Raktambar,' said Jack in Urdu, 'I want you to go the headman and tell him it might be best if the two men we're talking about left the vicinity fairly quickly, before the Soldier Sahib regains his strength.'

The Rajput nodded in approval. 'Yes, sahib. You do the right thing.'

'I'm not sure it's the *right* thing. I don't know what is, under the circumstances. But I certainly can't do else.'

'Yes, sahib.'

Raktambar rose from his bed and left the palm-leaf hut.

Gwilliams rolled over. 'Where's he goin'?'

'Call of nature,' replied Jack.

'What were you two jabberin' about in that tongue?'

'Urdu. We were speaking Urdu. Nothing much. Just going over the day's events. I don't have to account to you, Corporal.'

'Jeez!' exclaimed Gwilliams. 'Just curious, that's all.'

'All right. But get some sleep. We need to get out of here as soon as we can. Those rebels may be around here and we're now poorly armed and badly equipped.'

'Too right – my cartridge is a sodden mess.'

Later, Raktambar came back and nodded at Jack, who then tried to get some sleep himself. He must have nodded off, because the next thing he knew the cock was crowing on the maidan. A short time after a grey grisly dawn entered the glass-less window the headman came to see them. He told Jack a *moorpunkey* was coming down river.

'What's a *moorpunkey*?' Jack asked Raktambar. 'It mean's peacock's wing, doesn't it?'

'It is the name given to pleasure boats of important person-ages, Sahib Crossman. It would resemble the war boats of the Burmese, sahib. A large craft, certainly.'

'What in God's name is one of those doing coming down this dirty old river at the back end of nowhere?'

When asked this very question, the headman explained that merchants had purchased this boat from a local *zamindar*, a land-owner impoverished by the recent 'disturbances' to transport maize flour to villages along the river. Gwilliams immediately got up and roused King. Raktambar too was soon on his feet. The four men stumbled down to the jetty just as the *moorpunkey*'s crew was throwing out mooring lines.

The captain of the exotic but now beggarly craft, a small wizened man in a filthy turban, kurta and pantaloons, agreed to take them along to the next sizeable town. Jack and his men said their farewells to the headman and his villagers, who crowded to see them off. It was not often four such exotic people landed up in their backyard. However, as they were going up the gangplank to board, a naked man suddenly appeared on the deck and started shouting at them in a shrill voice.

'What's this?' asked Jack, eyeing the Indian, whose skin was marked all over with yellow river clay. The fellow's hair was stiff and stood on end in matted bunches, and it too was thick with the same ochre clay. There was black mascara ringing his eyes, giving him the appearance of a wild animal. Over his shoulder he carried a pole with a knotted piece of cloth attached, which appeared to contain his belongings.

The captain went to speak with this strange lean character, then returned to Jack and made a helpless gesture.

'He says you will bring the river demons down upon my boat, sahib, so I have to ask you to disembark.'

Jack growled, 'Who says?'

'The Holy Man, sahib.'

Jack could see the captain was upset with the whole affair and wanted it resolved as soon as possible.

'Who says he's a Holy Man?'

The captain turned and gestured. 'You can see it, sahib. Look how his eyes roll in his head. Listen to the harshness of his voice. The gods have entered his body. He has divine dreams. He tells me he dreamed you brought destruction on my little wooden boat.'

'Listen, Captain,' Jack said, firmly planting himself on the deck, 'you'd better cast off those mooring lines right now, because me and my men are staying right here. I am not a civilian. I am a lieutenant in the British Army. These men with me are soldiers of Her Majesty, Queen Victoria. We are not in uniform because we do not wish to be at this moment in time. You think we're going to be abandoned out here in the wilderness because some madman thinks he is a prophet and has bad dreams? Not a chance, Captain. I will hear no more arguments.'

The Indian captain looked from the determined man in front of him to the crazy man behind him, shrugged, and then finally gave the order to cast off. At this the so-called Holy Man went berserk. He ran up and down the deck several times, throwing his arms in the air and screeching at heaven. When he could see this was having no affect on the intruders he put his thumb in his mouth, but instead of sucking on it like an infant, he blew. What came out was the shrillest whistle Jack had ever heard. It hurt his ears and he found himself covering them up. The Holy Man was delighted and continued blowing until he ran out of breath.

'Let me hit him over the head?' implored Gwilliams. 'I could do it in a moment.'

The *moorpunkey* continued downriver. Jack believed they were heading vaguely towards Cuttack on the east coast. However, he intended to get off before they reached anywhere near that far downstream. Green jungle slid away on the either side of them, fresh at the edges, dark beyond. Jack felt satisfied that the worst was over: they had beaten the jungle, albeit they had not got their quarry. There would be explaining to do, but only to senior officers who understood the problems of a small unit sent out into the wilderness. Colonel Hawke and Major Lovelace were not exacting men, who needed their subordinates to provide every small detail of an expedition.

Throughout that day and into the night, the Holy Man kept up his persecution of the soldiers. When he was not trying to rally the crew and the rest of the passengers to his cause, he was directing those ear-piercing whistles towards his enemies. Jack was beginning to wonder whether this creature was a victim of the recent uprising. Perhaps the man had seen such terrible atrocities he had lost his reason? It was this consideration which kept him from releasing the fury of Gwilliams on that clay-covered head. Gwilliams would have brained him for certain.

The mutiny, and the retribution, had changed the people of India for good, and altered the attitude of the British Government towards the army of the East India Company. Jack could not see the Indian Army surviving under this momentous event. It had failed on all accounts. It had failed to see the mutiny coming, though the signs had been plain. It had failed to stamp it out when it was a mere campfire. It had failed to stop it spreading into a raging wildfire. Its officers could now be accused of being negligent, lazy and complacent. It had only survived by a whisker because the nationals were fractured into various sets of people who were rivals and enemies of each other, and some saw fit to remain loyal to the East India Company. It had survived by default.

He was sitting on a box of ropes on the deck when Raktambar came to him that evening. A white-breasted kingfisher, a beautiful bird, had been perched on the boat's rail and Jack had been observing it closely. Jack was not a great one for God's wild creatures but he had inbred in him the natural curiosity of a gentleman of his time. The birds of India were far-ranging and various, many of brilliant plumage, and it was difficult not to be impressed. Bee-eaters swept along gorges, brahminy kites littered the skies, flameback woodpeckers rattled at trees, and shrikes, bulbuls and oriols peppered the bushes of shrubland and forest. How could one ignore such sights and sounds in this strange and interesting land?

And it was not just the birds, or the sambur deer, mongooses, wild boars and tigers – it was people too. Such new and astonishing experiences. After Delhi had been taken, Jack had been passing through a bustling marketplace and had seen an elderly man painting. He had stopped, not just because the picture was worthy of a look, but because he was amazed by the delicacy of the brush the artist was using and the glittering permanency of the paint. His own father had been a very good artist, but he had never seen brushes such as this man was using. It had but one hair! On enquiry he learned that the brush was fashioned from the single eyelash of a camel. The paint, he was told, was made from the powder of ground-down gems: being precious stones the colours never faded.

Such wonders in this turbulent country!

The Rajput sat down beside him, saying nothing at first, but Jack could tell the man wanted to talk.

'Your wife can see those same stars, sahib,' said Raktambar, wrongly assuming that Jack was contemplating the swathe of sparkling gems in the heavens, 'even though she is many miles away.'

Raktambar, like a lot of Hindu men of his time, had not travelled beyond the shores of India. It was one of the grievances which had caused the revolt, the fact that the army required its soldiers to board boats and leave the sacred Indian soil in defiance of the rules of their caste. Raktambar had no idea of great distances. He could not know that Britain was still in daylight and would not have a view of the stars for a few hours yet.

'Yes,' he said in reply, 'that is a comfort.'

'Sahib,' said Raktambar, getting down to business, 'why did you let those two men go free?'

Jack knew he meant the men he'd suspected of being rebels.

'It seemed churlish to do otherwise – they saved King's life.'

'Churlish?'

'Wrong.'

'But were we not also wrong to let them go?'

Jack nodded. 'Yes.'

'So, where is the *right*?'

'Sometimes there is no black and white, only grey. I don't know what the answer is. I did what my impulses told me to do. I could be court-martialled for such a decision.'

Raktambar's expression showed that he did not think this likely.

'Who will tell?'

'It is the duty of men like Gwilliams and King to do so.'

'They know I would kill them first.'

Jack raised an eyebrow. 'Would you?'

'Of course. It is a point of honour. If they did such a terrible thing, they would have lost theirs. They would be dregs.'

Jack knew this would be the opinion of many.

'Well, I'm sure it won't come to that . . .'

At that moment Jack heard a splashing sound, down below on the river. There was a bump, as if the boat had hit a log, followed by a grunting sound. Both men rose and went to the side, looking down at the water. There was a glowing circle in the darkness below caused by a lantern which was being held up by the hand of a boatman. Its light showed a man in a European broadcloth coat leaving the boatman's canoe and climbing up a scrambling net which hung over the side of the *moorpunkey*. When the man reached the top, and he leaned over the rail, a 'wideawake' hat fell off his head and on to the deck. The man swung himself easily over and landed lightly on his feet, picking up his hat before he straightened. He placed it back on his head and stared into Jack's eyes.

'A European gentleman? Good evening, sir. I am Reginald Lee.'

Jack shook a proffered hand automatically, answering, 'Good evening – a rather unorthodox boarding?'

'But necessary,' replied Mr Lee, a Eurasian with some obvious Chinese blood in his veins.

The boarder began to look around him with keen eyes, when the Holy Man suddenly appeared from aft and on seeing Jack started his infuriating shrill whistling. Then Mr Lee moved under a lamp and, just as suddenly, the whistling stopped. The Holy Man remained standing there, naked as usual, with his thumb still in his mouth. He looked for all the world like an infant interrupted by a parent in the middle of the night.

Reginald Lee reached into his coat and said, 'Excuse me, sir,' to Jack, then shot the Holy Man between the eyes.

Jack stepped backwards, shocked, the noise of the gunshot ringing in his ears. The boat came alive. There was pandemonium for a short while as men came running from forward and aft, the captain of the craft amongst them, to stare first at the dead man, then at his killer. Mr Lee seemed quite unperturbed. He replaced his pistol in its holster, stepped forward, and took the Holy Man's bundle. Undoing it carefully he produced five thick discs the size of teaplates.

He held one up for Jack to see. 'Opium cakes,' said Mr Lee. 'This man was a thief. I have been chasing him for three days.' Then he said to the captain, 'Do you have a berth for me?'

The captain gasped, then closed his mouth, before opening it again to say, 'There is no spare cabin, sir.'

Mr Lee looked around. 'Then I'll sleep on this rope box, if I may. I will pay the fare accordingly.'

The corpse was dragged away and tossed unceremoniously over the side. It was obvious no one knew what else to do with it. These were not pleasant times and even if they were, India had corpses by the plenty. Everyone knew the body would start to deteriorate very quickly in the heat. The river was used to receiving corpses, both from funeral parties and from incidents such as this.

The captain told Jack, sagely, 'This man did not foresee *our* deaths, but his own – he had not the wisdom to know which from which, sahib. He must have been taking his own substances. He was not a wise man at all.'

Jack was more interested in speaking with Reginald Lee as the assassin arranged a borrowed blanket on the rope box.

'You work for the opium farmers?' asked Jack.

'For Sir Matthew Martlesham, yes. I am the runner.'

'The runner?'

Mr Lee gave him a smile. 'I chase thieves. There are many, sir. It is always thus. If they work in a diamond mine, they try to steal the diamonds. If in a gold mine, the gold. This pig worked as a labourer in the poppy fields – he stole my master's opium.'

Jack did not doubt the punishment for such theft was death.

'You are the judge, jury and executioner?'

'I have not the time, sir, to take a prisoner back with me – it is costly, is it not, to transport someone? And there is the chance he will escape. It is better to do it here and save a great deal of trouble.'

'Do you not find your work a little distasteful?' Jack asked with interest. 'A hunter of men?'

'It is very lucrative, sir. My master is a very rich man. Very rich. I am fortunate to have such an employer. He is very kind.'

Ever since the opium wars of the 1840s, when the Chinese

Emperor ordered the destruction of the drug which was destroying his people, Jack's brother James had been assiduous in his attempts to ban the commercial growing of opium poppies on British-controlled soil. James was a member of a political group (led by the Quaker Whig, Lord Holbrook) which was appalled by the devastation opium was causing throughout Asia and especially in China. Jack was aware that opium was still smuggled into China from estates in India.

'There is obviously a lot of money to be made in opium,' Jack said.

'Oh, sir, the riches are bountiful. Once upon a time my master grew tea, but opium is needed much more. Some people would sell everything they have for opium.'

'And do you use it?'

Reginald Lee smiled. 'Sir, if I were to smoke opium I would be sacked by my master. I am a runner. I must keep my wits about me. And you, sir? Do you indulge?'

Some ugly memories came to Jack. 'No, I was once obsessed with a tincture of opium – laudanum. It was not a pleasant experience. Well, at the time it seemed to be. It was only after I broke the habit that I could see what it had been doing to me. I never want to go there again and I pity the man who has been hooked into such a state.'

Jack recalled vivid dreams. So vivid it was difficult to separate them from events in real life. Having been an addict he could well imagine why others had trouble in separating dreams from reality. Those were times when he had dreams within dreams: when he fell asleep even though already asleep, and went down to a deeper level. Those dreams could be terrifying or enlightening. He sometimes wondered if there were even further levels to which a man might fall during unconsciousness: a place so deep it would be a struggle to surface again.

Lee shrugged. 'You and I, sir, are not the sort of men to participate in the idle smoking of opium. Those are worthless creatures who have no pride in themselves, no honour in them. You and I, sir, would spit on them in the street, they are so beggarly in appearance. It is no wonder they seek escape from this world, for their lives are lived in the company of low creatures like themselves. They have nothing else to live for. Many of them die in the filth of the gutter. They are of no account.'

'Yet they have made Sir Matthew Martlesham a rich man.'

Lee smiled. 'They can always find a coin for opium. It is a miracle that they do.'

Some of what Lee was telling him was undoubtedly true, however distasteful, regarding the determination of the opium fiend. And it was also a fact that such people managed, however short of money, to chase the next dragon. He had seen this in the Crimea, mostly amongst Chinese workers, but even amongst some British and French soldiers. What was dawning on Jack, an appalling thought, was that there must be tens of thousands of users in China, perhaps millions, to make so many men like Martlesham the wealth they were purported to own.

Reginald Lee got off the boat at the next stop, while Jack and his men waited for a larger town. Finally they were able to disembark at a place called Vidisha, on the river Betwa. There was a writer from the East India Company stationed there – a man called Fanthorpe who had been so long amongst the locals without European company he had trouble recalling his English – who helped them obtain horses. Once fed, watered and rested Jack and his men were ready to ride north again. King and Raktambar were much recovered from their fevers and were once again full members of the team. They encountered no insurmountable problems and were back in Gwalior within a few days.

Once back in a British Army stronghold, Jack shed his worries along with his dirt. He was in his bath, behind a screen of sweet-scented grass known as a *tatti* – when Rupert Jarrard paid a call. Throwing a silk robe round himself, an awkward business with only one hand, he went out to meet Rupert. The newspaperman grinned at him.

'Well, back safe and sound, eh?'

'Only just,' remarked Jack, pouring himself some gin. 'Would you care for a whisky?'

'No thanks – too early for me.'

'Well, I'm just catching up from a position of deprivation.'

'How was it? Out in the field, that is? I understand you left two men with a nawab on the way?'

'Well, a man and a boy. Wynter, and King's adopted son, Sajan. I trust they're still somewhere around.'

'Oh – ' Jarrard reached into his pocket – 'by-the-by, I picked this up at the mess. It was left for you – apparently a *choki* from some outlying village delivered it. Luckily I was around when the fellow arrived with it and no one else saw it.'

He held out a torn sheet of folded paper. Jack took it hesitantly, wondering if it was a note from Deighnton. He would not put it past that idiot to call him out just as soon as he was back in camp. But on unfolding it he saw that it was not from Deighnton at all. He read the note and his face twisted into what might have been mistaken for a smile.

'Trouble?' asked Jarrard casually.

'Oh, come on, Rupert, you must have read it – it wasn't sealed – and you a newspaper man?'

'Guilty – but who is this Captain Swing? Is he a somewhat illiterate friend of Deighnton's?'

Jack looked at the note again. It read:

> To Leftenant Crosman.
>
> Be ware of peeple who hav been put upon. Look to your bed that it dont get atention from insenderees. You hav not done rite by sertan peeple and that will be your undoing. You may be torched if you dont watch out and keep your wits about you. Be warned. Just becus your a criple won't help to save you from fate.
>
> Captain Swing

'You need to know English history, Rupert – especially the history of the rural poor in places like East Anglia. Captain Swing was the name used on letters written by anonymous incendiaries: labourers who burned down haystacks and farmhouses in the early part of this century. It's not commonly known but we in England were close to revolution during the first few decades. I remember the troubles as a boy . . .'

'Really? As in the French revolution?'

'Well, it didn't get to those proportions, but it was touch and go for a while, in the rural areas. I remember accompanying my father to London by coach and on the way we saw a young man – couldn't have been more than twenty years of age – being hung by the neck on some gallows at a crossroads. Apparently he had set fire to some corn sheaves. They had to almost carry him up to the noose he was so frightened. It made a marked impression on me, I can tell you. I had some bad dreams.'

'I'm not surprised. Hung for firing some sheaves, eh?'

The magistrates wanted to make a point. Farms had been attacked. Vicars had been beaten with cudgels and stoned out of villages . . .'

'Wait just a second,' interrupted Jarrard for the second time. 'Priests?'

'Certainly. The reason for the unrest was the poor wages paid to the farm workers by the farmers. The farmers themselves maintained they were unable to pay more because of the tithe. The tithe was collected, under the law of the land, by the clergy every year. It was supposed to be a tenth of the harvest, but vicars and farmers had long come to an arrangement whereby the farmer paid the vicar in cash, rather than cut away a tenth of his crops. Over the centuries this cash sum became a fixed amount and even though the yield might be poor – when the rains didn't arrive in time or were too much – the vicar got his money.'

'So the mobs blamed the clergy? Heck, you old-worlders live complicated lives, don't you?'

'Exactly.' Jack looked again at the note and then waved it in front Jarrard like a flag. 'This is of course from Private Harry Wynter. His father or grandfather was probably a Captain Swing in their time, I shouldn't wonder.'

'What will you do to him?'

Jack frowned. 'I don't know. If I reported it, he would probably be shot, of course. You can't threaten an officer of Her Majesty. Serious business. At the very least he would be severely flogged. The trouble with Wynter is he does things without thinking. I'm not sure what to do about this. If I ignore it, Wynter will only get worse and do something that really will have him climbing the scaffold steps.'

'Discipline him yourself.'

'I don't like it, but I might have to.'

The next day Jack rode out with Sergeant King to the nawab's palace. They stopped off at the house where Sajan was staying. King was reunited with his adopted son, while Jack renewed his acquaintance with Cadiz, his magnificent little Karashahr. The pair then left Sajan and continued along the road to Kashmar's hunting lodge.

After one night out in the open, they reached the nawab's province. Kashmar received them both royally and seemed genuinely delighted to meet with King again. After they had drunk tea and exchanged greetings, Jack asked about Wynter.

'He is alive,' said the nawab, 'but he complains a lot.'

Jack and King gave each other a sideways look, knowing that Wynter had probably not stopped whining since he had been well enough to give voice. Undoubtedly he would have tried the hospitality of a saint and most likely requested all manner of things which the nawab might have felt obliged to give him.

'I'm sorry for that,' Jack said. 'I hope he has not been too much of a burden. Unfortunately it is in his nature to complain about his lot. He feels God and the world is against him. I hope you did not feel obliged to give him alcohol?'

'Not that, nor the women he requested we supply him with. We have no alcohol in my hunting lodge, and the women . . .'

King was horrified at the audacity of his private soldier.

'Yes, yes, of course. I am absolutely mortified that he asked for . . . I shall take the man to task. You may rest assured, sir, that he will be made to pay for his insolence!' King then remembered Wynter's arrogance when dealing with natives of the country. 'He – he didn't insult you, I hope? He's a man of very limited intelligence.'

'Oh – ' Kashmar waved a hand – 'don't worry, I soon put him in his place. I'm not used to being spoken to as if I'm a servant. I told him I would open his wounds and let him bleed to death if he called me names.'

Jack gritted his teeth. 'He abused you?'

'Lieutenant, I did not *allow* it. He only did it once and I'm sure the fury with which I attacked him made sure it never entered his head to do so again.'

'I sincerely apologize for my soldier,' Sergeant King said, 'and would like to be shown the man so I can kick him in front of you.'

'Be my guest,' said the nawab.

Clearly he was not as forgiving as he appeared on the surface. Crossman and King did not blame him. They could only imagine what insults Wynter had flung at everyone once he had recovered. Wynter was a grovelling weasel who believed that in the natural order of things he was a lord in the presence of anyone he felt of lower status than himself. The fact that Kashmar was a nawab, the ruler of a province, would have meant nothing to Wynter. Kashmar was not a white man, and therefore he was classified in Wynter's book as his minion.

'I would appreciate it, sir, if you remained here,' said King to Jack firmly. 'I shall be back in a short while.'

Jack was about to protest, then thought better of it.

'Quite, Sergeant – I need to finish my cup of tea.'

Kashmar took Sergeant King to a cool room on the far side of the lodge. Wynter was lying on his bed asleep, dressed only in a loin cloth, while a punkah wallah fanned him gently. Kashmar indicated that the punkah wallah should leave the room, which he did. When he was gone, to the nawab's great surprise, King carried out his threat. He took a swinging kick, hard, at Wynter's thigh.

Wynter yelled, leaping from his bed, his eyes blazing. He swung instinctively at King's head with his fist. King blocked the blow and butted Wynter in the face, knocking him back down on his *charpoy*. Wynter tried to get up yet again, but his dead leg collapsed under him and he fell to the floor. He clawed at King's ankle. The sergeant trod on his fingers and pressed them into the stone flags.

'Ow! Ow!' yelled Wynter. 'What's all this then, eh? Attackin' a defenceless man in his sleep, eh? I'll 'ave you, you bastard.'

King ground the fingers into the stone floor.

'You will have no one, Private Wynter. You will get on your feet and stand to attention before your superior officer. If I get one more word out of you I'll knock you senseless, do you understand, you ungrateful cur? Now, soldier, *on your feet!*'

Wynter staggered to his feet, while Kashmar felt it prudent to look far away, out of the window.

'You do that to me?' shouted Wynter, suddenly realizing who was present, 'with that black sod in the room?'

King struck the soldier cleanly on the jaw and laid him out on the bed. A bucket of water was fetched and thrown over him. He came to his senses again and was again made to get to his feet and stand to attention. King walked round him and in a sergeant major's voice told Wynter exactly what he thought of him. Wynter was left in no doubt as to his deficiencies as a soldier and a human being. He was forced to apologize to the nawab for his foul manners and abuse. Then King told Wynter he was going to be flogged before they went back to Gwalior.

'What? I'm a sick man, I am. You can't flog someone on the sick list. What've I done to deserve it then, eh? Nothin'.'

'You either take your flogging like a man or I take you back to Gwalior to be shot like the cur you are, Wynter.'

Wynter now saw that none of the fury with which King had attacked him had dissolved in the violence. Normally men, especially King, came out of their rage once a few blows had been exchanged. King was clearly still white with anger. Wynter knew he was within an ace of being struck down dead on the spot. What he did not understand was the reason for King's anger. He knew the nawab and King were thick as thieves, but that surely did not account for such treatment as he was receiving. By now King's voice and manner should have softened, yet the sergeant was clearly only just on the edge of reason.

'What've I done, then? I'll answer for it, if you just tell me what I've gone an' done.'

'Do you deny you sent the lieutenant a threatening letter?'

'I never done no such thing,' Wynter protested vehemently. 'Who says I did? Whoever says it's a liar!'

'Captain Swing?'

Wynter stared at his sergeant.

King repeated his words, adding, 'You deny you've heard that name before?'

'Course I heard of it. But not in India. In England.'

'Enough of this,' snapped King. 'Will you take your punishment or will you take your chances with a court martial?'

Wynter quickly assessed his chances at winning a court martial. His normally dull mind was lively and alert when it came to such matters. The lieutenant obviously had hard evidence – no doubt the letter was in his possession – and Wynter came to the conclusion that he stood very little chance of walking away from a court martial, whether he was innocent or guilty.

'I'll take the floggin',' he said in a surly tone. 'Won't be the first.'

King led his man outside and requested a rope end from a stable boy.

Kashmar went back to where Jack was sipping cold tea. He sat down opposite the officer.

'You have a good man in that sergeant, Lieutenant.'

'Yes, I do.'

After a while, during which neither man said anything, Jack asked, 'Is King returning?'

'He is whipping your soldier.'

Jack straightened his back. 'What?'

'There was something about a letter. Sergeant King gave the soldier a choice – court martial or whipping. He chose the whipping.'

'Oh.'

Finally, King came back, grim-faced.

'Wynter is repentant, sir.'

'I expect he is, Sergeant.'

'Sir, shall we say no more about the matter?'

Jack was at a loss to think of any other course which would improve the situation. 'I think so, Sergeant.' He then went to see Wynter himself.

The private was having the lacerations on his back caused by the lashing treated with a creamy balm by a matronly looking woman with a very proud Roman nose. She looked a no-nonsense sort of female who was certainly not putting up with Wynter's complaints, for both were speaking at once and neither listening to what the other had to say. It was as if they were both talking to a separate crowd of people, their voices both loud and penetratingly insistent in their views. Finally the woman slapped Wynter's back to show she was finished and the soldier put on his shirt. Then he climbed slowly to his feet and went to attention.

'Sir!' he said, but without his usual tonal insolence.

Jack stared at the man before him. He was a very sorry-looking individual. One of his eyes was half-closed and crazed with whiteness. His hair was as grey and grizzled as that of a man twice his age. Hollow cheeks and sallow skin, covered in pock-wounds from the thorns, did nothing to improve his countenance, which was dry and cracked, especially around his mean-looking mouth. Wynter now stooped like a washerwoman with a heavy burden to carry, his thin frame bent and crooked. His shoulder blades stuck out and upward like stunted wings from his back, stretching the skin taut. His ribs formed deep furrows on his chest, between which were nasty sores. The bare feet were gnarled and corn-infested, the filthy toenails having cracked and split away in places to leave a rawness that must have been painful.

It was impossible not to feel pity for the soldier.

'Private Wynter,' said Jack in a softer tone than he had intended to use, 'stand at ease. Wynter, I'm sorry to see you in such a poor state. A man who has marched from the Crimea to India deserves that his body should be in a better condition. How is your wounded eye?'

'Blind, sir. Black as death.'

'Is it indeed? Well, that's a great pity.'

Wynter managed a crooked smile which was made more sinister by the stare of the milky eye. 'But at least *I* got both me hands, an't I?'

Jack shook his head slowly. There was, in his tone, the implication that at least he was not a cripple like Jack. The man's natural bent was to kick back at any authority, no matter what his condition. There was something rather tragic and strangely admirable in that. It was impossible for Wynter to shed his contempt, no matter how much punishment his body received, either by accident or from the army. He could be lying broken to the point of death and he would try to spit on the shoe of the man who had put him there. Wynter's bitterness was constant.

'You took your punishment, we shall say no more.'

'I never wrote no letter.'

Jack noticed the small single-shot pistol given to Wynter by the Dutchman. It rested by his pillow.

'I said we shall say no more on the matter. Your wrongs have been accounted for.'

'I never did no wrongs. You lot did. You left me to bleed to death,' said Wynter, his voice full of emotion with the memory of his night in the thorn bush. 'I was like Christ on the cross out there – the life just drainin' from me. Jesus Christ himself just wore a crown of thorns on his head – I wore 'em like a bloody greatcoat.'

'There was no help for it. We could not reach you.'

Wynter shrugged. 'Anyway, I didn't die, like you wanted. I got saved by that foreign bastard and his men.'

'Do not call the nawab names, Wynter, or you will be in serious trouble again. The nawab saved all our lives with his timely arrival, just when I had given up hope. I have had my fill of your insubordination. Be assured that if you anger me again you will spend the rest of your miserable life in prison.

I don't care what it takes, I'll have you behind bars. My patience is at an end. Am I understood?'

'But . . .'

'I mean it, soldier. Believe me.'

Wynter nodded. 'You got me, sir, you and your kind. You've always had me down and I an't now got the strength to fight it. But I'll always think I'm the better man. You can't take that from me. I come up from nothin' to be a respected soldier, while you was spoon fed from your cradle to your manhood. But I'll buckle, if it needs it. I'll buckle. When do we leave this heathen place? I'm fed up with bein' among pagans. I need to be back among Christians like meself again.'

Jack did not point out the obvious flaws in this speech, but allowed Wynter the luxury of believing himself to be a respected Christian. He pointed at the pistol lying on the hair-filled mattress.

'I hope you were not contemplating using that, Wynter – it's a tragic way to leave the world.'

Wynter glanced at the weapon which he believed elevated him above his normal station and then shrugged his shoulders.

'That? I already tried.'

Jack was puzzled. 'You've used it?'

Wynter's face twisted into a wry grimace. 'I missed.'

Jack realized Wynter was serious and he believed he knew what had happened. It was not rare. A suicidal man might put the pistol to his temple, even squeeze the trigger, intending to blow out his own brains. But at the last moment life-grasping reflexes thwart those intentions. He finds his hand has jerked the muzzle aside. Jack looked at the wall behind the bed. There was indeed a hole at the right height.

Jack nodded. 'Next time you'll have to put in a marker shot first.'

Wynter snorted with laughter at this attempt at humour.

'What, you mean practise on the left side of me head, afore doin' it to the right?'

'It could improve your aim.'

Jack could hear Wynter's snorting long after he turned his back and left the room and walked along the passageway. Maybe humour was the way to deal with this difficult and complicated man?

Ten

Captain Deighnton had arrived back at Gwalior just a week before Lieutenant Fancy Jack Crossman. Before his servant had had time to take off his boots and brush the riding dust from his coat, the captain was summoned to appear before the colonel of his regiment. The subaltern who delivered the message came in for a deal of abuse, but of course Deighnton's sword and pistol, along with his short temper, were feared amongst the younger officers.

An older man when challenged would simply remind Deighnton that duelling had been against the law since the second decade of the century and that they were in a no-win situation: if they were shot by their opponent they were likely to die, yet if they hit *their* target they would probably never be able to go back to Britain. Older officers knew that duels proved nothing. They knew their mettle having faced musket ball, cannon, grapeshot, canister and all manner of iron missile. They had cut and been cut with sabres, had horses shot from under them, had looked down countless barrels of death and had survived. They would not be likely to throw away their lives at the whim of a maniac duellist.

The young officers, however, were still more afraid of being labelled a coward than being run through or shot. They were still afraid of disgracing their family name. They were still afraid of losing the good opinion of others, especially loved ones back home in Britain.

Deighnton marched into the office of Colonel Weightmane.

The colonel was standing, leaning on a false mantle on which were photographs of his wife and children, all slaughtered in the uprising. He waved a piece of paper at Captain Deighnton.

'Is this your handiwork?' asked the colonel, who then let the paper fall to the floor.

Deighnton stared down at it. It was a letter. Deighnton's eyes were legendary. The eyes of an eagle. He recognized the handwriting as his own, even from halfway across the room. It was the letter he had sent to Jane Crossman, the wife of Lieutenant Jack Crossman. Deighnton said nothing. He simply stared in contempt at his colonel: a similar sort of contempt to the one Wynter bore towards his superior officer.

Finally, after a long period of silence, the captain asked, 'Where did you get that letter? Who gave it to you?'

'Why, are you going to call him out?'

The colonel's voice was calm, but his hands trembled as he reached for a glass of whisky on the mantle.

'Captain Deighnton, I have thoroughly investigated the claims you made in that missive to Mrs Crossman. While on the surface there have been some exchanges between the daughters of a corporal and this Lieutenant Crossman, deeper investigation revealed that they were in fact innocent exchanges. The officer concerned was actually plagued by the girls, whose father tells me they are difficult to handle.' He glanced at the mantle. 'I know what he's talking about. I had girls of my own.' The colonel then turned back to the captain. 'This is malicious gossip. I am amazed that an officer of your experience should sink so low. Even had the rumours been true, it was not your place to inform to a wife on a brother officer. You are a disgrace to your regiment, sir, and I want nothing more to do with you.' The colonel's voice was now taut with emotion. 'What have you to say for yourself, sir?'

Deighnton shrugged. 'I had the devil's own job to get him to fight. He kept shying off. This seemed a sure way.'

'And that's another thing.' The colonel slammed down his glass, bringing his servant running into the room. 'This damn duelling. It has to stop. Well, it *will* stop, because you, sir, are no longer welcome in my regiment. I would like you gone by tomorrow.'

The servant bowed out, very quickly.

'Gone? Where shall I go to, sir?' asked Deighnton mildly.

'Go anywhere, and I would sell out, if I were you.'

The captain said, 'You know of course that I have powerful friends back in England . . .'

'Damn your friends!' the colonel exploded, his eyes now steely with their own brand of contempt. 'God damn them, and God damn *you*! I'm sure he has already. You have several deaths on your hands. You may have had some friends, but you have also made some powerful enemies now that you have robbed families of sons and brothers. You think *I* care for your friends, now that my own family are all gone? Get out of my sight, sir. If you are here tomorrow I shall announce your misdemeanours to the regiment on parade. See then if you still feel you have behaved with honour! Gather then the true opinion of your fellow officers!'

Deighnton stared for a while at the trembling colonel, then turned on his heel and marched out of the room, his anger now at white heat. He strode towards his own bungalow. The warm wind of the evening was in his face and the foetid blown atmosphere of distant cesspits did nothing to improve his temper. Once he was on his own veranda he took a riding crop that hung on the doorpost. With this he began savagely to slash at the bamboo furniture, venting his temper. In the middle of this tirade his servant came out to see what the noise was about. Deighnton turned on the man and struck him several times around the face, causing bloody welts to appear. The servant was used to abuse, but never so bad as this, and put his arms over his head to try to protect himself. He cried out, 'Sahib, sahib, I have done no wrong. Please, sahib.'

But Deighnton was relentless. Someone had to pay. If he could not whip the man who was to blame for him being put in this position, he would whip this man just to hear him squeal. He laid about the servant's shoulders and back. The man crouched and cried out for mercy. Finally Deighnton's anger dissipated and he realized this was a silly occupation. Why whip a servant when one has to kill an enemy? First things first, though. He needed to find out who had given the colonel that letter.

The captain threw down the riding crop.

'Pick that up. Oh, come on, man, you're not badly hurt. Good God, I got worse from my schoolmasters for flunking Latin. Don't whimper like a baby, it disgusts me. If anyone calls tell them I'm out seeking the adjutant – I'll find out who carried that letter from England, if it takes me all night. And tell the cook I would like creamed chicken and sweet pota-toes. Come on, man, leap to the task. That's it! You'll be done with me by tomorrow. I'm leaving this damn hell hole for better pastures. Hah! That's brightened your eyes, hasn't it? You'll be out of a job tomorrow, but it pleases you. Human nature, it is a mystifying force . . .'

Later than evening Rupert Jarrard was in his room in one of the backstreet boarding houses when there was a rap on the door. Opening it he was confronted by a cavalry captain.

'Yes?' he said.

'Captain Deighnton. Mr Jarrard?'

'Yes.'

'I understand, sir, that you are a postman.'

'If that means a mailman, you understand correctly.'

'Ah, you know the letter to which I refer then?'

'Perfectly. Delivered by my own hand to your colonel.'

'In that case after I've levelled your friend,' said the captain, 'I shall be obliged if you will give me the satisfaction of doing the same with you.'

Jarrard opened his coat to show the captain his Navy Colt.

'Happy,' he said.

'Good. I was afraid that American gentlemen were not familiar with the European art of duelling.'

'Oh, we're familiar all right. A weekend sport with us.'

'Really? Until then?'

Jarrard nodded coldly and the captain left.

Unruffled, the newspaperman went back to writing his column.

He chewed the top of his pencil.

'Pervasive? Omnipresent? *Ubiquitous* – that's the word I want. Ubiquitous. Much more sinister in tone . . .'

Jack had not been back in Gwalior one hour when he received another summons, this time to attend to the major who had arrested him at Bareilly, Major O'Hay. It appeared the major had arrived the previous day and wished to speak with him urgently. Jack suspected more trouble: the business over his supposed desertion had still not been settled to the satisfaction of the senior staff at Bareilly.

Wearily he left his quarters and went to meet the major at the local headquarters. When he entered the building Major O'Hay failed to recognize him until he had introduced himself, then the portly field officer nodded. 'Ah, yes, Lieutenant

Crossman, isn't it? How d'ye do? Some refreshment?' This did not sound like the prelude to a court martial for desertion. Jack began to feel more comfortable with the situation.

'I was rather hoping to rest – I've had a long ride,' said Jack.

The major frowned. 'So have I, my boy. So have I.'

'Yes, sir. Yes, of course. How can I help you?'

'If I recall correctly you were the officer brought up in front of Colonel Boothroyde at Bareilly?'

So this *was* about the charge of desertion brought by Deighnton. Jack's heart sank once again.

'Look, Major, I still haven't had the chance to contact my superior officers – I'm sure they'll be able to clear up this misunderstanding once and for all . . .'

'I expect they can. Colonel Boothroyde is convinced of it – but we could progress from there without the word of your own colonel. During the inquiry you mentioned a civilian – Dutchman by the name of Hilversum?'

'Yes. I said he could verify that I had been abducted by rebel sepoys and taken over the borders of Chinese Tartary.'

'Quite, but you will recall I said the fellow was an unmitigated rogue, who sold guns to badmashes and dacoits? Other crimes too, that's a fact. Well, we have now located the fellow and want him arrested. You, sir, have been chosen as the arresting officer.'

Jack's heart sank even further now. 'Me? Why me?'

'Logical, ain't it? You're known to him. Friends – or at least acquaintances, ain't you? You can get close to him without being shot dead. Fellah's a sharpshooter, so I hear. Knock the pip out of an ace card from twenty yards. Wouldn't want to send an officer to his death just for the sake of arresting a blackguard. No, you're the man for it. Bring him back alive or dead and we'll forget the other thing.'

'And if I refuse?'

'Disobeying an order, old chap. Could be as serious as the charge of desertion. *Added* to it, no chance of getting off whatsoever.'

Jack knew he was being held to ransom. They wanted Hilversum for something more than a firearms charge, he was certain. They would not go to all this trouble just to get a man who sold the odd handgun to rich maharajahs and nawabs, for no one else could afford Hilversum's silver-mounted pearl-butted pistols. He was equally certain that he would not find out what it was until he asked Hilversum himself.

'Where will I find the Dutchman?' he asked.

O'Hay unfolded a map and spread it out on a table.

'Place here by the name of Narwar, further down the river Sinde. He's visiting a talukdar by the name of Chandra. Know what a talukdar is?'

'An Indian aristocrat, of sorts.'

'Quite. Back home he'd be called "landed gentry".'

'And Rudi Hilversum is staying with this Chandra.'

'Ah, Rudi. You know him by his Christian name, eh? Good. Knew we'd picked the right man. When we got orders from General Sir Matthew Martlesham to arrest the rogue, I recalled you knew him. Yes, guest of the talukdar. Selling him weapons, no doubt, with which to shoot the British. Never did trust the Dutch, not after that business with the nutmeg.'

The major was undoubtedly referring to the war over trading rights in the Spice Islands, an altercation that took place in the 1600s, centuries earlier.

Jack sighed. 'It seems I have little choice, sir. I'll do my best.'

'Of course you will,' cried the major jovially. 'Didn't expect any less, old chap. Now, will you have that noggin . . . ?'

Jack was given no time to see Rupert Jarrard before he was mounted yet again on Cadiz and riding for Narwar. He took none of his men with him this time. They were all still either sick or exhausted after their ordeal in the jungle. Wynter, the only man to avoid that long trek, was in no fit state after his flogging. Jack was having twinges of conscience about the punishment meted out to the private. There was growing doubt in his mind about the guilt of Wynter regarding the Captain Swing death threat. Still, he could not imagine who else would have written such a note and signed it with such a symbolic signature. In any case it would have been more than wearisome to drag Wynter with him; the man would be complaining every yard of the way.

As an arresting officer, Jack had reluctantly decided to wear his lieutenant's uniform. It was still a little dangerous out in open country, past villages where there was no army presence, for a British officer to ride alone. But order was

re-establishing itself throughout India and with that order
came fear of reprisals. Before the mutiny a white man could
travel anywhere in relative safety due to the firm action which
followed any attack. That kind of law enforcement was swiftly
returning and the rural communities were quick to adapt to
the norm.

After a long hard ride during which Cadiz did not once
falter or complain in any way, Jack arrived at Narwar. He
found a place to stable his horse and there asked directions
to the house of Chandra. The osler regarded this Hindi-
speaking British soldier with some suspicion and at first
showed reluctance to give Jack the information he needed.
However, two silver coins later and Jack knew where to find
the building.

Evening was coming on as Jack threaded his way along a
narrow alleyway looking for a house with two lamps, one
either side of a door studded with brass nails and bearing a
knocker in the shape of a tiger's head. Eventually he found
the place he was looking for. He hammered on the door with
the iron knocker and waited expectantly. Soon a little shutter
opened in the middle of the door and someone peered out.
Jack moved quickly up to the little window, so that only his
face was visible and his uniform could not be seen. He put
on an anxious expression and kept nervously looking over his
shoulder.

'Who is it?' came a female voice speaking Hindi. 'Who
are you?'

'A friend of the Dutchman, Hilversum,' Jack replied in the
same tongue. 'Chandra knows I am here. Let me in, quickly
– it is very urgent. Hurry, woman! A life depends upon it.
Quick! Quick!'

He had two pistols in his waistband and he now surrepti-
tiously armed himself with one of these.

There was a moment's hesitation, then he heard bolts being
withdrawn. He turned the handle, pushed the door and barged
in, past a startled young woman carrying a lighted candle.
She screamed something unintelligible, probably warning
those in the back of the house. Jack swept on, past empty
bedchambers that fronted a small courtyard. There was a light
in a room at the end of a short corridor. He ran down and
threw open the door, only to find he was in a kitchen with a

startled cook. Jack withdrew and turned left, towards another lighted room. The entrance to this one only had a beaded curtain, on which he nearly strangled himself as he flung himself through the doorway.

The two occupants of the room were already on their feet. One of them, the European man, was armed with a pistol. Jack pointed his weapon at Hilversum, for it was he, and ordered him to disarm himself. Hilversum blinked and then his face clouded over with annoyance.

'Lieutenant Crossman! How very uncivil, not to say impolite of you to threaten me with one of my own weapons.'

Jack glanced down and saw that he was indeed wielding the single-shot pistol which Hilversum had given to him as a gift.

'I apologize for that,' said Jack, 'but you are under arrest. I have been ordered to take you to Gwalior,'

'And there is a crime?'

'Trading in arms without a licence.'

Hilversum laughed out loud. 'Sir, do you honestly believe they would send a lieutenant to arrest me for that? Trading in pop-guns? I'm sorry, it doesn't make any sense.'

'No it doesn't,' agreed Jack, 'but I've still got to take you in – orders, you see. If there's a trial, I'll speak up for you.'

'You will? I understand you're not in a great position of authority yourself at the moment. Perhaps *I* should speak for *you.*'

Jack stared at the Dutchman. 'What do you know of my private affairs?'

'Major Lovelace said he had heard you were in some bother or other.'

Jack was greatly surprised. 'You know Major Lovelace?'

Hilversum was now smiling, as was the other occupant of the room, a slightly built Indian gentleman with dark-ringed eyes who twiddled a frangipani blossom between the fingers of one hand. The Indian was neatly dressed and had slicked his hair down with perfumed grease, the fragrance of which filled the whole room. This unlikely pair of criminals seemed to be enjoying some huge secret joke. Their attitude began to rankle with Jack, who believed he was on a serious business.

The Dutchman explained, 'We both do. We work for him. I tell you this, because I know you are also one of his spies.

Major Lovelace recruited me and the talukdar here just a few weeks ago. We are part of a cell of three. We know none of the other spies who work for Major Lovelace – he tells us this is best for us and them, in case we are ever discovered and questioned by an enemy.'

'And who is the third person?'

Chandra, still smiling, spoke now and revealed the joke. 'You are, sir. This is how we know you. You are the person to whom we must report if we cannot reach Major Lovelace.'

Jack's mind was spinning. 'I've not been told of this.'

'Have you seen the major lately? He's been very busy setting up his teams of spies.'

'That's not your business,' replied Jack, but he was losing ground rapidly. If none of this was known to him it *did* make sense. And Nathan Lovelace was such a shadowy figure in India it was unlikely these two characters would know of him and his work unless Nathan had indeed recruited them. Jack now dimly recalled Colonel Hawke telling him that Major Lovelace had been empowered to form an intelligence network, one greater than had ever existed before. At the time Jack had thought the colonel meant men like himself: British soldiers. Obviously not.

Hilversum put his own weapon down on a table.

'Well, are you going to take me to jail?' he asked.

'I don't know what to do now.'

'First, I would be grateful if you would lower that duelling pistol I gave you as a parting present – having adjusted the trigger mechanism myself I know it takes very little pressure to fire the weapon.'

Jack lowered the Wurfflain and then noticed that Chandra was staring at his left wrist.

'Yes,' he said, 'no hand.'

'I am sorry, sir – I don't mean to stare at your affliction. It must be difficult to load your pistol quickly.'

'You get used to it, tucking the thing under one arm and using the good hand to load. If you're wondering whether I would have managed to shoot the both of you, had it been necessary, I have to tell you I have another pistol in my belt. It is merely a matter of dropping this one after discharge and whipping out the other.'

'Ah,' said Chandra, nodding, 'of course. Tea?'

Without waiting for a reply Chandra went over to a kettle which was hissing on a stove. Jack watched him, still a little wary. It would be foolish to drop his guard completely, though he was fairly satisfied this pair were speaking the truth.

Once they were sat around the table, drinking and eating, Hilversum asked him, 'Who was it ordered my arrest?'

'Well, it was a Major O'Hay who gave me my orders, but they came to him from General Martlesham.'

Hilversum smiled broadly again.

Jack said, 'You seem to find a great deal of humour in all this.'

'Humour? Not so much. Irony, yes. I smile because of the irony.'

'Which is?'

'General Martlesham is the one who ordered Captain Deighnton to kill you in a duel.'

Jack was so taken aback he almost fell off his chair.

'Ordered – to – kill – me?' he repeated, haltingly.

'Yes.'

'But why would this Martlesham want me dead?' Jack tried to recall if he had ever met the general and given him offence, but could find nothing in his memory to advance that idea. 'I don't even know the man.'

'I don't know the details, but Major Lovelace does. When I spoke about your trouble with the cavalry captain – you do remember telling me about it when we were last together? – it's why I gave you the Wurfflein – when I spoke about this matter, Major Lovelace said under his breath, "Ah, yes, that's Martlesham's doing. He's the man who put Deighnton up to that business."'

'And why does this general want *you* arrested?'

'He doesn't just want me arrested, he wants me out of India, or just out of the way. Martlesham has business interests, vast estates, which actually conflict with his duties in the Indian Army. He is very jealous of those interests, even somewhat paranoid. I believe he will do anything to further his lust for wealth and power. If those interests are in any way threatened, he turns to unorthodox methods to remove the threat. Even a perceived threat is dealt with ruthlessly.'

'I would call Sir Matthew Martlesham a madman,' interrupted Chandra, 'but then I am a plain-speaking person.'

'Martlesham, Matthew Martlesham,' murmured Jack, the name nagging at recent memory. 'Where have I heard ... of course, the Chinese runner, Reginald Lee, on the boat coming down the river. Sir Matthew Martlesham is an opium poppy grower.'

'Precisely.'

'But,' said Jack, 'so far as I'm aware it's not illegal to grow opium.'

'There is a wider picture, Lieutenant. You are aware that China has been a powder keg of late? War with western powers only ceased in May. The Imperial rulers are about to sign the Treaty of Tientsin with several countries including America and Britain. The treaty will bring an end to hostilities and legalize the Chinese opium trade again. It is all very delicate and sensitive. It is in China that fortunes are to be made with opium. Martlesham is fearful of anything that might give rise to second thoughts. He is terrified this faction of Lord Holbrook will bring about a government change of mind regarding the opium trade.'

'How does this affect me?'

'Martlesham is convinced that there are spies out here gathering information which might be used against him by Lord Holbrook. You sir, are a spy ...'

'And,' interrupted Jack, the light dawning on him at last, 'my brother James is one of Holbrook's supporters. Martlesham believes I'm an agent for my brother.'

Hilversum said, 'I was not aware of your brother's involvement, but yes, that causes it all to fall into place.'

'And of course,' Jack mused in horror, 'young Faulks – the nephew of Lord Holbrook.' Jack's eyes opened wide and he found himself scratching his stump, a thing he did when he was extremely agitated. 'God, Hilversum, what it amounts to is that Deighnton is a paid assassin! He forces his victims into a position where they call him out – or they insult him so *he* can call *them* out – then disposes of them for Martlesham. It's monstrous.'

'Martlesham is a determined man who will brook no interference with his plans. Major Lovelace believes the killing of Ensign Faulks was a warning to Lord Holbrook that, if he did not cease his activities with regard to the opium trade, his immediate family would be under threat. I tell you, Martlesham is utterly ruthless. He will one day rule India – if he's not stopped.'

A lot of vague and misty things in Jack's head now became clear. No matter what Jack said to Deighnton, the captain was not going to let him off the hook. Deighnton was a killer. Yes, he risked his life each time he stood up against a victim, but Deighnton was probably one of those unusual men who did not fear death. Jack had met them before: they were one in ten thousand. They were of course as mortal as any man of flesh and blood, but they had no care for their own lives.

Naturally, since such men did not fear death, it became an inconsequential thing to bring death to others. If they did not fear it, why should the next man? Deighnton was doing nothing but hastening an inevitable event, the end of a man's life. Jack knew such men were estranged from feelings of remorse or pity, or any deep emotion. They probably enjoyed the quick thrill of seeing a man fall with a bullet in his brain, but then it became nothing, a hollowness.

'But what do I do now?' said Jack. 'I can't take you back, Hilversum. Who knows what will happen to you?'

'Thank you.'

'But I shall be castigated for it, I'm sure.'

Hilversum shrugged. 'Tell them you could not find me.'

'That will have to do,' said Jack, rising.

Chandra suggested, 'You will stay here for the night?'

Jack stared out of the window at the darkness.

'Yes, thank you, I will.'

Eleven

Captain Deighnton, still technically an army officer but one who knew he had to sell his commission, came away from his meeting with General Sir Matthew Martlesham in a cold and sober mood. When he had applied to the general for assistance in remaining in the army, more specifically the light cavalry, the general had turned him away. Deighnton needed the cavalry like a man needs his heart. Without it he would be an empty shell of a man with nothing to live for.

In his grand library the general had been in an imperious mood and less than sympathetic.

'You are on your own, sir. Your destiny is in your own hands. Tell me, do I owe you something?'

'I did your work, sir, thoroughly and efficiently.'

'I am aware of that, and I am also aware you were handsomely paid. Gratitude, I think, is not in either of our vocabularies.'

'I am not asking you to be grateful, General. I'm asking you to use your influence on my behalf. I shall still continue to do what is requested of me. You will have in me – ' Deighnton swallowed hard and uttered words which almost choked him – 'a good and faithful servant.'

Martlesham had then reached for a book from the bookcase, signalling that the meeting was over, but he added, 'I have no further use of you, Captain. The Treaty of Tientsin has now been signed.' He turned cold eyes on the tall cavalry officer. 'You may go.'

Deighnton stayed just a short while longer, then left as the servants came running.

The morning after the meeting with Chandra and Hilversum both Jack and Cadiz had rested and were refreshed. He was easier on his mount on the return to Gwalior, having nothing to race back to but possibly a prison cell. He surprised himself by talking to the horse, explaining his troubles, knowing of course that the beast could not understand one jot. But for once Jack imagined the tone of his voice was drawing feelings of sympathy from the impassive Cadiz.

And once back in Gwalior, the expected trouble was immediate.

Major O'Hay was incensed.

'What do you mean, you couldn't find him? I told you where to look for the man.'

'He was not there.'

'You're lying to me, Lieutenant.'

Jack flared. 'If I am, you know what you can do, Major.'

The major did it. He placed Lieutenant Jack Crossman under arrest pending court martial. Among other crimes he was charged with wilfully disobeying an order.

Jack spent a miserable time under close arrest. Sergeant King tried to see him, but was refused entrance. So was Rupert Jarrard. Private Wynter passed the building where Jack was being held and managed to jeer at his commanding officer before being grabbed and dragged away by the collar, courtesy of Corporal Gwilliams. So far as Jack's own senior officers were concerned Jack felt he had been abandoned. He had been told by Hawke that this happened to intelligence officers from time to time, but he was none the less embittered by the experience. Sitting in his lonely room, with no one to counsel him, Jack's hard feelings focussed on one man – Captain Deighnton. It raised all the fury of hell in him that this man had written lies to Jane – his beloved wife – and felt no remorse.

'I shall make him pay,' Jack resolved, 'if it's my last act on earth.'

Knowing Deighnton's reputation, he was aware that it probably would be Lieutenant Crossman's final curtain call.

His resolve had hardened to stone by the time Major Lovelace was standing in the room with him.

'Jack?'

'Nathan. At last.'

'Sorry, got held up. You know how it is. All been cleared up now. That idiot O'Hay has gone away ruffled, but the charges have all been dropped.' The major extended a hand. 'How are you?'

'A bit ruffled myself.'

'I can see that.'

'I'm sorry, Nathan, I have to do something. I made myself a promise.' Jack fingered the scar from the wound he had caused himself in order to escape the re-duel with Deighnton. Every time he looked at that scar he felt a flush of shame. It did not matter that Jack did not believe in great heroes or craven cowards, but believed men acted purely on impulse. He could no longer bear the thought that he had allowed Deighnton to bring scandal down on his marriage. 'Will you act as my second? Along with Rupert Jarrard?'

'I don't need to ask who the quarry is. Must you do this? It's all very unnecessary.'

'I know, I know. And I'm aware that though you, Nathan, can be . . . well, determined in your aims, you only employ your skills when it is absolutely necessary. You would never waste your obvious talents on a duel, which is by definition a destructive thing. However, I have borne more than most men could bear, and can no longer turn my back. It is regrettable, I'm fully aware of that, but necessary to my self-esteem and my mortal soul. I *cannot* go through life carrying this with me.'

'I understand. When?'

'As soon as possible. Will you explain to Rupert?'

'Certainly. I understand Jarrard has been offered the same, from the same source, once you have been disposed of.'

'In that case if I die I shall do so with the thought that my friend will surely make a better job of it than I have been able to. Rupert is no slouch with that side-arm of his.'

Lovelace smiled grimly. 'Let's not get too gloomy, Jack – you're no slouch with the pistol either.'

'I'm just all right, Nathan, nothing too special. But I have a sort of righteous fury about me, which may see me through. I keep telling myself this man can't win every time, even if he is best at it. No one can go through life without error. He has to make a mistake *sometime*.'

'Keep telling yourself that, Jack – and good luck.'

They had decided the duel should take place in a glade in a woodland not far from Gwalior. Men rode out separately and came together in that peaceful place of green plants and waxy fronds. Bees flew murmuring from flame tree flower to oleander bloom. Wide-winged butterflies carried their bright colours across open spaces. Brilliant birds trilled, screeched and chattered in the treetops of the lacy canopy. The first loud gunshot would shatter the natural order and bring a sudden shocked silence to the scene, but no wild creature even suspected such an event. They went about the business of life in quiet ignorance.

Deighnton had brought the same seconds who had attended him at the last duel he had fought with Jack. Jack was secretly pleased to learn this. Any witnesses who might have been suspicious of his courage were here today. They would go away knowing that Jack Crossman had not failed to meet the requirements of a gentleman. Honour was everything, in England, and in India. A man could not live without it and feel whole.

If Jack had believed he would feel any different at this duel – if he expected to be nerveless and carry a clear head – he was totally wrong. Righteousness did not banish his fear. He found he was still afraid, still had a racing heart and racing brain, and still wished himself elsewhere now that he was faced with death. He glanced at his opponent, now shedding his coat, and saw a man who looked calm and iron-willed. Deighnton appeared invincible and Jack felt entirely vulnerable. He tried to focus on the positive qualities of his tool for the task: the single-shot pistol he now owned, which was supposed to be so well-made, so accurate, that even a blind man could not miss with it.

Indeed, the Wurfflein felt comfortable in his grip. It was a well-balanced weapon with superior killing power.

'Are you ready, Jack?' asked Lovelace.

'Yes, I am,' he heard his voice saying.

'Jack, smooth and steady,' murmured Rupert. 'Don't fire too quickly. He's not a swift shooter.'

'Thank you, Rupert.'

'Gentleman!' came the call. 'Take your places!'

Deighnton strolled seemingly cool and untroubled towards the middle of the glade, while Jack found himself striding out. Very soon they were back-to-back. Jack could feel the heat of the other man's body through his shirt. Then followed the order to proceed, and the count began.

It seemed to Jack that his heart had already stopped. He

could no longer feel the beat. A parrot shrieked precisely on the count of ten, confusing things and making Jack start. He turned, quickly – too quickly – but took steady aim along the long-barrelled Wurfflein. He fired. The smell of burning gunpowder smoke filled his nostrils. Deighnton jerked backwards. Jack was momentarily exultant, but was then immediately despondent as his opponent remained on his feet.

A red stain was sweeping across Deighnton's white shirt around the left shoulder. He had been hit, but on the wrong side. *The wrong side.* Given the large calibre of Jack's pistol there must have been a hole in Deighnton's back as big as a fist, yet the captain was still on his feet. The man had unbelievable fortitude. Why had he not fallen to the dust? The shock and pain would be enough to drop a wild beast. Yet there he was, still able to lift his arm and take slow aim at Jack.

Deighnton's face was set in a hard expression. He seemed grim and taut as he squinted down the barrel of his pistol. Jack knew now that he was going to die. With all the time in the world at his disposal his adversary could not miss. Deighnton was a deadshot. Jack had to stand and wait for the ball to hit him. It struck him as peculiar that now the end was nigh, his nerves were steel. No shaking, no fear, no sorrow in his veins. He awaited the inevitable. All movements seemed remarkably clear as time came almost to a halt.

Jack heard a spectator shout as if from a long way off.

A cry of alarm.

'Look out!'

In a haze he saw a phantom-like figure stepping swiftly from the tree line wielding a sabre. The bright curved blade of the sabre swished through the sunlit air, flashing as it did so, decapitating Captain Deighnton with a single stroke. Then the shadowy swordsman was gone again, like a forest spirit, back into the trees from whence he had emerged.

Deighnton's head fell to the ground with the thump of heavy fruit dropping from a branch. It rolled like a ripe green coconut under a bush, disappearing from view. His body remained upright for a split second, standing on the spot, the right arm with the pistol still extended. Then the legs collapsed and the corpse fell forward, driving the muzzle of the pistol into the soft mossy earth of the forest clearing. Deighnton had fought his last duel, one he had been sure to win, if only . . .

No one moved for a moment. Then two officers, Deighnton's seconds, ran into the woods looking for the killer. The doctor took a cursory glance at Deighnton and pronounced him dead on the spot. He took Deighnton's coat and threw it over the body.

Jack felt two pairs of hands holding his arms, strong pillars on either side of him. He was glad for that, for he had been almost certain to collapse himself. Deighnton's gory end had shaken more than one witness to the beheading. There were others who were also quite unsteady. A death had been expected, but not the manner of it.

Even as Deighnton's two seconds returned, empty handed, a troop of soldiers had entered the glade led by Sergeant King. An arresting party, that much was obvious. Had King decided to inform the authorities about the duel? Jack could not think so. He could see that the captain in charge of the troop was surprised to see such a large party in the woods. The eyes showed puzzlement as they went from one pale face to another.

'Where's Captain Deighnton?' the officer finally asked.

Major Lovelace asked him tersely why he wanted to know.

'I'm here to arrest him – for the murder of General Sir Matthew Martlesham.'

Lovelace strode over to Deighnton's corpse and whipped away the coat to reveal a headless torso already swarming with ants.

'Here's the rogue you want. For the first time in his life he lost his head. You'll find it under that bush, Captain.' Then he added, 'For myself, I'm off to write a quick letter. A vacancy has just occurred at the Houghton Fishing Club and you never know your luck unless you try.'

Aware that the arresting squad was going to come to its senses and ask for the other duellist, Jarrard spirited Jack away to where Cadiz was tethered. The pair of them rode back to Gwalior in silence. Jack still appeared to be wrestling with his demons which left Rupert time to calculate calmly whether he would have survived a duel with Deighnton. Certainly Deighnton was one of the coolest duellists Rupert had ever seen, not rushing his shot, nor showing concern for the other fellow. That last was the trick: to ignore the fact that your opponent has a pistol in his hand and treat the whole affair as a target shoot. It would have been a close-run thing, he decided. He was by no means confident he would have come away from the duelling ground alive.

Two British officers and an American newspaperman were sitting on the veranda of Lovelace's bungalow with an Indian warrior. All except the Rajput were drinking long cool drinks with gin at the base. Raktambar had hot lemon juice laced with honey. They watched huge fruit bats gliding from palm to palm: giants of their kind. A red-sashed evening heralded the coming night and already the choirs of crickets were voicing their alarms and love calls. Charcoal-black tamerisks stood out on the plain, stark against the darkening sky. The *chowkidars*, those ever-reliable nightwatchmen, called to each other in soft voices as they took their posts, *chupattis* in their pockets, repast for the long middle hours.

India was laying down its head to rest.

Lovelace said, 'Deighnton's servant is missing.'

'It was he who killed his master?' questioned Raktambar, not without a note of approval in his voice.

'So it's believed,' Lovelace replied. 'A lot of servants are mistreated, of course. I used to be disgusted by what I witnessed but unhappily one becomes inured to the ill-treatment of the natives. After a while it seems normal. Then occasionally one runs amuck.'

'Officers can abuse and humiliate servants to a point, then sometimes it's like a stretched wire has snapped in their heads,' Jarrard said.

'Does it happen with the slaves in your country?' asked Jack.

Jarrard had to think hard about that. 'Not so often. Not so's I recall. Maybe it's something to do with being in one's own land. The slaves back home have nowhere to run to. Here, they can vanish into the millions of others like them. They'll never catch this one.'

'Deighnton would have hung anyway, of course,' said Lovelace, 'for the murder of Martlesham. His servant saved the state the cost of the execution. Two snakes gone with one blow, eh? Not that it'll make any difference. The opium trade will flourish without Martlesham, the army will still have its bully boys like Deighnton, and the world is only marginally a better place for their absence. Now, Jack, what will you do about this soldier of yours? Wynter? Shall we send him back to the 88th? You must be tired of his insolence and insubordination.'

Jack sighed. 'It would kill him to rejoin the regiment. At best he'd be in the stockade within days – at worst before a firing squad for striking a senior rank. He has survival grit though. He walked over a subcontinent and lived to tell the tale. He spent a night in a bush of three-inch thorns and came out of it ugly but alive. He has a bitter gall flowing in his veins, that man, but I'll put up with him, as I always have. Sergeant King keeps him off my back for a good part of the time.'

'King's a good man, then?'

'We have our differences, but in the main, very steady. I just wish he could shoot. It's very inconvenient having a sergeant who can't hit a haystack from two yards.'

'You have Gwilliams though – a sharpshooter, I understand.'

'And good with the knife, when necessary. Rupert here can't stand him, but I think that's like the Irish and English, or the Irish and Scots, or the Scots and English. And the Welsh and everyone else. There's nothing so abominable as one's close neighbours.'

'Amen,' added Jarrard, swilling his drink round his glass.

Raktambar said, 'Yes, it would be good if we were not neighbours for too long, sahibs.'

Jack threw a warning glance at the Rajput for revealing his dissentious ideas. Jack could cope with them, but he was not sure Lovelace could. Raktambar simply raised his eyebrows. There was no solid friendship between Jack and his reluctant bodyguard, only a truce. They respected one another, they would probably die in defence of one another, but they could not be bosom friends. That could only happen when Raktambar was released from the servitude placed on him by his maharajah and he was free to choose. Who knows, thought Jack, perhaps he would remain by my side if such a thing happened?

Major Lovelace appeared not to have heard Ishwar Raktambar's remark and was simply staring out at the oncoming night.